A
PICTURE
OF HER
TOMBSTONE

Also by Thomas Lipinski

The Fall-Down Artist

A
PICTURE
OF HER
TOMBSTONE

THOMAS LIPINSKI

St. Martin's Press ✖ New York

Just like the first time,
this book is dedicated
to my parents.

A THOMAS DUNNE BOOK.
An imprint of St. Martin's Press.

A PICTURE OF HER TOMBSTONE. Copyright © 1996 by Thomas Lipinski. All rights reserved. Printed in the United States of America. No
part of this book may be used or reproduced in any manner whatso-
ever without written permission except in the case of brief quotations
embodied in critical articles or reviews. For information, address St.
Martin's Press, 175 Fifth Avenue, New York, N.Y. 10010.

Design by Nancy Resnick

Library of Congress Cataloging-in-Publication Data

Lipinski, Thomas.
    A picture of her tombstone / Thomas Lipinski.—1st ed.
      p.   c.m.
    "A Thomas Dunne book."
    ISBN 0-312-14390-7
    I. Title.
    PS3562.I574P53   1996
    813'.54—dc20   96-6487
                                               CIP

First Edition: July 1996

10 9 8 7 6 5 4 3 2 1

A
PICTURE
OF HER
TOMBSTONE

SPRING
1986

1

For most of the crosstown trip from South Side, Dorsey was pre-occupied with searching for a comfortable position in the van's passenger seat. His trick knee was aching, and it wasn't until they had passed through the Downtown area and into the Strip Dis-trict, a valley floor along the Allegheny River populated with threadbare warehouses and wholesale distributors, that he secured his leg firmly between the seat and dashboard. Al Rosek was at the steering wheel, grinding away at the van's standard transmission at each stop sign. Pulling onto Penn Avenue, heading east into the working-class neighborhood of Lawrenceville, they were brought to a stop by the traffic light at the merger of Penn Avenue and Butler Street.

"Can't say that I recall you ever mentioning it," Al said. The light went green; he worked the transmission, then veered left onto Butler. "But seriously, your mother's people, they're from around here, from Lawrenceville?"

"Don't sound so surprised." Dorsey watched the light early-evening traffic through the windshield. "What's surprising to me is that Al Rosek of Rosek's Bar and Information Exchange wouldn't have a full dossier on my entire lineage."

Al slowed the van to a crawl, negotiating his way around some crater-sized potholes. "Every spring," Al said, gesturing with his chin toward the road surface. "Every spring, these things come up as regular as dandelions. The van's scheduled for a wheel realignment next week."

The white van rattled along Butler, and Dorsey studied the sidewalk through the passenger window, looking at the small huddles of men, both young and old, who seemed to gather at alternate street corners. The sidewalks were cracked and grainy, and the spring evening's lingering light highlighted the grime of empty store windows. Once past Thirty-seventh Street, the groups of men turned from black to white; Dorsey could see little difference in them beside race. But the number of active storefronts increased: mostly discount stores, pizza shops, and bars. Dorsey thought of it as South Side's slightly poorer relative.

"Anyway," Dorsey said, shifting his weight in the passenger seat, facing Al, "your previously unknown limitations not withstanding, my mum's family is from around here. They're a little farther out Butler, around Fifty-second Street. It was mostly Irish out there."

"I've got a feeling that it ain't mostly Irish where we're headed." Al took a hard right up Forty-forth Street, again playing with the transmission as the van tried to cope with a sudden and steep incline. They crossed an alley, and Dorsey was taken aback by the neighborhood's abrupt transition. Going away from the rundown business district, one side of Forty-forth was lined with well-tended rowhouses fronted by black wrought-iron fencing. On the far sidewalk was an enormous reddish-brown brick church. *Some people can live pretty well here,* Dorsey thought, then remembered the scene on Butler. *Yeah, they live here; they just don't shop here.*

"Polish church over there." Al pulled the van to the opposite curb and considered several row houses. "That one, I think; third one up."

Dorsey watched Al put the van in park and flick off the ignition. "Still sounds strange to me," he said. "Ziggy has to be, what? Maybe in his early sixties? And this is his aunt were supposed to be seeing? Can this be right?"

"All I know is what Ziggy told me." Al slipped out onto the sidewalk, and Dorsey came around from the passenger side, meeting him as he undid the gate latch. "Like I said, Ziggy comes to me because he knows I'm friends with you. Said his aunt wants to hire a detective, and you're the only one he's ever heard of. Not a great recommendation, but just remember, you were kind of famous for a while. And you've been hungry because of it."

Don't remind me, Dorsey thought. *Bust the wrong guy and then have it turned around into a public lawsuit; that's not so good for a supposedly* private *detective.* At the door he reached over Al's shoulder and pressed the doorbell. From his height of six four he gave Al the once-over and laughed to himself, recalling that Al was wearing what Dorsey referred to as the bartender's summer uniform. The black synthetic fiber pants were good year-round, but at the first sign of warm weather Al broke out the short-sleeved white shirts. The long-sleeved ones went to the cleaner and on vacation until October.

The door opened just a crack, and against the background of a dimly lit interior Dorsey could discern half of an aged face, the eye of which was level to his belt buckle. "You the men my Ziggy send?" The woman's voice was weak, but the Slavic tones of Eastern Europe came through to Dorsey. *My God, Ziggy does have an aunt. And a live one, too.*

Al introduced them both, and the old woman undid the security chain and opened the door the rest of the way, reminding them to close and lock it once they were in. Dorsey trailed Al and the old woman through a small vestibule and inner door into a living room, where the old lady motioned them around a coffee table and onto a sofa beneath the front windows. As she left through a small passageway for what he took to be the kitchen, Dorsey took in the room. Opposite the sofa were two easy chairs, both with doilies on the arms, similar to the ones protecting the sofa's armrests. Two of the walls were adorned with golden crucifixes, and the third held a large portrait of the Virgin Mary done in a variety of golds and with a black face. Dorsey elbowed Al in the ribs and gestured toward the icon.

"Czestahowa," Al said, "Our Lady of Czestahowa. The black face is because some invaders burned it. Swedes, I think. Like I said, that's a Polish church across the street. Holy Family."

The old woman returned carrying a tray with three cups of coffee, a creamer, and a sugar bowl. She was so short that Dorsey could barely discern any bending of her waist as she lowered the tray to the coffee table. With the window light, her hair was the metallic gray of unfinished steel, pulled back in a bun and thinning. Her worn, sleeveless housedress accentuated the flaps of skin hanging from her upper arms. *Late eighties,* Dorsey thought, *but don't rule out ninety.*

"You are Mrs. Leneski, right?" Dorsey took one of the cups and sipped at the rim. The coffee was hot and very strong. "You're Ziggy's aunt?"

"My brother's boy." Mrs. Leneski handed a cup to Al, who added cream and sugar.

Listening to her, Dorsey decided that her English wasn't broken, like an immigrant's. *The woman doesn't have a Polish accent,* he figured, *she's got a Polish tone.* The flavoring one heard in the voices of first born Americans, the echoes of parents from the Old Country.

"He's gone now." Mrs. Leneski sat in one of the easy chairs, taking the last cup of coffee. "Ziggy's father, I mean. Thirty years in Heppenstall's mill and raised Ziggy and four sisters. And he helped out my mother, too. Ziggy is good, too. Like his father. Always worked real hard."

6

"He said you might want to hire my friend," Al said. "Said you had some trouble. Didn't say what, but Ziggy said you needed a detective."

"You a good one?" Mrs. Leneski turned her attention to Dorsey. "Good detective? If I pay good money, I expect something to get done. So, you good detective?"

Dorsey rested the coffee cup on the knee of his khaki slacks and wondered if Ziggy had told her anything and hoped that he hadn't. It had been eighteen months since his own trouble, and he hoped that the woman's eyes had weakened to the point where she no longer bothered with the papers or TV news. There's still the radio, though. "My workload has been light lately," he said. "Referrals have been down, you might say. But I've done some good work in the past. Over all, I think I can promise you my best."

Mrs. Leneski set down her coffee cup and cut her eyes at Dorsey. "You was the one had the run-in with that priest and his people. Roughed you up a little? Year before last, wasn't that when?"

Well, Dorsey thought, *at least the radio got the message through.* "Didn't care much for the publicity," he said. "Your trouble is most likely different. Yours I can probably keep out of the newspapers."

"Big shot priest, he was," Mrs. Leneski said. "Led those people and got them in all kinds of trouble—and for what? Not like a good parish priest, the kind you got to respect. That trouble is long over. I need your help. I pay you good."

It had been a long time since he had been hired without reservation, without a kind word from a well-placed friend, and Dorsey felt as though he had just been taken off the blacklist. "Tell me how I can help."

Mrs. Leneski rose and fished around in the pocket of her housedress. First she produced a chain of rattling rosary beads, quickly transferred to her other hand, then found a folded sheet of paper that she gave to Dorsey. Straightening it out, he saw it was a handbill with a reprinted black-and-white photo of a very attractive girl, about seventeen or eighteen, by Dorsey's judgment. Below the photo a caption asked for help in locating the girl, who had been missing for two months. An unspecified reward was offered.

"My granddaughter, Maritsa. These are all over the neighborhood." Mrs. Leneski retook her seat. "The junkies, they got her."

2

Seated in the office swivel chair, the back support pushed to the give point, Dorsey just sat and enjoyed the room, enjoyed his continued ownership of the room. He enjoyed the bookshelf that held his undisciplined collection of jazz and the photos that showed him as he moved successfully through the city's Catholic basketball hierarchy: parochial school team, Central Catholic High School team, and eventual stardom at Duquesne University. Beneath the two windows that fronted on Wharton Street was a cushioned chaise he had accepted as payment from a bankrupt client. And behind his chair was the office midget refrigerator, stocked with Rolling Rock beer. *Thank God,* he had told himself again and again, *thank God they were wrong. Refreshing isn't it? Real estate agents can be fuckups, too.*

Oh, he remembered, how they had tried. But the place just wouldn't be sold. "It'll move fast," the agents had told him. "It's this gentrification thing you're always hearing about. You know, rich young guys who like to think of themselves as urban pioneers, they buy up these places and sock a lot of money into them so they can look cool living next to poor folks." Until, Dorsey had told the agents, their rich friends caught wind of how good these places were supposed to be and started in buying all the other houses on the block, moving out what you guys called the poor folk. Move them out and right into subsidized housing projects. Where they got the living shit kicked out of them.

The house just hadn't moved. Not as a "Must See", not as a "Starter Home," and not as a "Bargain." The realtors had suggested, to Dorsey's humiliation, that it be billed as a "Fixer-upper," and that's when he decided to stay put. A second mortgage was taken out, and for sixteen months he had worked as Al's afternoon bartender to pay the legal fees that came with defending himself against the priest's lawsuit, the result of his last big case. The suit was eventually dropped when both sides lost their taste for the fight and when the newspapers and television lost their interest in both of those sides.

Pulling himself upright in his chair, Dorsey returned to the work at his desk, typing the notes of his interview with Mrs. Leneski. He cranked a blank sheet of paper into the Olivetti portable, recalling the old woman's strength. She had gone on for over an hour, telling a terribly sad story but without a tear or a stumble, as if she had lived through worse and was prepared to do it again. *She wants her granddaughter back home. Good thing I'm on her side.*

Dorsey began his notes with a brief history of the missing girl. Maritsa Durant, the seventeen-year-old daughter of Catherine Leneski and Teddy Durant, now divorced, had lived with her grandmother for the last twelve years. "Because," Mrs. Leneski had explained, "my Catherine was no damned good as a mother. Because of all the dope she took with that goddamned Teddy. Never worked, neither of 'em, and where they got the dope money I don't know. Spent all their time with the junkies in that park over on Forty-sixth Street. Catherine's on the metha-something now— methadone, I think—but she's half crazy most of the time. Even when she's feeling better she's no damned good for anything."

Where the father might be was anyone's guess, Dorsey remembered, pecking away at the Olivetti and manually returning the carriage. In the following lines he recorded that Maritsa was a junior at the local Catholic high school and, according to her grandmother, an excellent student. Topnotch grades in all subjects and active in school clubs, primarily community service clubs. Very compassionate, Dorsey had concluded, based on Mrs. Leneski's comments. Reluctantly, however, the old woman had admitted that for the last few months before her disappearance, Maritsa had become secretive and had avoided her usual school companions. Her grandmother had suspected drug abuse, and Dorsey hadn't been able to argue with that. "The junkies have her," Mrs. Leneski had insisted. "The junkies in that park two blocks away. She'll end up like her mother if we don't get her back soon."

Dorsey finished the notes with a brief list of people to contact and slipped the papers into a manila folder. Listening to Bobby Short singing from the tape player crammed into the bookcase, he took a pencil and scratched out the name of a former client from the folder's edge, replacing it with that of the missing girl. From the far left corner of the desktop blotter he took the handbill with the girl's picture. The photo was faded, showing the result of being duplicated through a poor-quality copier, probably at a local bank for five cents a copy. But the image was still striking. How had the grandmother described her? Dorsey asked himself. "She's beautiful but dark," the old woman had said. "Dark like a Jew, like one of those real pretty Jewish girls. She's Jew dark." Dorsey didn't know about the Jew part, but yeah, the girl was a beauty. Her hair was dark and coarse, and the eyebrows were elegant. The nose was straight and free of imperfection, and her smile was wide and radiant. It worried Dorsey that she might be an attractive victim for someone other than a dope dealer.

Turning in his chair, Dorsey pressed the tape player's stop button, and Bobby Short was cut off as he hit the high end of the scale. He crossed the converted living room–office and put the girl's

11

folder in the metal file cabinet's middle drawer. Through the front windows he checked Wharton Street, sunny and empty at midday, and decided to walk to work.

Once his vision had adjusted to the dim barroom light, Dorsey recognized the man behind the bar as Henry Antos, Al Rosek's brother-in-law. *The one who never works,* Dorsey thought, *except when he tends bar for Al. If Henry's back, and it sure as hell looks like he is, then you're out.*

Dorsey crossed the room and rounded the bar, crouching low and looking beneath the bar for the clean linen apron that normally awaited him. The shelf was empty, and when he straightened up he saw Henry, squat and bald and wearing a white shirt that Dorsey could have sworn he'd seen on Al the day before. Around his waist, in the bartender's classic double wrap, was a white linen apron that was just beginning to show the stains of a few hours' use.

"So," Dorsey said, "let's hear it. The hell's the story on this?"

Henry served a beer to a customer seated midway down the bar, then used his bar rag to work at a streak at the countertop. He was bent forward, intent on his work, and Dorsey noticed that Henry had gathered what little fringe of hair he had into the smallest of pigtails. *Yeah,* he thought, *what the hell is the story?*

"Sorry, man." Henry turned his attention to Dorsey. "Al's in back, in one of the booths, working on yesterday's totals. He said for you to head straight back there. For a talk."

Descending the three short steps to the back room, which had in years back served as a dance floor, Dorsey could feel his pulse quicken. *This job, and some simple-ass insurance inspections, have been carrying you,* he reminded himself. *And this Henry, talk about a flighty bastard. First he lives with Al and Rose; then he lives off them; then he disappears for a year and a half. But now he's back in town. And in need. And being Rose's brother, her asshole brother who takes some looking after, he's in.*

"So, he's back." Dorsey slipped into the booth, facing Al. Between them was a Formica-topped table covered with stacks of coins, folding money, and an ancient-looking adding machine. "Tough way to find out you've been canned. Show up for work and someone else is doing your job."

Al pulled at the arm of the adding machine, waited for the total, and wrote the figure on a scratch pad before looking up. "Temporary—we agreed to that when you started. This was only to be for a while. You needed help staying afloat, and I needed an afternoon barkeep because Henry was off on another of his adventures. And because Russie is gone."

Thanks, Dorsey thought. *Thanks for the memory. Russie's gone. Gone dead. Because a guy who took it upon himself to come after you with a stretch of pipe got it all wrong and crushed Russie's skull instead of yours. Russie's been gone almost two years now. God, it's been a long two years.*

"Think I'm happy about this?" Al asked. "Keep something in mind. A guy never marries just a girl; he marries the girl's family. Nine out of ten times—for me, anyways—that's been a pretty good deal. Rose's mother, she was a saint. That's all you can say about her. And her father, he did a lot of repairs to this place, once he took his retirement from the post office. Put down floor tile, looked after the kitchen stove and the coolers. And he did it all on Sundays when the place was closed. But then you come to Henry."

Dorsey propped his chin in the cup of his right hand and sighed, disgusted. "Yeah, Henry. Tell me about it."

"I never have," Al said, "but if you feel like you're losing out to him, maybe you're entitled. You guys, you and Bernie, you always figured him for a bum."

Dorsey's eyes fell to the tabletop, but he thought of Bernie, not Henry. Like Russie, he had been a casualty of the big case that went wrong. And being Dorsey's friend while being on the staff of a law firm that was up to its ass in hot water, Bernie had had to find new work. And the only place where his name wasn't shit was a firm in Harrisburg. *God Almighty, what a costly mess.*

13

"There may be some truth to that," Al said, "but believe me, the guy's had a bad time of it." He craned his neck out of the booth to check on Henry, and Dorsey followed the motion. "Won't know it from looking at him, but what we have here is one of the first nonconformists. An original beatnik."

"You're shittin' me? Henry?" Dorsey asked, then remembered the pigtail. He twisted back to face Al. "Beatnik, huh? Like-wow-man beatnik?"

Al snorted a laugh and continued. "Always been a real bright guy. Flaky, maybe, but bright. Liked to read a lot and talk things out. Worried the hell out of his father; the old man thought he had some kind of mental problem. Anyway, he was over in Korea during the war there, I think with the army, for about two years. And when he came back to the States, he didn't go home. Got off the troop ship in San Francisco, took his discharge, and stayed put. He actually knew those two guys they talk about sometimes on PBS. Ginsberg and Kerouac, I think. Spent a few years hanging out at some bookstore out there."

"City Lights," Dorsey said. "Name of the bookstore you just mentioned. It's called City Lights." He gave Al a thin smile. "Kind of famous because of the two guys from PBS."

Al nodded, impressed. "That's pretty good; but, then, you read some, too. So, Henry is out there I guess until about '62, maybe early '63. Spent a little time at a state farm for marijuana and some stuff that goes with it. Then in '63, that was the first time he worked for me. Can you believe that? All these years I've been taking him back."

"Just comes and goes, huh? All this time and he's still the same?" Dorsey watched Al shake his head, but he couldn't help but feel some new respect for Henry creep into his thoughts. *Takes some nerve,* he told himself, *some real guts. To try a different path, even if it turns out all wrong. And to do it again and again and never lose the heart to try. Also doesn't hurt to have Al and Rose to fall back on. You know that last part yourself.*

14

"Never changes." Al took a worn leather bank pouch from the seat next to him and removed a packet of deposit slips. "And these last few times he's taken off, me and Rose haven't had any idea where he's been. Thought about having you look for him—but, I guess where he goes is his business. Had a suspicion that Rose really knew where he was but didn't want to say. Which is okay with me. She knows best sometimes."

Dorsey watched Al scribble some figures on a deposit slip that he put into the pouch before scooping in the coins and cash. "Ah, well," he said, "regardless of the family history lesson—interesting though it was—I'm out of a job. Still, there's a few calls I could make; somebody might have a spot for a part-time field investigator."

"You've got a full-time job already," Al said, shifting his weight to get at something in his back pocket. "Mrs. Leneski's granddaughter, remember? You're supposed to find her?"

"That's a case," Dorsey said. "It's not a career."

Al produced a thick letter-size envelope and slid it across the tabletop, where it dropped into Dorsey's lap. "Ziggy left that off this morning. It's from the old lady. She wants you on the job full time, so Henry's timing couldn't be better."

Dorsey took the envelope in hand, opened it, and fingered his way through a wad of bills, all hundreds. *Jesus Christ,* he thought, *you haven't seen this much money since you paid that attorney. That bastard attorney.*

"It comes to seven thousand," Al said. "I went ahead and counted it for you."

"You're a pal."

"I am." Al took a second, thinner envelope from his shirt pocket. "Something else, your last paycheck. With a little severance. Get the little girl home."

3

Dorsey moved the Buick along Butler Street, letting the turn at Forty-fourth Street—and his client—pass by. Mrs. Leneski could hold for a few minutes, he figured, although the thickness of the cash envelope teased at the corners of his thoughts. Seven thousand; that's a big payday. Especially when there's no more scheduled.

Stopping for a red light at Forty-sixth and Butler, listening to Diane Schur sing "How About Me?" from the dashboard radio, Dorsey scanned the green lawn that fronted the park. *This is it,* he told himself, *the junkie haven that supposedly swallowed Maritsa whole. Doesn't look the part,* he decided. The lawn, sea green and well tended, led to a swimming pool with basketball courts and a baseball field beyond. Children chased and tackled each other on the lawn, and Dorsey spotted two teenage boys practicing free throws on the basketball court. *So, where's the dope?* he asked himself. *Where's the danger and what is it that attracts the dopers?* The traffic light went green and Dorsey hit the accelerator. Continuing along Butler, his questions were answered.

The far end of the park butted up against Allegheny Cemetery,

16

square acre after square acre of headstones, mausoleums, stone crosses, and woods. Virgin woods, Dorsey had heard it called, as wild and uncharted as the Louisiana Purchase. Safe haven, he figured, every time the city narcotics squad raided the park. There was a tall cyclone fence, weathered and rusted, separating the park and the graveyard, and Dorsey could picture the huge gaps in it, preplanned escape routes cut with tin snips. *Yeah, lose yourself back in those trees and it would take Lewis and Clark to fetch you out.*

On the radio, Diane Schur gave way to Dave Brubeck, the kind of mix Dorsey had come to appreciate on WDUQ. He continued on Butler, moving past the high stone walls of the cemetery until it gave way at Fiftieth Street and the storefronts resumed. Like those of lower Butler, they held secondhand stores, a butcher shop, and several bars. Only a few of the names were familiar to Dorsey, and he tried to recall how long it had been since his last visit. High school graduation? Maybe college?

After a few more blocks he took a right, climbed a slight incline, and took another right onto Carnegie Street. Again, Dorsey was taken by the contrast of a failing commercial thoroughfare and its well-cared-for residential surroundings. Three-quarters of the way down the block he pulled to the right-hand curb. Resting an elbow in the open window, he took a long look at St. Kieran's, his mother's parish church. Built into the hillside, the church was long and brown-orange bricked, and the building flowed seamlessly into the grade school, rectory, and parish hall. He remembered a cousin's christening, another's first communion, and a wedding that had gone on far too long into the night. The only disturbing memory was that of the morning after. A whole family he had seen only in spurts and not at all for too many years.

Dorsey was about to turn over the ignition when the church's side service door opened and a man, only a few inches taller than five feet, backed his way out. Dressed in a white T-shirt and work pants, his full head of hair the rust color of a graying redhead in his early sixties, he clutched a long metal tool chest to his waist and kicked the church door closed. Dorsey took the keys from the ignition and stepped out onto the street's asphalt topping.

"Uncle Davey!" he shouted, heading toward the man as he reached the middle of the street. "C'mon, you don't recognize me?"

Balancing the tool chest against his hip, the man in the T-shirt stopped in midstride and took a hard squint at Dorsey. It took a moment or two, but the light of recognition eventually crept across his face. "Carroll? That's you? The hell you doin' around here?" The tool chest slipped when he glanced back at the church, apparently hopeful that the bricks had not noticed his cursing.

Dorsey rushed across the asphalt and caught the tool chest as it began its slide down his uncle's pant leg. Working a grip at its edges, he swung the tool chest under his arm, appreciating its heft and his uncle's struggle.

"The priest, I'm givin' him a little help with the plumbing," Uncle Davey said, as if reading the questions on Dorsey's face. "Saves him some money, and I up my chances for heaven. Besides, retired guys have to fill their time. C'mon over the house for a little while."

"Sure," Dorsey said, following his uncle. "I've some time on my hands."

The house was opposite the church on Carnegie, three doors down from where he had left the Buick. Freestanding, but with strings of row houses to either side, it had the distinctions of the street's original homes. Instead of a two-step entrance, the house had a wide front porch enclosed by four feet of brick wall. An arched picture window, in three sections with dark wood dividers, dominated the front wall. Once on the porch, his uncle took the tool chest and gestured Dorsey into one of two folding chairs, then opened the metal screen door and went inside. Dorsey settled in and propped his feet atop the wall.

"Been one hell of a long time," Uncle Davey said, returning to the porch, letting the screen door bang shut behind him. He handed Dorsey a glass of iced tea and sat across from him. "So, just flyin' through the old neighborhood on your way somewheres else? Or maybe you've just been dying to see your uncle again?" Uncle Davey waved off any attempt at an answer. "Either way, it's good to see you."

Dorsey sipped at his tea and watched his uncle's eyes dance. *Clear blue,* he thought, *the same ones you've seen in those old photos of your mother. The Sullivan eyes.* The eyebrows were the same mix of white and rust as his hair, and Dorsey wondered if, had she lived, his mother would have looked the same.

"To be straight with you," Dorsey told his uncle, "I'm working on something local. And, well, anyways, it got me thinking about how I never seem to be around. So, thought I'd just drop by and take a look at the church, see the house. Didn't expect you to be around, but I'm glad it worked out this way."

"Me, too," his uncle said. "I'm glad, too. And that other stuff, the not-being-around-much business, forget it. That was your father's doing. He never was much for our side of the family, especially after your mom passed on. How's he doin'? Your father, I mean. Seen in the paper where he was sick."

"Doing better." Dorsey sipped at his tea. "His speech came all the way back, but the left side is still pretty weak. The neurologist, he wants him in extended care a little while longer, maybe a week or two; then he goes home. I suppose the therapists can come to him after that."

Uncle Davey's gaze wandered out to the street, and he seemed to study a solitary blossoming tree planted at the curb. "That's good. Everybody deserves good health. Even him." He turned to Dorsey and gripped his shoulder. "Sorry. It's got nothing to do with you. Old business just dies slow sometimes. Christ, him and that snooty bitch, that Boyle woman."

"Ironbox?" Dorsey asked.

"What do you call her?" Uncle Davey laughed and again

19

checked the church walls to see if the irreverence had left an impression in the brick. "Yeah, that's good. Fits." He laughed again and wiped at the corners of his eyes. "Anyways, the hell with them for now. You say you're on local business, anything you can tell your old uncle? Strictly between us?"

Dorsey worked on his tea and recounted his meeting with Mrs. Leneski. Uncle Davey told him that he had seen the handbills and recalled how pretty the girl was.

"That's down in the ninth ward," his uncle said, and Dorsey could see the perceived distance in his face. *As if it were a foreign land,* he thought. *As if you needed a stamped visa to cross Forty-ninth Street.* "If she's mixed up with that park crowd," Uncle Davey said, "heaven help her. And you, too. If it's the dope, she's lost for good."

Dorsey finished his tea, gave his uncle the empty glass, and began his farewells. "There's a few people I need to see," he said.

"So stop by once in a while, okay?"

"I'll be around." Dorsey gave his uncle a parting smile. "Especially now that I know I'm welcome. You being such a staunch Catholic, thought you might not be too happy with me. After what's happened the last year or so."

"The business with you and the priest?" Uncle Davey pointed across the street. "For me *that's* the Church—the parish I was born into and where I drop off my weekly envelope and where I help out the priest when I can. The bishop and his crowd, they're Downtown people. Don't mean nothin'."

4

The kitchen was the same one Dorsey had seen in a thousand working-class homes, on a thousand interviews: Formica-topped table with chrome legs and matching chairs. Over the bare sink, four steel hanging cabinets, spray painted white. In the corner, a standing metal pantry, also painted white, but still reminding Dorsey of a school locker. Mrs. Leneski took the coffeepot from the front burner of her white porcelain gas stove, pulled a hot pad from the pantry, and placed them on the table. From the refrigerator, white, she took a half-gallon of milk. The sugar bowl was already on the table.

"Pretty hefty envelope Ziggy dropped off this morning," Dorsey said. Sitting at the table, facing the open back door, he could see the sparse spring grass in the long fenced-in yard that reminded him of his own. For a moment he thought about putting in a garden that year. The moment passed quickly. "It's more than is necessary, even if it's the original reward money."

Mrs. Leneski, again wearing a housedress, poured coffee for them both and sat. "It won't break me, if that's your worry. Worked all my life, except for the three years I was with my George.

Worked at Kress Box, down on Smallman Street, pushing cardboard along conveyor belts. For thirty years. I got plenty."

Yeah, Dorsey thought, *maybe even the first buck you ever made. Stitched onto the bottom of your mattress.* "George, he was your husband?"

"My George," Mrs. Leneski said, mixing a generous dose of milk and sugar into her coffee. "He worked at Kress Box, too. We married during the war, 1943. He was a little older by then, we both was, so he didn't have to go into the service. Three years after we was married we had Catherine. And then George drops over dead coming home from work. Just down the block from here, he drops over dead. People used to do that."

"Then you went back to work?"

"Kress took me back," Mrs. Leneski said. "Pretty nice of them to do it. Didn't have to. My mother looked after Catherine, so did my brothers and sisters, and so did Ziggy. He was just a boy, but my sister would send him over after school."

"So," Dorsey said, "no second thoughts on the money? Sure about it?"

Mrs. Leneski fit her cup into the saucer and placed her hands, palms down, on the tabletop. "I want Maritsa back and you gotta work on it. So you gotta get paid. I want you to work hard, so this is what I pay. You like to get paid?"

Dorsey grinned and nodded his agreement. "Very much," he said. "Money's one of my favorites."

"Good." Mrs. Leneski took hold of her cup. "So, you got some kind of plan?"

Dorsey moved his cup of coffee aside, thinking it was strong enough to clean the tap lines at Al's place, and fished a pen and memo pad from the pocket of his jacket. "I need a few things from you. Like the names of Maritsa's girlfriends. And of any boyfriends."

"No boyfriends."

"This may seem out of line," Dorsey said, "but I've had a look

22

at the girl's picture. If she didn't have a boyfriend, it wasn't because the boys were rejecting her."

"After I seen what happened to her mother," Mrs. Leneski said, "I don't let any boys in the house when they come after her. Tried to keep her a good girl."

"Okay with me," Dorsey said, both palms out to deflect her anger. "Just give me the names of the girls. And I'll need a letter from you—a note, really—to introduce me to the principal at the high school."

"Sister Bede? Why her?"

"Never can tell," Dorsey said, pushing the pen and pad across the tabletop. "She might have something worthwhile to say. She or one of the teachers. Never can tell."

"Some plan." Mrs. Leneski wrote as she spoke. Finished, she looked up at Dorsey, and from the steel in her eyes he knew she didn't care for the possibility that someone at the high school might know something about Maritsa that she did not. "What a plan," she said, "talking to some nun. Told you, the junkies got her."

"Could be," Dorsey said. "It's something to look at, and I plan on doing so. But first, after I leave here, I'm headed downtown to the Public Safety Building. There's still a cop or two there that'll give me the time of day, and one of them I think is still in Missing Persons. He might be of some help."

Mrs. Leneski lifted her coffee cup and pointed it at Dorsey. "Check out that park, check out those junkies. I still say they have her."

Detective Phil Strobec ground out a cigarette in his hubcap of an ashtray. A minute engine whirled in its center, vacuuming in the residue smoke. Bending forward, he exhaled a cloud at the ashtray, causing the engine to whine at a higher pitch. "I get caught smoking in this office, it'll be my ass," he said. "Anyway, we started out with the possibility that one of the girl's parents took her somewheres. You know, like maybe the grandmother did something to piss off one of them. Which is easy to believe with her having sole custody of the girl."

Strewn across the desk in Strobec's tiny cubicle of easily ignited fabric walls, were the photos and investigator's notes contained in Maritsa Durant's case file. Huddled next to Strobec, Dorsey fought for elbow room and fished through the interview reports. "Not much from the parents," he said.

"As I understand it, the mother has visitation rights, but she doesn't make much use of them." Strobec pushed back in his chair, shifting his considerable weight to get his cigarettes from his hip pocket. "And the father, he's not to see the kid at all."

"What's with the mother?" Dorsey asked, reshuffling the reports and photos and placing them in the file jacket. "She's supposed to be clean and sober these days."

Strobec lit another cigarette. "Catherine Durant, she's off street drugs, but she's far from being okay. I don't have the actual diagnosis, but there's some kind of psyche problem. Matter of fact, she was on the ward when I interviewed her, which sort of ruled her out as a kidnapper. Suicide attempt or gesture after the girl turned up missing. Didn't say a word worth recording."

"And the father? I saw where you talked to him, too."

"Once I found him." Strobec aimed a stream of smoke at the ashtray. "Bumped into him by accident, really, just cruising Butler Street. Still into dope and moves all over Lawrenceville. No address, but there's a few bars and apartments he shows his face in, once in a great while. I checked with Narcotics and there's nothing outstanding on him as far as wanteds go."

Dorsey asked if the father had anything to say.

"Says he hasn't seen the girl for years, just like the court ordered. Is he telling the truth? Shit, we're talking about a drug user who's been through the system God only knows how many times. This is a polished liar we're talking about here. Sets his mind to it, Durant could lie his way out of the electric chair. And he's one of those

24

nervous junkies, always scratching at something when you talk to him. His crotch especially. I had to warn him to be careful about scratching off his dick."

"Mrs. Leneski," Dorsey said, turning from Strobec to avoid a few wisps of errant smoke. "Mrs. Leneski, she's got a thing about this park at the bottom of Forty-sixth Street. Figures that the girl fell in with some dopers who hang out there. Maybe Teddy Durant is connected there?"

"Could be," Strobec said, "but let's see if the narc squad can help with that. They've got a thing about Lawrenceville just now."

Dorsey rode the elevator down to the next floor and followed a long corridor painted in whitewash to the far end of the building. Bordered in adhesive tape on the second to last door was a cardboard placard indicating the office of an unspecified Combined Task Force. To Dorsey, the term suggested a World War Two film complete with U.S. Navy destroyers picking off kamikaze pilots as they threatened our aircraft carriers. Inside were four metal desks, three empty, the fourth occupied by a dark-haired man about Dorsey's age. Dressed in jeans and a carpenter's work shirt, he had a telephone receiver cradled between his ear and shoulder.

"He's here, Phil. Just stepped in." The man took the receiver in hand, clearly wanting to hang up. "Sure, Phil, I heard of the guy and his old man. You say he's a friend, I'll see if I can help."

Without invitation, Dorsey slipped into a plastic scoop chair next to the detective's desk. "Heard of the family, huh? Anyways, Phil sent me to you. And he's a good man."

"It's not just who your old man is," the detective said. "I remember your name from that big hoopla you were in a while back. Didn't care much one way or the other about it. But yeah, Phil says you're all right. He also said you were interested in Lawrenceville and the park. Talk to me about it." The detective pulled out a desk drawer and planted his feet on the edge. "I'm Jimmy Labriola, in case you're interested. Been with this task force business for a few years now."

"Good to meet you, Jimmy." Dorsey told him about the missing girl, and Labriola nodded several times in the telling, as if taking mental notes, zeroing in on the meat of the tale.

"The old lady, she could have things half right," Labriola said. "Teenage girls do tend to float in and out of that park. The dopers up there, along with everyone else in that park, they got a hell of a line. They get these girls feeling sorry for them about how they're just some sort of nonconformists being harassed by the police. And these girls, they're easy pickings. A little dope and a lot of dick and before you know it they're part of the gang. But they float out eventually and surface somewhere. Although your girl has been out of sight for a while now."

Dorsey stretched his legs, working the kinks out of his knee, and slumped deeper into the chair. "So the old lady, she's right then, when she says there's dope in that park."

"She should be a narc," Labriola said. "Although you don't have to be one to figure out what's going on there. Along with the dope—and that could be smack, pot, or any pill that happens to be in fashion—there must be God only knows what in the way of stolen goods. Mostly little stuff—car radios, shit like that. But then again, who knows?"

"I've been by there," Dorsey said. "The lay of the land has to make it tough for a raid. Unless you gather up enough cops to surround Allegheny Cemetery. And that would take an infantry division."

Labriola went silent and Dorsey felt the air get heavy. *He wants to be asked,* Dorsey told himself. *He's got something to say, but he wants to be asked first, at least.* "Something else is happening, right," Dorsey asked. "So, what's the real problem?"

Labriola shifted his weight and dropped his feet to the floor. He made a slow production of closing the desk drawer, and Dorsey wondered if he was saying a reluctant good-bye to something inside.

"Ah, shit. Phil gives you the okay, so I guess it's all right." Labri-

26

ola's eyes met Dorsey's. "We're sort of taking a break from Lawrenceville. For a little while, you know?"

"How's that?"

"Not my idea," Labriola said. "And by the way, I know Durant, the little weasel. He's like a lot of guys up there. When they hit twenty-one, they partially graduate from the park to a couple of bars on Butler Street. If you plan on checking things out, try the bars first. More your age group."

"That's good to know," Dorsey said. "But c'mon, what's with this give-Lawrenceville-a-break stuff?"

"Know anything about a Dr. Novotny?" When Dorsey shook his head no, Labriola continued. "He's a GP with an office along Butler. Looks like a nice, fat old gentleman from the Old Country. The kind of guy you used to see in the summer when you were a kid, sitting on his front stoop, maybe gave you a piece of candy? Well, my friend, he's the pill connection for the boys in the park."

Dorsey laughed. "Old gramps has a sideline, huh?"

"Wrote so many prescriptions that he had the neighborhood pharmacists working overtime and tripling their Valium stock." Labriola shook his head. "Novotny's really something. Drug company reps, they load him up with free samples and he sells them to the neighborhood druggies. About eight months ago, we finally cracked him. Us and a couple of state narcs, we had him cold. A few of the druggies turned on him, and we had the lot numbers on the samples from the drug reps."

"So, what are you telling me?" Dorsey asked. "The old doc goes behind bars and it's time for you guys to move elsewhere?"

Labriola left his chair and went to the office window, his back to Dorsey. "Novotny isn't going anywhere," he said over his shoulder. "Except maybe to his office every morning."

"He got out from under?"

"Things got a little crazy around here." Labriola went back to his seat. "Some of the druggies—our testimony—disappeared. And the drug companies' records were lost. Two sets. One from our files—or the DA's files, depending on who you asked—and the drug companies set went south, too."

Dorsey shifted about, the rough edge of the plastic seat pinching his pant legs. "You're serious? Somebody at the companies helped fix this? Big drug companies gave that much of a shit about a neighborhood GP?"

"Oh no, shit no," Labriola said. "This isn't Eli Lilly we're talking about, just a couple of local distributors. One had a fire and just happened to be the only company in the western half of the state without fireproof cabinets for their hard copy records. The other was a guy who worked out of his house. He had a burglary, like we did, I guess."

"So Novotny walked."

"He walked," Labriola said. "He walked right into his attorney's office and filed for false arrest, defamation, and a whole lot of other shit. So, we look like hell—and feel like it, too. And when shit like that can happen in a neighborhood, it's time to move on for a while."

"So, not much you can do for me, right?" Dorsey asked. "Kind of on my own?"

Labriola took a sheet of paper from the desk's center drawer and dug a pen from his shirt pocket. "This I can do. Let me write down the names of a few bars along Butler and thereabouts. And the names of a few locals you might lean on, if you're the type. Can you do that?"

"It's not my first preference in handling a case," Dorsey said. "But then again, well, if I gotta, I gotta."

Labriola looked up from his writing. "Really think you can find this girl?"

Dorsey was motionless, his thoughts trailing back to one of his first cases as an independent. He was working for a local attorney whose case needed the support of a witness that Dorsey had been hired to find. And like any rookie, Dorsey had asked the attorney what he should do if he couldn't locate the witness. The attorney had simply grinned and said if Dorsey couldn't find the guy, just bring him a picture of the tombstone. Then he'd be satisfied. And Dorsey might just get paid.

"Yeah," Dorsey said to Labriola. "I think I can find her."

5

Spread across the desktop, the mail held little promise at first, just a few utility bills and a come-on to buy into a new resort community in the Allegheny Mountains. Listening to a tape of George Benson giving Bobby Darin a run for his money on "Somewhere Beyond the Sea," Dorsey continued picking through until he found an envelope from Blackwell Insurance. *Finally,* he thought, *thank God and just in time. Payment for the last few interviews, the only type of work they'll trust you with. But you gotta be careful,* he reminded himself. *When you have so few customers, you can't be pissing them off by sending overdue notices.*

The date and amount of the Blackwell check was entered into a ledger kept in the desk's center drawer, and Dorsey made out a deposit slip. The other mail was pushed into the drawer on top of the ledger, set aside for another and perhaps better time. Dorsey pulled back in his chair and sipped at his second Rolling Rock. Before reviewing the mail, he had checked his telephone answering machine and had heard two female voices. He couldn't decide if he loved the one as much as he hated the other.

"Carroll, I need you to take me to see your father," the older and much more authoritative voice had said in the message. "I've no other way of getting there, and you haven't been there but once. He'll be coming home in a week or so, according to the doctor, but you should still get over there. I'll be ready at six-fifteen."

"What a set of nuts on that woman," Dorsey had muttered, listening to the tape. Ironbox Boyle has spoken. No suggestion that you might call back to confirm or of the remotest possibility that you might have other plans. And after all that'd happened. What a set of nuts.

The second message had brought a different reaction.

"It's me. Sorry I didn't call back last weekend." Gretchen's voice had been hurried, and he had been sure she was calling from the hospital. "Things have been hectic, both here and at home. I forgot how big of a job moving into a new place can be. Anyway, sorry about last weekend. What I wanted to say was that I'm coming down to Pittsburgh on Saturday, day after tomorrow. There's a little get together for Dr. Riddle, some recognition award from this year's crop of residents. I thought we could go. Also, I was hoping to stay at your place. Call me so we can talk. Okay?"

Dorsey rubbed the beer bottle against his cheek, letting the chill slice through his jaw, looking for physical pain to ride roughshod on his emotions. It had been mutually arrived at, he reminded himself, like all proper and costly decisions. All the publicity with the priest and his lawsuit was sure to eventually find her doorstep. And what might it do to her medical career? Nothing good; that was the only conclusion they could reach. Better make some space, get a little distance, until this blew over. So they had packed up whatever clothes, books, and toiletries she had kept at his place and hauled them across town to her Bloomfield apartment. And then, possibly out of the blue, Dorsey had never been sure, the offer had come in from Franklin Hospital.

"It's only up the Interstate, north on seventy-nine," Gretchen had told him that evening. They had been in her apartment, sitting at the kitchen table with a half-eaten pizza between them. "The trauma chief says it's ninety minutes to two hours from here. Not far at all, when you think about it."

"Yeah, sure, I'm thinking about it," Dorsey had said. "I'm thinking that geographically we'll be a lot farther apart than we are now. Which is not what we planned when you cleaned out your closet at my place. I'm also thinking something else. You don't need this position, but you sure do want it. Am I right?"

"The trauma center is new," Gretchen had told him, lifting a slice of pizza and then, thinking better of it, dropping it onto the wax paper lining the bottom of the box. "State of the art, from what I can tell. And the title, Assistant Trauma Unit Chief, is something I couldn't hope to get here in the city. Not at this point in my career." She started again for the pizza, stopped, and leveled her eyes at Dorsey. "Yes, you're right. This is a job I want."

"So, take it." Dorsey ran his hands along either side of his jaw line. "Ah, shit, I don't know. Let's see what works out."

"Is that all?"

"No," Dorsey had said. "The other part is to try like hell to see that something does work out."

He finished off his Rolling Rock and headed back along the hallway to the kitchen, washed out the empty bottle and dropped it into a blue plastic garbage pail for recyclables. Looking out the screen door at his back yard, so much like Mrs. Leneski's, he considered having another beer and telling Ironbox to take the bus. He decided against both. There's no defeating the power of a sick relative, he told himself. No matter how estranged he is, and how much you just might hate him.

This last year and a half hadn't done her any good, Dorsey concluded, watching Irene Boyle from the corner of his eye as he drove. His contact with her over that time period had been minimal and, to Dorsey, her aging had been dramatic. He was sure that the bend in her back and the liver spots on her hands and forehead were newly acquired. *It's been a bad time for everybody,* he reminded himself. *Even for a fool like you.*

They were headed northward on Allegheny River Boulevard, hugging the riverbank and moving away from the city. The stretch they were passing through was lined on either side by tall trees that bent inward to form a canopy above the Buick, dappling the early-evening sunlight across the windshield. Mrs. Boyle asked if Dorsey had ever traveled in Italy, perhaps while he was in the army.

"Never left the fifty states," Dorsey said. "Thought you knew that. It was my father's doing. And he does so little without your help."

"Don't start up again." Mrs. Boyle wiped a handkerchief at the tip of her nose and looked out the passenger window. "Your father had the best of intentions when he made those arrangements. I only ask about Italy to make conversation. This bit of road, with the trees and river and all, it reminds me of a road that runs along the Arno, just as you come into Pisa."

"You've been to Europe?" Dorsey asked, halting at a stop sign. Just past the stop sign he turned left, traveled a few yards down an access road, and pulled into a parking lot. "Italy you say? Never knew you to take a vacation in your life."

Mrs. Boyle checked her appearance in the rearview mirror and gathered her purse to her side. "Just the one time. In the '50s, maybe 1960. I forget who the president was at the time. Went alone, as a matter of fact. Italy, Greece, and a little bit of southern France. I suppose the one trip was enough."

Dorsey got out of the car and made for the passenger door, but Mrs. Boyle stepped out before he could offer his assistance. He figured the hell with it, remembering he didn't like the woman in the first place. He trailed a few steps behind her, crossing the gravel lot toward a one-story building that overlooked the river. To Dorsey, the Ryder Extended Care Center had the institutional look of a public school retooled for a student body of advanced age.

"No thank you, miss," Mrs. Boyle said, dismissing the receptionist's offer of help and turning to Dorsey. "I, for one, have been here several times before."

Dorsey smiled an embarrassed apology at the receptionist, then caught up with Mrs. Boyle at the entrance to Room 127. She cautioned him to be quiet, and led the way in.

Martin Dorsey was asleep in his hospital bed. In place of the customary gown, he was dressed in royal-blue pajamas, and a matching robe was folded at the foot of the bed. Mounted above his head were several exercise pulleys; the nurse's call button was pinned to his pillow. The curtains were drawn against the light, and it was a moment or so before Dorsey spotted the tripod cane standing at the far side of the bed.

What had happened to him, the way it had happened, must have been a terrible embarrassment, Dorsey was sure. Martin Dorsey, grand old man of Pittsburgh politics, had been halfway through an after-dinner speech when his words began to garble. For the first few moments, Dorsey had been told, his father had appeared bewildered, listening to his own words as they drooled out from the only corner of his mouth still working. He had remained at the podium, his expression turning shamefaced, until his left leg buckled and he dropped from sight.

"I hated that hospital, all those monitors." Mrs. Boyle held her voice to a whisper, leaning into Dorsey's shoulder. "I hated those things. Always made me feel like he was at death's door." She moved to the bed and gently nudged Martin Dorsey's shoulder. "Mr. Dorsey? It's Irene."

Dorsey's father awoke slowly, smiling at Mrs. Boyle and softly taking her hand. They exchanged some hushed words before he looked past her and acknowledged his son with a nod. *The imperial nod,* Dorsey thought, *the formal granting of an audience. Now you can approach the altar.*

"Carroll drove me here," Mrs. Boyle said. "I thought it was good of him. Once I had asked."

34

"Pleasant drive?" Martin Dorsey asked. His voice was weak and there was the slightest trace of a lisp at the mouth's left corner. But the eyes, Dorsey saw, those eyes still held command. He could still pull in a hundred thousand votes. From a sickbed.

"Nice evening," Dorsey said. "On the way up here we talked over Mrs. Boyle's world travels."

"Pardon me?" In a jerky motion, Martin Dorsey turned to Mrs. Boyle. "You've been where?"

"Oh, nothing," she said. "Just some idle talk about that trip I took way back when. The road up here reminded me of a favorite part of Italy."

His father rested on his pillow for a moment, and Dorsey wondered if he was having trouble processing Mrs. Boyle's comments or remembering the trip. The doctor had mentioned the possibility of memory lapses.

"You're working, I hope?" Martin Dorsey asked his son. Gripping the mattress with his right hand, he pulled himself into a sitting position. "You've had a dry spell. And debts, I assume."

"You do more than just assume. Always have." Dorsey moved from the door and took a chair near the bed. "A few things have been coming my way. There's a job I'm working down in Lawrenceville right now. Looks like a good one. A money maker."

"Should you need any help down there, let me know," Martin Dorsey said. "I have friends."

"Yes," Mrs. Boyle said. "Your father always had a lot of support in that neighborhood. And he did a lot of things, favors, for people there. If you need help, ask."

Dorsey slowly shook his head at his father then turned and did the same to Mrs. Boyle. *Oh, no,* he thought. *That's how it started last time.*

"I can only offer." Martin Dorsey shrugged a shoulder.

"Please don't," Dorsey said holding his father's eyes with his own. A moment passed between them, filled with the disappointments of a son and the betrayal by a father eighteen months past, until his father turned to Mrs. Boyle, asking if anyone had been in contact since her last visit.

"Only Judge Nixdorf and that black state senator." Mrs. Boyle consulted a list she had taken from her purse. "The usual messages. Hope you feel better soon and that they're thinking of you. The state senator, he had one of his aides make the call. I thought you'd want to know that."

"He needs to appear respectful," Martin Dorsey said, "but at a distance. Can't look like he's paying homage to an old white man, even if he needs me. Understandable." He held his thoughts for a moment, then spoke to his son. "This business in Lawrenceville, is it an insurance matter?"

"Missing person," Dorsey said. "Seventeen-year-old girl. Pretty little thing. No one's seen anything of her in a couple of months."

"Such a shame," Mrs. Boyle said. "A child just disappearing. Things happen so easily in some parts of town. Like in that Lawrenceville."

"I don't recall any unusual happenings in that part of town," Martin Dorsey said. He seemed to study Mrs. Boyle's face. "I don't see the connection you're trying to make."

Dorsey didn't see it either.

6

St. Ambrose High School sat at Butler and Thirty-seventh Streets, an area trying to complete a partial conversion from Catholic white to Baptist black. Dorsey figured that like most fleeing whites, the St. Ambrose parishioners wished they could just lift the school from its foundation and cart it along with them to the far side of the Allegheny. *You can pack up your bags,* he thought, *but not your lives.*

He left the Buick at the curb on Butler, opposite the school, in front of a building that housed a small appliance repair shop. Next to the storefront was a doorway that, Dorsey expected, led to upstairs apartments. An older black man edged open the door and asked Dorsey if he cared to visit the girls upstairs.

Holy shit! Dorsey thought, laughing. "No thanks, man. I've got business across the street. At the school."

"Ya'll's choice," the black man said, closing the door. "But dem girls over there ain't got the 'sperience what they's got upstairs."

Don't bet on it, Dorsey thought, recalling his own Catholic-school days. *Just don't bet on it.*

The school consisted of two long floors of yellow brick and sash windows, and as Dorsey made his way through the main entrance, he spotted a dedication placard dated 1956. A sign for the principal's office led him along a corridor lined with bulletin boards and religious icons. Next to the office door was a statue of the Blessed Virgin, a green serpent withering beneath her foot. He fenced with the school secretary across the office counter, a short woman who appeared to be in her midfifties, until she finally admitted that the principal wasn't really all that busy and actually could take the time to talk to him.

"You say that you're some sort of detective?" The principal, who introduced herself as Sister Bertram, didn't rise to meet him but instead waved Dorsey into a chair before her desk. *Jesus Christ,* he thought. *Unbelievable. This woman hasn't updated her habit for years. A cardboard forehead—you haven't seen one of those since eighth grade.*

Nothing of Vatican II showed in the nun's appearance. And as far as Dorsey was concerned, she was a throwback to the Catholic Dark Ages—about the time the school was founded. Her veil was secured by a cowl of black cloth, and white cardboard framed her face at the chin and just above the eyebrows. Her eyeglasses were what Dorsey considered to be standard nun issue: perfectly rounded lenses held together with steel wire. *You frisk this woman,* he told himself, *and I bet you'll find Kleenex, a metal-edged ruler, and a pitch pipe stuffed up her sleeves.*

"Yes," Dorsey told her. "That's right, Sister. I've been retained to look into Maritsa Durant's disappearance." He passed her an envelope containing Mrs. Leneski's letter of introduction.

Sister Bertram read the letter slowly, so much so that Dorsey wondered if she were silently correcting the grammar. She folded the letter, returning it to the envelope before speaking.

"Well, the girls will love speaking to you." The nun clasped her hands on the desktop. "Oh, don't let it go to your head. I'm just suggesting that on a Friday these girls will welcome any break from class. Although I can't say that I like it, disrupting class schedules. No, I don't care for that at all."

"It's sort of important," Dorsey said, already tired of the old fuss-budget. "Could be one of them knows something. Something that might help."

"The police have already spoken to the three girls mentioned in the note." Sister Bertram held her breath for a moment, then sighed. "I suppose we could arrange a talk with each of them. But I'll have to be present. As if I had the time."

"Any way you want to work this," Dorsey said.

"I'll be present. It'll be better that way. I'm the guidance counselor, too, you know."

What a surprise, Dorsey thought, *she's the guidance counselor. Tough job. Smart girls go to college and dumb ones go to typing. Have to wonder how many girls she's sent over the edge and up to that second floor apartment across Butler?*

The first two girls had little to say, and their giggling led Dorsey to cut the interviews short. The nun was right. It was Friday, and Friday called for a diversion. The third girl, very slight and with strawberry-blond hair, was different.

"I guess; I don't know. Maybe I shouldn't say anything." The girl sat in a metal classroom chair with an attached desktop; Dorsey and Sister Bertram had squeezed into similar chairs on either side of her. She was dressed in a school uniform of blue blouse, pleated plaid skirt, and knee socks. *You used to love that combination,* Dorsey reminded himself. *Twenty-some years ago.*

"You just tell us what you have to say," Sister Bertram said sternly.

Thanks for all the help, Dorsey thought. *Let's just put her at ease and see what she has to say.*

"I just think you need to talk to Janie Neiman," the girl said. "The police didn't bother. Janie used to ride home sometimes with Maritsa."

"They took a bus?" Dorsey asked. The school was less than nine blocks from her home, and he couldn't believe that Mrs. hard-as-

39

nails Leneski would come up with carfare for a commute of less than five miles.

"No, not the bus," the girl told them. "There was some guy in a car. Last winter, he used to ride them home sometimes."

The plain ones latch on to the pretty ones, Dorsey thought as Janie Neiman entered the classroom. Carrying a bit of extra weight, she had dull brown hair, eye glasses, and a hostile attitude. Her major concern seemed to be making sure Dorsey was not with the police.

"You've been told twice already!" Sister Bertram slapped at the desktop. "This man is *not* with the police. And regardless of whether he is or not, you had better just tell us who this fellow was, giving those after-school rides!"

Janie held the nun's gaze, then turned on Dorsey, impressing him with her defiance. *This one's okay,* he thought.

"Maritsa," the girl said, "she made me promise not to tell anybody about the rides. So I kept it to myself."

Sister Bertram struggled out of the desk, her face filling with blood. "Kept it to yourself! What do you think this is?" She went into a windup and swung at Janie who blocked her with a leisurely, almost contempt-ridden, forearm. Sister Bertram fumed and turned to Dorsey.

Great, he told himself, *and you thought you had lousy partners at the DA's office.* He pulled his seat a little closer to Janie and waved off the nun. Janie spoke before he had the chance.

"Maritsa's still my friend, whatever's happened to her." Her voice maintained a steady tone, as if the physical attack had never happened. "The rides were supposed to stay a secret."

"A secret from adults, right?" *The hell with it,* Dorsey thought, *let's get on her level.* "Well, the secret's out now, like it or not. So cut the shit; I've gotta know about these rides. Your friend may be dead and cold already, or maybe she's just on her way to that happy state. If it's the latter, you might still be of help. If she's dead, then she'll never be pissed off at you for breaking a promise."

Janie leveled a thin smile at him, and Dorsey felt he had sparked a connection. *Christ, this girl is damned scary.*

"Who's the guy?" he asked. "Some boyfriend she wanted to hide from her grandmother?"

"It wasn't some guy," Janie said. "It was her dad."

Dorsey couldn't remember how many years it had been since his last trip to the psychiatric wing of St. Francis Hospital, but he recalled the visit's purpose. He had still been with the DA's office at the time, and his then partner wanted to interview a patient about a string of convenience-store hold-ups in the north end of the county. The patient was a twenty-two-year-old shrimp of a fellow, calm and reserved, who confessed to the robberies. He also confessed his involvement with the Watergate burglary, which he explained was a crime he had committed in an earlier life, during which he was a registered Republican. This time Dorsey hoped to keep politics out of the discussion.

Leaving the Buick on a neighborhood street zoned for resident parking only, he crossed Forty-fifth Street and entered the hospital's East Wing. A security guard at the front desk checked his identity, took the patient's name, and made several phone calls. A few moments passed before a blond woman in her midthirties came down the hallway beyond the security desk and introduced herself as Peg Malloy.

"I'm the psychiatric social worker assigned to Catherine," Miss Malloy said. Dorsey compared her appearance to the photo ID card pinned to her blouse and decided he liked the real thing better. She was medium height, not overweight and not slim, and her blond hair was done in a short, over-thirty cut. The healthy farm girl with a master's degree and a business wardrobe, he concluded.

She asked that he follow her and led him past the security desk

41

and along the corridor from which she had come. The walls were painted a dull yellow, which Dorsey took as the latest therapeutically neutral shade for psyche wards. "This is a good time to see Catherine," Miss Malloy told him. "She's really stabilized now. A week or two back, I think you would have been denied access." At the end of the hall they turned right, passed three doors, then stopped while the social worker unlocked the fourth, ushering Dorsey inside to her office.

"What's her condition?" Dorsey asked. "The diagnosis, I mean." The office was small, made cramped by a desk and two guest chairs. The walls were the same pale yellow but were almost completely covered over by posted announcements, schedules, and charts. Dorsey took a seat while Miss Malloy rounded the desk.

"Confidential information," she said, settling into her seat. "When you called, you said the interview was to be about her missing daughter. Sorry, but the conversation should be confined to the daughter, not the patient."

"It might help."

"Sorry," Miss Malloy said, "some things can't be discussed."

Dorsey shrugged it off. "One other thing, though, that might not be confidential. Her husband—or ex-husband, whatever—has he been around to visit lately?"

"Not that I'm aware of." Miss Malloy paged through several documents on her desk. "Matter of fact, the only time Teddy Durant's name ever came up was in my initial interview with Catherine. She said that her contact with him is almost nonexistent. Which is probably the best thing for her."

But not for me, Dorsey thought. *You've got to find him,* he told himself again. *Because he may lead you to Maritsa.* Durant was taking a hell of a chance hanging around that school. Not with the law. With Mrs. Leneski.

There was a soft knock at the door, and before Miss Malloy could respond, the door was opened by a male orderly. "Catherine's with me," he said. "You two ready?"

"Please, Catherine. Come in," Miss Malloy said, and the orderly stepped aside. In the woman who entered, Dorsey saw all of Maritsa's fine good looks at a later age. Her hair was almost black and very thick, with eyebrows and lashes to match. But something was missing, and he decided it had to be the sense of good health. The eyes themselves were vacant, and the jeans she wore were baggy and gaped at the waist, suggesting a severe weight loss. Dorsey figured she had been denied a belt for her own safety.

Catherine took the seat next to Dorsey, and Miss Malloy introduced the two. "Mr. Dorsey has been sent by your mother. He's trying to locate Maritsa." Catherine began to speak, but Miss Malloy continued. "Catherine, you've been doing well lately. But I don't have to remind you that your daughter's disappearance helped to necessitate your being here at St. Francis. If this gets too stressful, let me know and we can end the conversation."

"Please, it's okay," Catherine said. She seemed focused on the meeting, but to Dorsey her voice had a drowsy, distant quality to it. *The medication list,* Dorsey thought, *that must be confidential, too.* He cautioned himself to consider the drugs as he listened to her.

"Catherine, I've taken this job with the hope of finishing it." Dorsey spoke slowly. "You've got a beautiful girl; looks a lot like you from the pictures I've seen. Your mother is the one who hired me, and, as I understand it, things aren't the best between you two. But believe me, I plan on helping."

"My little girl," Catherine said. "I'd really like her to be safe."

"Talk to me about her, just a little bit." Dorsey shifted in his seat, settling his weight against the armrest nearest Catherine. "You used to visit her once in a while, right?"

"Every couple of weeks. At my mother's place, mostly. Otherwise, maybe we'd meet at a pizza shop, one of the ones on Penn Avenue. Maritsa loved anchovies. They're so salty, and, uh, slimy I guess. Lord knows where she learned to like them."

"How about the last time you saw her?"

Catherine's face showed the effort of thinking through her drug haze, and Dorsey again speculated about her medications. "Lemme see," she said, pushing her hair from her temples. "It was at my mother's for dinner. We had a roast."

Dorsey shot a look at Peg Malloy who returned it with a shrug. "How was Maritsa that night?" he asked. "How long was that before she disappeared?"

"A day or two. Maybe three." A tear formed at the corner of Catherine's eye. She made no attempt to wipe it away. "She seemed fine. This has been real tough, ya know? Her bein' gone and all?"

"Catherine, this is square business," Dorsey said. "I seriously doubt I could even imagine how you must feel." Peg Malloy handed him a box of Kleenex. Dorsey offered a tissue to Catherine, who failed to take it, so he went ahead and dabbed at her eyes and the edge of her nose. She responded with neither thanks nor resistance, and Dorsey again wondered at the value of her comments. *But she's the mother,* Dorsey told himself, *and the rules of the game say that you talk to the next to kin. So push on, my friend, push on.*

"Miss Malloy and I," he said, returning the Kleenex box to the desktop, "we spoke very briefly before you came in. One of the questions I had was about Teddy. She said he hasn't been here to visit."

"No, no," Catherine said. "He hasn't been around. Hard to say when I saw him last."

"Those last few times you saw Maritsa, did she talk about her father?"

Again, her face showed the strain of her response. "Teddy's not allowed to see her, but she remembers him from before my mother took her. But she always asked about him. But not so much lately, come to think of it. Not the last few times we talked."

Why should she? Dorsey asked himself. *Why ask a question when you already have the information?* "I'd like to talk to Teddy. Any ideas about where I can find him?"

"Sort of," she said. "Not where he lives, 'cause he moves around a lot. But there's some places on Butler Street you can try."

Labriola's list, Dorsey thought. "There's something else," he said. "When I first spoke with your mother, she was afraid that Maritsa had fallen in with some people. The ones who hang out in the park on Forty-sixth. Your mother thinks she might have run off with someone from there. Any chance of it being true?"

"It's me all over again," Catherine said and again she started to cry. This time she took the tissue that Dorsey handed her. "That's what she thinks. It could be true, I suppose. Happens sometimes. Hope not, though." Catherine focused on Peg Malloy. "Is it true? Is it me all over again?"

"Catherine, please," Miss Malloy said. "You and your daughter, you have to think in terms of two distinct individuals. Even if there's some similarity, there's no evidence to suggest that you are responsible for the disappearance. Please keep that in mind." She swiveled in her chair to face Dorsey. "What do you think? Let's try to bring this to a close, okay?"

Dorsey shrugged and addressed Catherine. "It's a lead I have to follow, this business with the park. But I'm pretty old to go poking around down there and not be suspect. Does anyone come to mind, someone who could help me check this out?"

Catherine smiled. "Outlaw could."

"Outlaw?" Dorsey turned to Peg Malloy for help. She shrugged and motioned for Catherine to continue.

"Sure," Catherine went on, still smiling. "Outlaw. Jeez, he was the park's mayor. The mayor of Butler Street, they used to call him. He'd know what was going on. And I bet he would help find my girl."

Peg Malloy telephoned for the orderly, who arrived within a few minutes. After a tearful plea to help find her girl, Catherine thanked Dorsey and left with her escort.

"This is for real?" Dorsey asked, resettling into his chair. "There's a guy running around this neighborhood calling himself Outlaw?"

"She's not delusional," Peg Malloy said. "Not now. And her blood work shows her medication to be at a therapeutic level."

"Just seems a little dramatic, don't you think? She isn't embellishing a bit?"

"Possibly some exaggeration," Miss Malloy said. "Seems unlikely, though, considering how she's been lately."

Okay, Dorsey thought, *now there's two guys to find. Teddy and the Outlaw. There's a song in that somewhere.* "Well," he said, "Friday night on Butler Street awaits me. Any chance you'd like to come along?"

Peg Malloy smiled and toyed with a paper clip. "I'll pass, but stay in touch and let me know how it turns out. And if you find this Outlaw, send him around for an evaluation. Sounds like an interesting case study."

7

Just before eight that evening, Dorsey entered Al's Bar and was surprised to find Henry still manning the taps. Crossing the room, he checked his appearance in the bar's back mirror. Stained painter's pants, a worn maroon T-shirt, and work boots. *Just another laborer,* he thought, *through for the week and out for a Friday. Hope it passes muster on Butler Street.* Taking a bar stool close to the taps, Dorsey asked for a Rolling Rock.

"Only got the little ones, the seven ouncers," Henry said. "That okay with you? It's all the distributor had."

"It'll do," Dorsey said, then asked for Al.

"Supposed to cover for him till about nine-thirty." Henry set the beer and a short glass on the bar. Dorsey pushed a dollar toward him, and Henry sent it back with the heel of his palm.

"On me," he said and returned to washing glasses. "Wasn't my intention to knock you out of a job. When I got back in town, I figured my job would be waiting on me, like always. Maybe I stayed away a little longer than I realized."

"Oh, just long enough," Dorsey said. He poured his beer and recalled what Al had said about Henry's timing. *He shows up and so does Mrs. Leneski's cash envelope. Maybe he brings you luck,* Dorsey told himself. *That's if you believe in that kind of shit.*

"Sounds like you're still a little pissed about the situation." Henry dried a glass with a thinning dishtowel and racked it beneath the bar. "Way I heard it from Al, you're too busy for this job anyway."

"Temporarily," Dorsey said, sipping at his beer. He set down his glass and shrugged. "Nah, I'm not pissed, not anymore. Just getting used to the change. This was my bread and butter the last year and a half. Saved my house with this job. For a while, before it looked like I could keep the house, I was planning on moving into the upstairs apartment here. But it never came to that. You know, Russie's old place?"

Henry went to the far end of the bar, checked on some customers there, and returned to the taps. "Oh, I know the place all right," he said, drawing a large Iron City draft. "I'm up there now. Kinda nice. Looks out over the street and the basketball court. Used to have some good games there in the summer time. Played some, didn't you? At least that's what Al says."

"Some," Dorsey said, watching Henry take the beer to one of the customers at the end of the bar. "Sounds like you kind of like the game," he called after him.

Henry rang up the sale and turned back to Dorsey. "Like it real well. Especially this time of year, NBA finals. First game's tomorrow afternoon. I like Boston. Looked a little weak against Detroit, but they can take L.A. With some trouble."

"You know something," Dorsey said, smiling, "you are definitely not what I was led to expect. Being hot for basketball doesn't fit well with the picture Al paints of you."

"Surprising, huh?" Henry returned the smile.

"Yeah, it certainly is," Dorsey said. "You're my first counterculture hoops freak."

Henry put his hands to the small of his back and stretched up through his shoulders. "There's a couple of sides to most people, I find. I dig the game, but I just might roll a joint at halftime."

"Up there?" Dorsey gestured to the ceiling and the apartment beyond. "Under Al's roof?"

"It can happen." Henry looked over the group at the end of the bar. "Just calls for a little discretion. Maybe you want to stop by some time?"

"Not for smoke." Dorsey finished his beer. "But maybe for one of the play-off games. Have my doubts about Boston this year, despite past miracles. But it'd be nice to watch with someone who appreciates the game."

"Tomorrow's good for me."

"Not for me." Dorsey pushed back on the bar stool and started for the door. "I've got a houseguest for the weekend. Kind of important."

On the crosstown drive to Lawrenceville, Dorsey's mind wandered back to thoughts of his houseguest. Gretchen was due late the next morning. The award dinner was scheduled for the evening, but the afternoon was free, and Dorsey saw it as a chance to find some balance, to see where things stood for the present and the foreseeable future. *As if any of the future is foreseeable,* he told himself. His pact with life, for the protection of his sanity, was for the here and now. You took what came your way and tried to mold it into a shape that suited you best. *Gretchen,* he thought, *we'll be together while we're together. Let's hope that's a long time.*

As for Outlaw, he had only a physical description. "Big sumbitch," Labriola had told him in a brief telephone conversation that afternoon. "A little taller than you, maybe, but he's got these forearms like tree trunks. Kind of a gut growing on him, but not much. Lemme see, his hair is long and usually in a ponytail."

"Anything in the way of an arrest record?" Dorsey had asked.

"Not much, as I recall. Juvie stuff. We never had him on any-

49

thing, but there was kind of a difference of opinion about him among the task force members. He never impressed me as anything too important. More like a local guru than a dealer, from where I stand."

Dorsey dropped below Butler on Forty-third Street and pulled the Buick to the curb. The failing sunlight sent long shadows across the row house fronts, partially obscuring Dorsey's view as he checked the doorways and front steps. In front of what seemed to be every other house, elderly couples sat on folding lawn chairs, curing a winter's worth of cabin fever. The women wore sleeveless housedresses, and the men were dressed in white T-shirts and work pants. From hand-held transistor radios came the voices of announcers calling the Pirates game. Dorsey knew that just a block away Mrs. Leneski was taking the evening air in the same manner. And just like these folks, she could spot a stranger and his car six blocks away. *Let's hope,* he thought as he climbed out of the car, *that this trait hasn't been passed on to the next generation or two.*

Up on Butler, Dorsey went left and passed a pizza shop and two variety stores before entering Budnar's Bar. The room itself was standard: long and thin with the bar and booths on opposite sides of a center aisle. The booths were empty but Dorsey had to search awhile to find an available barstool, finally settling for one next to the men's room door. Thinking he would complete his disguise, he flagged down the bartender and ordered an Iron City draft.

The bartender, like his patrons, was in his late twenties, maybe thirty at best, Dorsey figured, with the look of a displaced day laborer. His back muscles strained his Penguins T-shirt, and his dark hair was slicked back from his forehead, giving Dorsey the impression that he was waiting out his latest layoff from wherever. A little bartending, take a few numbers, and you've got a nice supplement to the biweekly unemployment check.

A jukebox planted near the entrance kicked out one rock tune after another, each of them lost on Dorsey who longed for something by Ellington or Basie. Huddled over his beer, elbows pinned to the crowded bar, he tried his best to pick away at the conversations that whirled about him. Talk of home repairs, bosses who didn't know jackshit about getting the job done, and local ball clubs that didn't stand a chance in hell and let me tell you why. A few paces down the bar, the bartender listened to a guy in a Pirates cap tell why he should have sued.

"My mom," the guy said, "she's the same way—like all them old bashas. 'Don't start no trouble,' that's what they all say, as if they was words to fuckin' live by. She don't know what's goin' on with her, doesn't even fuckin' know how long she's got. But 'don't start no trouble.' For Chrissakes!"

The bartender refilled the guy's beer and poured a shot of Imperial. While the bartender made change, Dorsey watched the guy in the cap sip off the head of his beer and then dump in the whiskey. Dorsey winced at the ruination of an innocent brew.

"She has this pain," the guy said as the bartender took up his position with one foot propped on a beer cooler. "This pain and a lump, ya know, on her tit. He looks at her in the office, some kind of an examination, and tells her not to worry. Just some calcium or some such shit. She went back a couple of times 'cause it was really hurting, and he tells her the same thing. So anyways, it gets to be too much, so she goes up to St. Francis, the emergency room. That was three weeks ago. Now these doctors are calling it cancer, spread to the bone. But my mom, even after she's been fucked over like this, she says the same thing. 'Don't start no trouble.' "

"Who's this doctor again?" the bartender asked.

"Fuckin' quack just down the street." The guy in the cap sipped at his beer. "Novotny. From the Old Country. One of the old countries, anyway."

Dorsey studied his reflection in the liquor bottles standing on the back bar. *This Novotny,* he thought, *must be some piece of work. Too busy with the pharmaceutical trade to pick out one breast lump and schedule a mammogram. And he slides on that one, too. Because his patient load consists of first generation Poles, Slovaks, Czechs, and Croa-*

51

tians who carry the outlooks and attitudes of their peasant origins. "The doctor's a brilliant man, too smart for us to grapple with. Don't start trouble." And if a guy did start trouble, maybe sued, what difference would it make? If Novotny can undo a drug case, he can surely kick the shit out of some old lady, her blue collar son, and the neighborhood attorney (probably a relative) that they were sure to hire.

He sat through three more drafts and a dozen partial conversations. An older, heavyset fellow told a younger friend about a demolition site where used brick could be lifted after dark. A skinny fellow with long blond hair who didn't look old enough to be in the bar mumbled something to his buddy about a girl he had coaxed into a drive through the cemetery and all that went with it. A third fellow, badly scarred from acne, asked several patrons where he might score some speed. Dorsey finished off his beer and motioned for the bartender.

"One more?" the man in the Penguins T-shirt asked, taking away the glass.

"Nah, that's all for me." Dorsey pulled himself from the barstool. "One thing, though, you might help me out with. Tryin' to find a guy I used to work with. I got laid off about a year and a half ago, ain't seen him since. I remember he used to talk about runnin' the bars along Butler Street. Shit, never even knew his real name, but the guys used to call him Outlaw."

It was risky, Dorsey knew, showing your cards so early in the game. You had to pick the right opponent, and when the bartender grinned, Dorsey knew he had chosen well. *This is a young guy,* he told himself, *wants to be part of things on the street. And you can't be part of things on Butler Street unless you're tight with Outlaw. This bartender might not know much, but what he does know, or thinks he knows, he'll tell.*

"Sure, Outlaw," the bartender said, hanging on to his grin. "Worked with him, huh? He's a good guy. I know him; we hang out sometimes."

Yeah, Dorsey thought, *every time you pay for the drinks.* "Seen him 'round? Know where he might be?"

"Not in here," the bartender said. "Sometimes he might come in with a friend, but I'd try up the block. Dodo's Place or Zima's. Just up the block. Zima's the best bet, though."

Out on the sidewalk, the sky had gone black and the mercury vapor streetlamps gave a glow that Dorsey could only describe as misty. The city air was freighted with humidity, and the lamp's emissions seemed to move through a fog at the top of the stanchions. Across the street a municipal parking lot broke the string of storefronts, and teenagers occupied a bench between the exit and entrance ramps. Four girls had two boys showing off for them in voices just a little too loud. Dorsey wondered what effect Maritsa's disappearance had had on them, deciding that it had none. *It's dark,* he thought, *and they're on the streets—the streets with Maritsa's handbill stapled to every other telephone pole.* Maritsa Durant, portrait of a missing seventeen-year-old, was yesterday's news.

Dodo's was a dive. Arranged like Budnar's, it lacked maintenance and attention to hygiene. The floor tile was cracked and missing in places, and the worked tin ceiling, the kind that Dorsey admired in so many South Side bars, was grimy and ripped away in spots. The few patrons, at first glance, looked older to Dorsey. But while ordering bottled beer to protect his health, he came to another conclusion.

These boys weren't old, just worn out. He guessed their ages to be in the early to midforties, and they had the look of so many men he had questioned in their jail cells. Men whose lives of hard drinking and dope had left them careless about themselves. Deodorant every morning but showers rationed to once every three days. And a set of clean clothes after every second shower. *Can't call them junkies,* Dorsey decided. *That just doesn't capture it.* Alkie burnouts was the best he could do on such short notice. Guys who got up in the morning thinking about the bar and how the first couple of beers would be rough on their stomachs, but afterward it would be clear sailing back to oblivion.

Two barstools to Dorsey's left was a man hunched over his beer, his rough fingernails chipping away at the bottle's label. His hair was long and stringy, revealing an extra length of forehead. Wearing jeans and a numberless basketball practice shirt, he looked up at the television mounted at the end of the bar and shouted at the Pirates.

"Fuckin' niggers! It's a fuckin' nigger team!" He turned to Dorsey. "Fuck you lookin' at?"

Dorsey turned from him and stared at the back bar. Just above two bottles of Calvert whiskey, Maritsa Durant stared back at him. It was the same handbill, a little less worn, that Mrs. Leneski had given him. The photo was clearer and the printing had less of the cheap copy machine blur. *Oh, you Jew-dark beauty,* Dorsey thought, *where the hell are you?*

"That girl never had a fuckin' chance."

Dorsey pulled back from his thoughts and whipped his eyes to the man with the stringy hair. "What'd you say?"

"You was lookin' at the girl," the man said. "Like I says, she never had a chance.

"At what?"

"At life. Fuck ya think I'm talkin' about?" He hooked his hair back behind one ear and took a pull on his beer. "Not from the get-go, not with those two for parents. The old man was Teddy Durant. Ever know him?"

"Maybe a little," Dorsey said. "Just from around, ya know?"

The stringy-haired guy rapped his knuckles on the bar, and the bartender at the far end of the room waved him off and concentrated on the baseball game. "Prick," he said, then turned back to Dorsey. "Went to school with Teddy. What a fuckin' rat. It was up at Holy Family School. One year he steals the milk money. Another time he sets part of this classroom on fire after gettin' into the altar wine. Last thing I remember was him stealin' all this money a couple of fuckin' nuns collected for the missions. These nuns, they must've been on our asses for months collectin' that money, sayin' how good we had it here and how shitty it was in New Guinea. Anyways, the nuns finish the collection and Teddy steals the whole stash. Got caught, too. But it wasn't bad. Juvenile probation and he had to go to public school."

"See him around anymore?" Dorsey asked.

"See everybody around." He rapped again for a beer and again was ignored. "Including people that ain't even there."

That I don't doubt, Dorsey thought. He drank off the last of his beer and made his way outside.

Dorsey passed an Isaly's dairy store and had to negotiate his way among shoppers, most in their sixties and seventies, laden with brown grocery bags. *People,* he thought, *who looked after families, homes, and themselves—whether or not it was Friday night. People like Uncle Davey.* Dorsey wondered if he'd ever make the grade himself.

On the far side of the next intersection, Dorsey saw the purple neon sign for Zima's. The sign itself was on a side street wall, in script with a directional arrow hanging from the tail of the *S,* prompting the foot traffic to continue along Butler to the front door. At the bar's facade, Dorsey found a matching neon sign mounted above the doorway and two small windows, each framing an Iron City beer logo. *Looks like a step up,* he thought, *the spot on the street for the better, more accomplished drinkers. Or maybe it's the place for self-delusion, the holding area for drunks and still casual dopers waiting for the final slide to Dodo's.*

Just before entering the bar, a refurbished storefront a few doors down caught Dorsey's eye. A slate-colored facade had been laid over the building's red brick, and two large casement windows filled the space that, by Dorsey's figuring, had once held a single enormous piece of plate glass. In the window nearest the metal and glass security door, five-inch slate lettering gave the telephone number and office hours of ANTON NOVOTNY, MD, GENERAL PRACTITIONER.

Stepping along the windows, Dorsey studied the bland interior of the reception area. Neutral beige wallpaper, earth-tone sofas, and a blond-wood receptionist's desk with white telephone—all of which Dorsey pegged has having been selected from the back pages of a physician's business journal. He took a guess at which sofa the old woman had sat on while waiting to be reassured that her breast lump meant nothing. If the drunk in Budnar's was to be believed. And if Labriola was right, the neutral decor of the waiting room masked an illegal drug dispensary. *Hold on,* Dorsey advised himself, *back to the work at hand. Stick to things you know. Like missing girls and barflies.*

The interior of Zima's showed the results of well-spent remodeling money. Normally, Dorsey cared little for the remodeled and refurbished, preferring the well-kept old to remain just that. But to Zima's he took a liking. Configured like the others with a long bar and opposing booths, and the worked metal ceiling gleamed. The walls had been replastered, not drywalled, and had a white-wash finish. Fresh stain showed on the knots and swirls of the back bar's wood. Passing through a healthy crowd to a seat at the far end of the bar, where he could observe the entire room, he took notice of the framed photographs mounted above each of the booths. The photos, some sepia, dated from early in the century with hand-printed captions identifying the subjects as neighborhood landmarks. A home for Polish Army veterans, a wooden bridge across the Allegheny, two pictures of Sodality Circles at local Catholic churches, and an early landscape of the park on Forty-sixth Street.

Dorsey went back to his Iron City draft and watched the crowd. Similar to the one at Budnar's, he decided, but with the look of better times financially. The piles of change on the bar counter in front of each drinker was larger and rich with tens and twenties. The haircuts on the patrons were a bit fresher and more polished, and with two bartenders the place was hopping.

"Oh, sure, yeah, they got niggers living there now." The fellow on the next barstool, heavyset and just starting to bald, spoke to a friend standing at his side. "It was my grandmother's place. Just before you get to Thirty-sixth Street. Nice place when she was there; my uncles used to do all the work around the place for her. Not no more, though. The place is going to shit. Since the niggers, I mean."

"You expectin' something else?" his friend asked, signaling to one of the bartenders for a refill. "White people move farther up Butler every year and the spades follow. Before ya know it, we'll be in the tenth ward."

Better warn Uncle Davey, Dorsey thought, *let him know these two dorks might be moving in. Maybe he can get a good price on his place before the neighborhood goes stupid.*

The companion of the half-bald fellow took his fresh beer and seemed ready to continue when the front door opened. "Ah, shit," Dorsey heard him say. "Here she is."

Dorsey twisted about in his seat, and his first thought was that this woman had to be three inches taller than Gretchen, who stood a full five ten. And she was beautiful. Dressed in jeans, running shoes, and a long cotton blouse with the tails out; her hair was the black of shoe polish and cut short. Her skin had a much more than healthy sheen and smoothness, and Dorsey's inspection could not come up with a single blemish. Most of her height was in her legs, and her breasts were full but proportioned to her long frame. *Ah, shit, is right,* Dorsey thought.

But the crowd's reaction was not that of half-drunk men to a good-looking woman. Thoroughly hushed, the bar patrons seemed to withdraw into themselves, heads turned to their drinks and away from the woman. She made her way down the center aisle without interference, men carefully stepping out of her way, and Dorsey realized that he alone was looking directly at her. Seeming to conduct an inspection, she came even with Dorsey who found himself as uncomfortable as the others. *Christ,* he thought, *this woman is in charge.*

She gave Dorsey a thorough study, a solemn nod or perhaps a

warning, then made an about-face and left the bar. The noise level in the room returned to normal, and to Dorsey it seemed as if all suspended motion had been restored. *The hell was that?* he asked himself. He was tempted to pose the question to his neighbor but feared he might reveal his ignorance.

Dorsey signaled to the closest bartender for a fresh beer but the man turned to a door behind the bar. He opened it just a hair and whispered something. When he turned back, he was smiling, and was followed by a man large enough that he had to duck coming through the doorway wearing a grin that outshone the bartender's. He had long gray hair hauled back into a ponytail and a strong chin that showed just the earliest signs of sagging. He wore a black T-shirt, and his arms—especially the forearms—were heavily muscled. Several groups along the bar began to cheer and clap, and Dorsey knew he had just made the acquaintance of Outlaw.

"What a pain in the ass!" Outlaw said, rounding Dorsey's end of the bar. He moved a few paces down the bar, and space was automatically made for him by several male admirers. The bartender set him up with a shot and a short beer chaser. "If I was up to something," Outlaw said, addressing the entire crowd, "if I was trying' to pull some shit, I could see the interest she takes in me. But this is horseshit. Harassment." The crowd erupted in a cheer.

Dorsey's beer arrived while he sized up Outlaw. Just as Labriola had said: big and strong with the first signs of middle age. *Your age,* Dorsey reminded himself, comparing his softening middle with Outlaw's. This guy was the leader of the pack, that was clear. So why hide out from a woman, whatever her size? The woman was tough, that came through like a beacon from an airplane nose, but this was Outlaw, the hard-ass's hard-ass. Maybe women did really run the world.

The big man made fast work of his drinks and weaved through the crowd for the front door. His progress was impeded again and again by packs of drinkers who shouted his name, slapped his shoulders, and, Dorsey figured, hoped to be acknowledged in return. The delays allowed Dorsey to finish off his beer without a show of haste and begin his own journey to the exit, once Outlaw stepped outside. He hoped the big man would remain on foot since his own car was several blocks away.

Back out into the night, Dorsey checked the street and spotted Outlaw's tall figure on the far side of the street, heading toward the park on Forty-sixth Street. Dorsey stayed on his side of Butler and fell into step a half block behind. *Stay out of the park,* Dorsey willed him, hoping somehow to influence Outlaw's actions. *There's more than one bar on this street. Why not pick out another and have a shot? Hell, I'll even buy one, eventually.* It had been Dorsey's hope to tag along as Outlaw barhopped, letting him loosen up and even springing for a few drinks. And then getting down to business about Teddy and Maritsa. But getting the park into it, that Dorsey didn't care for. If half they said was true, the idea of traipsing around in there after dark had no appeal.

Outlaw passed below the lighted sign of a funeral home, crossed Forty-sixth, and entered the park along an asphalt pathway cut through the front lawn. He was soon lost in the darkness and Dorsey hung back, considering his options. *I've got only two,* he told himself: *Go into the park or go home.* Recalling which one he was getting paid for, Dorsey scanned the intersection of Butler and Forty-sixth, found himself alone, and crossed into the park.

The change in lighting was abrupt as Dorsey moved along the pathway, leaving the street's mercury lights behind. The park held several small spotlights, one above a play area with swing sets and climbing bars, several others near the swimming pool entrance and the basketball court; but the pathway and lawns were black, conceded to the night. Dorsey could hear distant voices from beyond the pool and basketball court, figuring it for a party near the cemetery fence—positioned for a fast getaway. Near the pool entrance, a few feet from the edge of a puddle of light cast by a fixture over the door, a woman spoke.

"Business with Outlaw?"

She stepped into the light from a flight of steps leading up to the basketball court. Despite the harsh light she was as striking as she had been in Zima's, but Dorsey instinctively took a few steps backward before noticing the man to his left. Not Outlaw, he was short and wiry with a reddish beard that matched his hair. *These two are anything but junkies,* Dorsey thought, *although what difference does it make when you're on a dark path and there's two of them and one of you?*

"I suppose you know who we are," the woman said. "Most people around here do. And if you're here for Outlaw, then you know for sure."

"Hold up for a second," Dorsey said as the woman stepped closer. "Whatever your problem is with the guy is your business. This Outlaw guy did something to piss you off, take it up with him." Dorsey turned to the small man with the mustache. "What's the deal? She your sister? Outlaw the boyfriend?"

The woman took Dorsey's arm and turned him about. "Here's the deal," she said sticking a badge in its leather case under his nose. Her voice was soft, a purr. "You're coming with us."

8

A spring rain had begun, and Dorsey watched the drops strike the outside of the diner's window, each one a quick splat with a trailing streak. He sipped at his second cup of coffee and across the booth's Formica tabletop the woman dunked a teabag into a cup of hot water. Her partner worked a fork into a pile of bread, hot beef, and brown gravy.

"The Durant girl was seen around the park several times, by us," the woman said. "Didn't mean anything to us until she came up missing. She could be anywhere." The partner grunted his assent through a mouthful of food.

Troopers, state narcs, Dorsey thought as he watched cars glide by in the wet night. He couldn't see what business they had in the city. *Well, business must be expanding.*

It had taken Dorsey a half hour of explanation and a review of all his identification before they bought his story. And he had given them the whole story. Mrs. Leneski, Maritsa, her parents, Labriola, and Outlaw. Client confidentiality carried little weight against state badges—as if it existed at all for a private detective. Satisfied that Dorsey was what he claimed to be, State Troopers Janice Manning and David Lyle finally identified themselves. It was

Trooper Manning who had suggested they have a little discussion of mutual interests.

"Was she getting high?" Dorsey asked. "The girl, I mean."

"Wasting her time down there if she wasn't," Lyle said through his last bite of food. "From what I've seen of these young girls, even the so-called bright ones, they go for these guys. Element of danger horseshit. So maybe she wasn't using; she could have just had a thing for one of them. Like she was gonna save him. Happens a lot. Either way, she's most likely gone."

"Gone where?" Dorsey asked. "Like dead gone?"

Lyle wiped at his chin with a paper napkin. "Don't rule it out; I wouldn't. Most likely, though, she probably took off with some guy from the park. Maybe they're just around the city, but then again, who the hell knows?"

"More I think about it," Janice Manning said, "I recall her being one of Outlaw's girls. One of the many."

"Little hard to buy," Dorsey said. "The man looks to be about my age, and he's got a shrewd look about him. Doesn't seem the type to take a chance on seventeen-year-old jailbait." As he spoke, Dorsey flashed on Maritsa Durant's snapshot and thought again.

Janice Manning set down her teacup and gave Dorsey a warm smile he would have never guessed she had in her. "You're right, he's a shrewd one. He's been operating on the fringe of things, maybe, for a long time. And you have to understand about him; maybe you do. From what you've told me, it seems like you've had a good look at him. To most of these guys he's a hero, the master operator, personification itself of giving the cops the finger with a smile. And to the girls—the younger the better—he's an updated swashbuckler. Brave, dangerous, with a little mystery thrown in. What the hell, these girls think he rides a black stallion and disappears into the mist every night."

Dorsey sipped at his coffee and found himself unable to disagree. Back with the DA's office he had been into more than a few wretched apartments looking for suspected burglars or dealers only to find some young girl cringing in a corner, pleading the innocence of her boyfriend. The boyfriend who had just dropped out the window, leaving her holding the bag and most times a kid. "Let him go," she'd say. "He's good and didn't do nothing." And then three days later you'd find him in another apartment, with another girl, bouncing an infant on his lap.

"So, you figure Outlaw is the guy to follow up on?"

"Best bet." Lyle pushed away his plate and glanced at his wristwatch. "Time for that call, Jan. Gimme a minute; I'll be back." He slipped from the booth and made his way to the public phone mounted by the cash register.

Dorsey swallowed the last of his coffee. "There's another possibility. The father, this Durant. He's barred from contacting the girl, but I'm hearing that he got in the habit of chauffeuring Maritsa and a friend home from school. Supposedly just before she disappeared."

"Doesn't sound right." Janice Manning shook her head and looked around. "Believe me, you couldn't miss him. Built like a toothpick; that's what's left from the dope. Always has half a beard, and he must have a permanent crick in his neck from spending so much time looking over his shoulder."

"I know the type."

Janice Manning again gave off that warm and unexpected smile. "Anyway, as I said, we know Teddy pretty well. What I've heard is that he had to take off because he owes a bundle to somebody. Maybe he owes child support to the grandmother."

Dorsey thought of Mrs. Leneski and that mattress filled with every dollar she ever made working the production line at Kress Box. She wouldn't take a dime from Teddy, unless it was to put into a savings account for his future funeral expenses.

"He must owe a dealer," Dorsey said. "Or just someone who is pissed off enough to do him some real harm."

"Regardless," Janice said, "keep after Outlaw. He's your best lead. Tell you what. I have some background notes on him. I'll get 'em from my files for you. Maybe we can help each other out."

"We'll see." Dorsey nodded at the possibility. He watched Janice glance over her shoulder, as if checking to see if her partner was still on the phone. She turned back to Dorsey and mixed some charm into that smile. *Jesus,* Dorsey thought, remembering her performance at the bar. *Which one is she? Hard-nosed narc or manslayer? Or both as she pleases?*

"Mind a personal question?" she asked.

"Ask and we'll find out."

"Married?" she asked. "Now or ever?"

"Nope."

"Seriously involved at the moment?"

Dorsey stared into his empty coffee cup. "Now, that's not easily answered. I was for a while, but things aren't so certain these days." He looked up into her smile and beautiful eyes. "To be honest, this weekend may tell the tale."

"Hope for the best." She never took her eyes from his.

Trooper Lyle slipped back into his seat and told his partner they had to get moving.

"Before you take off, "Dorsey said, fishing his wallet from his back pocket, "I have a question. It's my understanding that Lawrenceville wasn't a narc priority." He again mentioned his conversation with Labriola.

Trooper Lyle lit a cigarette, whipping the match in the air until it was out. "We know Labriola. We were part of that half-assed task force. We got fucked over on that Novotny business, too. Whatever went wrong didn't happen on our side of the table. So as far as laying off Lawrenceville, fuck that."

9

The alarm was set for six o'clock, but Dorsey pulled himself out of bed and a ragged sleep twenty minutes before the hour. The sun was up and strong through the bedroom windows, combining with his anticipation of the day to rob him of sleep. From the floor of his walk-in closet he took his gym shorts, a paint-splotched Duquesne University sweatshirt, socks, and canvas-topped Converse sneakers. Dressed for the late spring morning, he stepped out onto the pavement of Wharton Street and let his arms and legs fall into action for his morning walk west to the foot of the Smithfield Street Bridge, eighteen blocks away.

By the third block his injured knee began to loosen, the long lazy S surgical scar no longer pinching at the joint and putting a hitch in his stride. His thoughts were jumping about from last night's business to the business at hand for today. *Teddy Durant has left town, Maritsa Durant is still out there in a void, and Gretchen Keller will be here this morning. And Janice Manning, for some unknown and unlikely reason, thinks you're pretty. Maybe she just has trouble finding guys her own size. She sure must have trouble finding ones that look as good as she does.*

With the about-face at the Smithfield Street Bridge, sweat ringing the neckline and cuffs of his sweatshirt, Dorsey forced his concentration solely on to Gretchen. She was due at ten that morning, and he had built a mental schedule for cleaning his house. His own cleaning practices, greatly superior to Gretchen's, had gone downhill for a time when she had first moved to Franklin, and it had taken some effort to regain the lost ground. He'd be ready for her, that much was sure, but maybe not for what she had to say to him. Long distance telephone lines had done nothing to disguise the growing distance in her voice.

At the row house he began with the front-room office and made his way backward. The tape player worked over a worn tape of Ella Fitzgerald, scat mixed in with classic lyrics, while Dorsey cleared the desk of the Durant case notes and dropped the dustcover over the Olivetti. He made quick work of the kitchen, then moved upstairs to scrub out the shower, replace the curtain, and attach a fresh roll of toilet paper to the dispenser. It was in his own bedroom where he was brought to a staggering halt. He was clearing the walk-in closet, taken aback by how quickly he was completing the job. *Because it was half empty to begin with,* he thought. No so long ago it had been bursting at the seams, trying to accommodate two wardrobes. All of Gretchen's jeans, khakis, broadcloth blouses, and lab coats. Now he had enough wire hangers to go into the dry cleaning business.

Dorsey backed out of the closet and sat at the corner of the bed. *It may be time,* he thought, *for the practicalities, the personal protections required by a breakup. When you clean out the closets and change the snapshots in the picture frames.*

The telephone rang in the office, and Dorsey pulled back from his musings and hustled down the steps. He lifted the receiver a moment before the answering machine would have clicked in.

"Hello?"

"Your father came home yesterday. Where were you?"

Ah, shit. Ironbox. Dorsey dropped into his desk chair. *This I need like a third nut.* "What's that supposed to mean? So he came home—by ambulance, I'm sure. With attendants for you to boss around and aggravate. You make it sound like I forced the guy to take the bus."

"You should have been there," Mrs. Boyle said. "You should be here now. I'd like to see you here this afternoon."

"Not today," Dorsey said. "I have plans."

"More of this chasing around Lawrenceville?"

Jesus Christ, Dorsey thought, *does every detective have two elderly people sitting around a sickroom critiquing his work?* "That and some other things," he told her. "Which reminds me, I should call my client with an update. Right away."

"Well, we'll expect you soon." There was a moment's silence on the line. "This Lawrenceville, can't say I know much good about it. Not since I was young."

She sounded strange to Dorsey, regretful. But then he remembered that Ironbox had never been young. She had always been Ironbox and nothing else. By choice, he figured.

"I'll get there soon." He made a quick good-bye and hung up. From the case file he retrieved Mrs. Leneski's phone number.

"That son of a bitch, where could he run off to? Who would have him?" Mrs. Leneski said after Dorsey had brought her up to date. "You should know better by now. No-good bastard like him got nowhere to go."

She's got a point, Dorsey conceded, *of a sort. Guys like Durant aren't know for having old buddies and pen pals scattered across the country. He was the kind that never left home, that got lost taking the bus downtown.*

"If he ran off and took that girl, you find him," Mrs. Leneski told him. "You find out where he is so I can go there and kill him."

Gretchen arrived three hours late. Dorsey was at his desk running through his checkbook, trying to decide who would get what part of Mrs. Leneski's seven thousand, when the doorbell rang: He wondered what had happened to her house key, the one he was sure she still had. It was a relief when he heard the lock being worked and the sliding of metal on metal as the bolt shot back.

He met her in the hallway and took the garment bag she held across her shoulder, carrying it into the office and draping it across the chaise. Gretchen was dressed for the weather: khaki shorts and maroon T-shirt. Her jewelry consisted of a single gold strand around her neck, and her hair was cut short in tight curls with the telltale wisps from a razor at her neck. Dorsey took her softly by the shoulders and kissed her, wishing he could better read her response, settling for neutral. The smile that followed was more promising.

"No changes worth mentioning here." Gretchen stepped around the office, peeking over the desk at the midget refrigerator. "Good, your personal home entertainment center is still in place. Little early for a Rolling Rock, but it's a comfort to know it's there."

Dorsey returned her smile and asked if she could stand a little lunch.

"Sounds good," Gretchen said. "As long as we avoid fried bologna and onions."

"It's out of season." Dorsey took her hand and led her along the hall to the kitchen. "It's May; everybody knows you're only supposed to eat fried bologna during months with an *R* in them."

Gretchen took a seat at the far end of the kitchen table while Dorsey crouched at the open refrigerator door. "So," he said, "run this past me again. This business tonight."

"Dr. Riddle, you remember him?" Gretchen said. "He's getting the Resident's Recognition Award. It goes to the doc who is the best role model—or something along that line. The award ceremony itself is at the hospital, but I'd rather not bother with that. Now the reception, that's at the William Penn and should be worthwhile. The ballrooms are supposed to be pretty nice. Besides, I always liked Dr. Riddle. The man was always good to me. That's really why I came down."

"And then there's me," Dorsey said, taking several jars and storage containers to the kitchen counter. "The opportunity to spend the weekend with me. That's also part of the drawing card that brought you down from Franklin."

"That's right, I wanted to see you." Gretchen turned and looked out through the back screen door. "I wanted to see you for the weekend."

"That I can settle for." Dorsey abandoned the food and reached across the tabletop for Gretchen's hand, turning her toward him. "I'll settle for that, so don't make it difficult. You're not saying anything new."

He released her hand, pulled back a chair, and dropped into it, lacing his hands behind his neck. "It wasn't my expectation that you'd show up here and all would be well. It's been a hell of a time, this last year or so."

Gretchen smiled, her eyes shining. "It really has. Things can be a strain, can't they?"

"True," Dorsey said. "But as I said, let's settle for a weekend. We'll make it a good one."

"So forget the food and let's get started." Gretchen rose from her seat. "The bedroom still at the top of the stairs, turn left? Or have you gone and rearranged things on me?"

Dorsey returned to the bed holding two bottles of Rolling Rock, handed one to Gretchen who was stretched atop the sheets, and worked his way out of the gym shorts he had worn for the trip to the office refrigerator. "And so," he told her, "there's this Henry."

Gretchen sipped at her beer, holding the bottle with both hands, the bed sheet double wrapped at its base, and cradling it in the shallow hollow between her small breasts. "You could stand a new friend. Al's still number one with me, but you know I always had some reservations about Bernie. So I can't say I'm sad about him taking a job out of town. Make new friends is what I say—not that it's as easy as it sounds. But I'd take the guy up on his offer to go over for the ballgame."

69

Dorsey sat at the foot of the bed, stroking Gretchen's leg. He gave the kneecap a quick peck of a kiss. Nipping at his beer, two fingers pinching the bottleneck to protect his damaged hand from the cold, he gave her an accounting of the Maritsa Durant case.

"She-devil policewoman!" Gretchen laughed. "Now, *this* is interesting. Kind of like Modesty Blaise with a badge. All I can say is be careful. Sounds like she eats 'em up."

"Strictly business," Dorsey said.

"Strictly business. Sure."

Dorsey grinned and swirled the beer in its bottle. "We shall see what the new week brings, when it brings it."

Gretchen laughed and, using Dorsey's shoulder for support, pulled herself into a sitting position. Dorsey noticed how her slim waist formed only the slightest crease in her skin as she sat. Softly, she kissed Dorsey's cheek. "We're a mess, aren't we?"

"More or less."

"This Dr. Novotny," Gretchen said, returning to the Durant case, "he certainly doesn't speak well for my profession. Have you had the pleasure of meeting him?"

"No reason to."

Gretchen got to her feet, apparently headed for the bathroom. "From the sound of it," she called from the corridor, "this Novotny should be about the same age as Dr. Riddle. And Dr. Riddle knows all his contemporaries. When these guys were young, there just weren't that many doctors around. I could ask him about Novotny."

"Couldn't hurt," Dorsey shouted back. *That's right,* he thought, *it couldn't hurt to have something on Novotny, something to give to Manning and Lyle. In return for their help in finding Maritsa.*

The evening was clear, with a lingering sun, and the thin Saturday traffic made for a quick ride into Downtown and the William Penn Hotel. Dorsey left the Buick at home, opting to drive Gretchen's new Integra Vigor, looking forward to a parking valet who wouldn't laugh at him when he pulled the car between a BMW and a Lincoln.

Inside the hotel lobby, a classic room of arched ceilings built with old steel and coal money, sofas and chairs were grouped in scattered pockets for quiet conversations. It was the kind of living museum that Dorsey loved, and he stalled for a few moments as he and Gretchen passed through to the concierge station, where they were directed to a third-floor ballroom. Gretchen wore a black formal dress and Dorsey had taken the dry cleaner's plastic wrap from his lightweight olive suit for the first time that spring.

"Those pants look a tad loose," Gretchen told him as they stood at the reception table, getting their assigned dinner seats. "Tough winter?"

"Nuts and berries I stored up last fall ran out in late February." Dorsey took the name card and table number and led her into the ballroom. "I almost had to eat one of my fellow chipmunks to stay alive."

They shared a table with two other couples, strangers, and the dinner of prime rib, twice-baked potato, and vegetables passed in near silence. Gretchen explained, to Dorsey's sincere relief, that all of the speeches had been made at the award ceremony and that only drinks and dancing followed the meal. "You remember how to dance, I hope?" she asked. "Right? Dance?"

"I still have the seventh grade two-step down pat." Dorsey sliced a piece of beef and grinned. "They stick with the slow numbers long enough, and you and I'll drill a hole clean through to the lobby."

"Nothing more adventurous?" Gretchen asked. "I knew it. We should have taken those ballroom dancing lessons we talked about. Then we could at least keep up with the old folks."

"Al could teach us," Dorsey said. "In the back room of the bar. In fact, he's offered a few times. Him and Rose. Ever see that old jukebox back there? Disconnected most of the time, but Al hasn't changed the records since 1951. I can see us now, gliding across that checkered floor. Me in my double-breasted, you in chiffon."

71

"Get your eyes checked, fella," Gretchen said. "Chiffon?"

Waitresses cleared the dishes, and a twelve piece orchestra took over the area formerly held by the head tables, leaving space for a dance floor. Dorsey led Gretchen to the floor, and at his lead they shuffled through the first three songs. The floor began to crowd, and Gretchen suggested they sit out the next few, saying that going in circles made her dizzy.

Dorsey went to the bar for a Rolling Rock while Gretchen drifted through several conversations with her former colleagues. Beer in hand and with his elbow planted on the bar, Dorsey gazed through tall windows down onto Grant Street, brick paved and divided by well-chosen trees. *Settle for a good weekend,* he reminded himself, and for the first time he really accepted the situation. *It's okay and it's all you've got. Stick with reality; it hasn't led you wrong yet.*

Dorsey felt a not-so-gentle nudge at his elbow and turned to find Gretchen and a tall elderly gentleman, whom he took to be Dr. Riddle. His white hair was full and allowed to grow thick at the sides, smoothly patted back behind the ears. The eyes and skin were clear, and Dorsey saw him as the poster boy for patrician WASP doctors. Gretchen made the introductions.

"She used to mention you," Dr. Riddle said, his voice as authoritative as his appearance. "When we worked together at Mercy." He turned his attention to Gretchen. "We always had high hopes for you, and I still wish we could have found a staff position for you at Mercy. It's getting to be an old story, but my power has been usurped by administrators. Still, you've done well for yourself."

Gretchen shifted her feet uneasily, then asked Dorsey to order her a white wine. "I mentioned that Carroll was interested in that GP in Lawrenceville—Dr. Novotny. You said you knew him?"

Dorsey handed Gretchen her wine and turned again to Dr. Riddle, surprised to find his face captured in a scowl. He hadn't expected much from the doctor, figuring him for just another lodge member who wouldn't speak ill of a brother or the brother-hood. *Maybe he's different,* Dorsey told himself. *Older and accomplished, so his ambitions are fulfilled. So maybe he figures the truth can't cause him any harm. Let's find out.*

"From what I hear, Dr. Novotny has had his share of recent legal problems." Dorsey sipped at his beer, watching the doctor's face turn red.

"You must be referring to Eliot Ness."

"How's that?" Dorsey asked.

Dr. Riddle laughed and Dorsey could see it wasn't out of joy. "Eliot Ness," the doctor said, "the man has to be one of the Untouchables. He must be untouchable; certainly no one has ever been able to lay a hand on him."

"Please," Dorsey said. "You can't stop now."

"There have always been rumors, on a variety of issues, even his taxes, but he always seems to get out from under any charge or investigation. Surely, I thought, they had him on this drug matter. But then again, poof! He is exonerated and his accusers are under attack. He must have some very special friends, ones that owe him dearly."

"The rumors," Dorsey said. "Could you be more specific?"

Dr. Riddle, with apparent effort, worked a sly smile across his face. "Please, it's a party we have here. A party for me, no less. I say we enjoy it." He gave Gretchen a light pat on the hand, nodded a farewell to Dorsey, and was soon lost into a crowd of well-wishers.

"Rumors," Dorsey said, tilting his eyebrows at Gretchen.

"On a variety of issues," she replied, wiggling her eyebrows back at him. "Detectives love a mystery, I suppose."

Dorsey laughed and finished off the last of his Rolling Rock.

His morning walk behind him, Dorsey climbed the stairs to his bedroom, pulling off his soaked sweatshirt, and found Gretchen's packed garment bag folded at the foot of the bed. He heard her coming down the hall from the bathroom and checked his watch. Nine-thirty. *Short weekend,* he thought. *Looks like I get to appease Ironbox and see the old man.*

"Early start?" Dorsey watched Gretchen brush roughly at her hair as she entered the bedroom. "Figured you as a breakfast guest, anyway." He dropped into an old armchair near the window.

"Just thought I'd get on the road."

"Makes sense." Dorsey wiped at his forehead with his sweatshirt. "I'd do the same. Wouldn't want to get caught in one of those nasty late May snowstorms we're always hearing about."

"Not fair," Gretchen said, pulling on the khaki shorts she had driven down in. "Monday morning comes early, and I'd like to take it easy today."

"Didn't even get in your morning run. That's not like you. I thought the run was a ritual."

Gretchen slipped a raspberry Izod shirt over her head and shoulders, leaving the tails untucked. She sat herself at the edge of the bed squarely in front of Dorsey. "We settled for a good weekend. That was the deal. So, hold up your end of the bargain."

"Trust me, I am." Dorsey pushed back into the chair and draped the sweatshirt across his midriff. "It's just that I figured Sunday as part of the weekend. Took me by surprise is all. Ending so soon."

"I know," Gretchen said, her head lowered as if inspecting her lap. "I know, but I'd like to get back to my place. My home. It feels different now, having my own place. Before, when I was working here, it was just a couple of rooms across town in Bloomfield and most of my stuff was over here anyway. You've seen my place. Nice little house and lawn. And it feels like mine, even if it's only a rental. You like having your own home, don't you?"

Dorsey smiled, inwardly and outwardly. *Settle for what you've had and how it is now,* he told himself. *You stick with the real.* "Your home's up in Franklin," he said, still smiling. "And home is where the heart is. No problem."

Gretchen returned the smile and took his hand, gliding a finger across the disfigured knuckles. "And like good sensible people they said good-bye for now."

"Not sensible," Dorsey said. "More like reasonable. The sensible seem to do things as a matter of course. I like reasonable. Sounds like we put effort into keeping things civil."

"Reasonable it is."

10

The red bricks of the driveway had a thin coating of gray dust, the remains of mortar cracked and scattered in the winter freeze. Another sign of his father being laid up, Dorsey decided. When the lord of the manor can't saddle up and survey his holdings, the serfs tend to slack off a bit.

He had left the Buick at the curb on Wilkins Avenue, disregarding the no parking signs, knowing the cops held this house and its visitors immune. After hitting the doorbell, he turned and gave the garden a once-over and saw that it, too, had the look of neglect. The grass was unseeded and the ground had yet to be turned for flower planting. And the far wall was overrun with tangles of ivy, which his father hated for the small animals he claimed would next be there. *Something's way out of whack,* Dorsey told himself. *Even with the old man sick, he's still got Ironbox as his overseer. But this place is run-fucking-down.*

"Oh, good. You came." Irene Boyle opened the door and Dorsey turned to her.

"Oh, good. You came"? What's this shit? he thought. *No contempt? Not even a trace of it? First the garden's gone to hell, and then Ironbox has a sudden lapse of bad manners.*

76

"My schedule had a sudden change thrown at it." Dorsey stepped inside, allowing Ironbox to close the door. The air-conditioning was running, and it took Dorsey a moment to adjust to the chill. "Bedroom or office?"

"He says he's been stuck between two sheets for too long." Mrs. Boyle led him through the living room to the closed office door. "I get frightened over it. He should be resting more than he is. You could talk to him about it. I'd appreciate it if you would."

This is no lapse, Dorsey thought. *The woman is undergoing a distinct change in personality. She acts as if she likes you. Don't you start liking her.*

Mrs. Boyle lingered for a moment at the door, one hand on the knob, the other poised to knock. "Your father's getting older and so am I. We'd both like to spend the rest of our time in peace. Just left in peace. Not much to ask, is it?"

"Not from where I'm standing." Dorsey studied her face, wondering if he had recently done something to disturb these two. But that wasn't what he saw in her eyes. This wasn't a plea for some consideration; it was just a sincerely asked question.

She knocked at the door and opened it without waiting for a response. Dorsey entered and found his father seated behind his dark-wood desk, dressed in pajamas and dressing gown. Hanging on the wall beyond were the familiar photos of his father with visiting dignitaries. On the wall itself he could find none of the gouged plaster caused by his last visit to this room.

"At first the repairmen thought a little Spackle and paint would gloss over the bullet holes," Martin Dorsey said, apparently reading his son's thoughts. "In the end, though, we replaced several sheets of drywall. By the way, the beer's in the usual place."

Dorsey took a green bottle of Rolling Rock from the corner bar's refrigeration unit and chose the wingback across from his father. Sipping at the beer, he noticed his father was making notations in a checkbook register. "Catching up on bookkeeping now that you're home?"

Martin Dorsey appeared confused for a moment, then gathered himself, sliding the checkbook into the desk's center drawer. "Thank you for coming to visit. And I am doing rather well now that I'm home. I'd like to rid myself of this thing, however." He gripped a metal cane in his left hand, giving it an angry shake.

"Someday, maybe," Dorsey said, swirling the beer in its bottle. "So what's with Mrs. Boyle? She's not her usual acerbic self."

"I've taken notice of that myself." Martin Dorsey reclined deeper into his chair. "Menopause had to be ten, twenty years ago for her. She has her moods, I suppose. Some women do. Your mother did."

"Moods?" Dorsey said. "She's flat out depressed. I'm no shrink, but that's my diagnosis."

Martin Dorsey pulled forward and rested his elbows at the edge of the desk. "You're right. You are not a psychiatrist. Just a law school dropout."

Dorsey let the insult pass, but not out of charity for his father. *That ran out a while back,* he reminded himself. *But he mentioned your mother. When was the last time he did that?*

"Mum was a moody type, huh?"

"Mum?" Martin Dorsey asked. "Oh, yes, you did call her that. It surprises me that you remember."

"I don't remember much, really," Dorsey said. "I just happen to think of her as Mum. Mother is too refined for Lawrenceville Irish, and Mommy just doesn't do it for me."

Martin Dorsey spread his hands out across the desktop and heaved a sigh. "Lawrenceville Irish. I was from this end of the city, too, you know. I met your mother at work, first floor of the City-County Building. She worked in some office as a clerk, and oddly enough I can't remember which one it was. I was across the hall in the Clerk of Courts, filing sentencing reports and other such nonsense. We were introduced at lunch by a mutual friend, Gus Meyers. He was from North Side, around Avery Street."

Dorsey smiled encouragement to his father, hoping he'd go on. He'd heard so little about his mother, her death in his early grade-

78

school days now just a blur. He felt he couldn't miss the chance. Martin Dorsey returned the smile and continued.

"After that I made sure I ran into her all the time. Even on the trolley. Which wasn't easy. She took one that came along Butler Street, and me being from East Liberty, I took one along Penn Avenue. As you know, I believe, those two streets merge halfway to Downtown, and I thought it would be too obvious if I transferred cars there every morning. So, I would get off my trolley at the top of Forty-fifth Street, by St. Francis Hospital, and hurry down to the bottom of the hill and catch your mother's trolley on Butler. That took some timing at first, but eventually she got in the habit of saving me a seat."

"Politics, war, and love." Dorsey finished the last of his beer. "All is fair."

"Always," Martin Dorsey said. "In a good cause, always."

He rose to leave, but a soft knock at the door kept him in place. The door opened partway, and Mrs. Boyle poked in her head.

"I'm leaving now," she said.

"For where?" Martin Dorsey asked. "Have you made any arrangements for my dinner?"

"There are a few stops I'd like to make. I think one of the priests at Sacred Heart hears confession now." She started to close the door, then paused. "Your son is here. I'm sure he can get something for you."

The door closed, and Dorsey went for another Rolling Rock. "What priest hears confession on Sunday?" he asked. "Unless he hears them on the third green. You better have her checked out; that woman is not herself. And with you in your condition, this is no time to have a lunatic on your hands."

"Lunatic is a bit harsh," Martin Dorsey said. "Besides, I would have thought the change would be to your liking."

Dorsey shrugged and dropped back into his chair. "There is comfort to be found in the constants of the universe. How would Einstein have taken it if the speed of light changed?"

79

"Good point," his father said. "Well, now that you're my only hope, what's for dinner?"

Pounding at the bar's locked door, Dorsey again wondered why Al had never installed a separate entrance for the second-floor apartment. The problem caused by this oversight had been even worse when Russie lived there, he recalled. Russie, who had never gotten his own phone, who took ten rings on the bar's pay phone before he made it down the steps. Fifty-some years on this earth and not even an entry in an old telephone directory to mark his presence.

He heard someone rushing down the steps and then metal on metal as the deadbolt slid free. "First quarter just ended," Henry said. "Lakers held the ball for the last shot, that's why you had to wait."

"It's okay." Dorsey watched Henry reset the lock, then followed him through the back room and up the stairs. "What's the score? Couldn't find the game anywhere on the radio."

"Celtics by three. Like I said, the Lakers held for a final shot, but the best they could get was a real ugly hook shot out of Kurt Rambus. You know, the guy who looks like he's got tape all over his glasses?"

The stairwell opened into a long and thin living room, matching the dimensions of the barroom below. At the rear were two doors, which Dorsey assumed led to a kitchen and a bedroom. He figured the bathroom was hidden back there as well.

"First time I've been up here," he said, his attention now drawn to the far wall where makeshift shelving of bricks and plankwood held older stereo components and a mixture of hardcover and paperback books. He had never seen similar construction outside of a college dormitory.

"First time, really?" Henry adjusted a large box fan that sat on the floor, allowing the stream to cross the two unmatched easy chairs he had pointed at the television set. "Wouldn't have thought that. Al makes out like you and Russie were close."

"To a degree, to a degree." Dorsey crossed to the shelves and ran through the book titles. There were a few by Burroughs and Kerouac, and a thin, shopworn copy of *Howl*. John Clellon Holmes's *Go* held an apparently prominent spot on the top shelf. The most current volume was a book by Abbie Hoffman with advice on how to live on the cheap.

"Game's back on." Henry gestured toward the easy chairs and made for the far doorway. He returned with two long neck Rolling Rocks as Dorsey took a seat.

"Christ, it gets hot up here," Henry said, handing a beer to Dorsey and taking a seat of his own. "Al has the bar rigged for air-conditioning but he never extended it up here. It can get bad. August and September, they must be killers in this place. I'm not looking forward to it."

Dorsey took a pull on his beer and smiled thinly. "You mean, of course, if you happen to stick around that long."

"You got a point," Henry said, returning the smile and then letting out a laugh. "There ya go! Now you're in the spirit of things."

Dorsey widened his smile and settled back. For a few minutes they concentrated on the game. The score seesawed, but the play was getting rough. Mitch Kupchak's elbows put Danny Ainge on the floor, and on the next exchange McHale flattened James Worthy as he spun from the low post to the basket. Fouls were called but the damage was done. Dorsey rubbed at his mangled fingers and was glad he had never made the pros.

"Nasty stuff," Henry said, reaching back to lift his pigtail and wiping the sweat from his neck with a handkerchief. "I played some ball, ya know. Nothing organized, like they call it. But I thought that the reason behind organizing a sport was to get rid of shit like that. Like the idea was to keep it clean."

Dorsey took a hit of beer. "That was the original idea maybe. Along with turning a buck. Pros and college."

"Hell, yes," Henry said. "Get that buck. I can get into that some. Part of the time, anyways."

81

"Really?" Dorsey smiled and turned back to the game. Magic Johnson connected a look-off pass to Jabbar, who rammed it home. "Henry Antos, a capitalist?"

"I need financing just like the next guy." Henry leaned forward and watched the ball game as he spoke. "You said it yourself with that crack about me not being around for August. I try to put a little bankroll together every now and then, and there's not too many ways—legal ways—to do that. And I'm not doing it any other way. No more. Fuck that shit; I took my fall."

"How's that?" Like Henry, Dorsey concentrated on the game as he spoke. "Al made some mention of something once."

Henry pulled on his beer and shrugged. "It's cool with me, Al mentioning it. Wasn't much of a fall, anyways. Just eleven months in what they called the county farm. It was this county in Oregon. Minimum security, shit like that. I think I remember there being a fence, and I'm not even sure the gate was locked." Henry laughed. "The guy who manned the gate was more of a receptionist than a guard."

"What was the charge?" Dorsey asked, recalling Al's speculations. "That's if you don't mind me asking."

"Illegal Chinese." Henry laughed again. "No shit, really. You used to be able to make a good dollar doing that, running them in from Vancouver. It was like a taxi service. The truck—and it was a real piece of shit—we'd run it across the Canadian border, which, at least back then, had more back roads than the state of Alabama. When they say that the U.S.–Canadian border is unfortified, they ain't kidding. So, anyway, once we got out of the wilderness, we'd drop those little yellow guys in a couple of places. Some in Portland, but eventually we finished the route in San Francisco. Good money, but all ill-gotten money has a price in the end."

"How'd you get cracked?" Dorsey asked. "Highway patrol pull you over for looking suspicious? Inspection sticker expire?"

"Bullshit," Henry said. "Looked that way at first, but face it, man, the cops don't catch anybody without a tip-off. I just figured we were protected by payoffs, things were going so easily. Later on, we found out that, yeah, that was the case, but the guy who was taking the dough needed a favor from somebody else. So our operation was sold to the cops."

"Do anything about it? After you got out?"

"Like what?" Henry turned to Dorsey and grinned. "The hell I look like, Sam Giancana? I can't hold a grudge, let alone pull off a vendetta. No, I didn't get mad and I didn't get even. I just got eleven months. And then went home."

They went back to the game in silence for a time, and worked on their beers. The last thirty seconds dragged on with time-outs and fouls, and Dorsey longed for the halftime horn. *Gretchen is home by now,* he thought. *In her little house in the country. Maybe in a few weeks she'll suggest you make a visit, spend the weekend. Including Sunday afternoon. Maybe you'll get up there, if things aren't too hectic. If the Durant girl finally shows.*

At the half, Henry popped from his chair and took Dorsey's empty, heading for the rear of the apartment. On his return he handed a fresh beer to Dorsey and set his own on the floor by his chair. "Let's have a taste," he said, then went to the shelving unit and removed a fat, black-bound novel. From behind it he produced a plastic bag and cigarette papers.

"Don't mind, do you?" Henry asked, taking his seat. With the book on his lap, he moistened the papers with his tongue and then dripped the pot from his fingertips across them. He worked the papers into a thin cylinder and sealed them with a quick stroke across his lips.

Dorsey laughed. "Not as long as my taking a pass doesn't offend your hospitality." He had never been much for smoke and remembered a time during his years at Duquesne when he had the label of juicer applied to him by friends. Not much fun when you can't master the skill of inhaling without coughing up a lung or two. So, if you didn't get anything from it, why suck on the joint?

"Nah, it's cool." Henry fired up with a disposable lighter and made a rushing noise as he pulled in the smoke. He inhaled so deeply that Dorsey thought his face might collapse and his eyeballs merge into one. *The hell with smoking,* he thought. *It's more fun to watch.*

"Tell me," Dorsey said with the ignorance of a dope outsider, "where do you buy this shit at?"

"Anywhere and everywhere."

"You can be more specific," Dorsey said. "It's been years since my highly acclaimed departure from the county police."

Henry released a billow of smoke, filling the room with the harsh scent that reminded Dorsey of burning dung. "Sorry, I wasn't jaggin' you off. It's the truth. There's even a guy who comes in downstairs who moves ounces. Me, I usually buy from a few guys I know. Over in Polish Hill."

"Polish pot?" Dorsey asked. "Does it give you a Hunky high?"

"That's good. Hunky high." Henry tapped ash from the tip of the joint into his open palm. "Seriously, those guys over there have good shit. And I've known the guys for years. I catch up with them at the Falcon Hall by the playground there or maybe at this private club by the boulevard. There's a lot of pot up there and more. Has been for a long time."

Dorsey flashed on Polish Hill. Mostly long-ago immigrant housing. It was only half of a hill, the neighborhood abruptly ending at a boulevard that slashed midway up the incline, another of the city's immediate boundaries between white and black. But it was the lower end of Polish Hill that Dorsey saw, where again the neighborhood suddenly halted. There was a hollow with railroad tracks and a spur line that had once served the Pittsburgh Brewing Company. A bridge for both cars and pedestrians spanned the hollow connecting Polish Hill with Lawrenceville.

"Al mention anything about the job I'm working on?"

"You mean the little girl?" Henry doused the joint with quick bites of his thumb and forefinger. "It's okay, right? Me knowing about it, I mean. You know Al talks things over with some people.

84

But he keeps it to a small crowd. And he keeps a secret when it has to be kept. He's got your best interest at heart."

Dorsey focused on the TV screen, watching the teams take warm-up shots. *You don't have to be told Al has your best interest at heart, he reminded himself. He's your best friend, so he takes liberties. Ones he figures he's entitled to, like counting your money, saving you the trouble. Son of a bitch is a good friend. A sometimes very annoying friend, but he finds ways to make up for it.*

"So," Dorsey said, "you know the case is in Lawrenceville. And anybody that knows Polish Hill must know his way around Lawrenceville."

"You'd think that," Henry said, "but it ain't so. What I know about Lawrenceville is 1963, the last time I was there. No call to go there. Far as I'm concerned, you could bomb the bridge, drop it right into the Iron City Brewery. A sentiment I'd think you'd share."

Dorsey hoisted his bottle of Rolling Rock and agreed. "But this girl I'm looking for," he said, "both parents are into dope, heavy into it. The mother seems to get hers by prescription, but the old man works the streets. Who the hell knows what he's on."

"Nasty shit," Henry said, slipping the saved half joint into his wallet. "Dope can be nasty shit."

11

Dorsey beat the next morning's cross town rush-hour traffic by getting away from the house at six-thirty, but a spring rain had him going slow. Not a shower, it was a downpour, steady lines of gray that battered the asphalt in sharp pinpoints. The Buick's defrost unit had seen better times, and Dorsey kept his windows cracked, keeping the windshield fog to a minimum. Rain sprayed in across the rear seat, catching the edge of his left shoulder, adding to his annoyance, but he stuck to his plan and schedule. He wanted to check out the other side's home field, and he wanted to do it early before the team showed up for practice.

He left the Buick at the curb on Forty-sixth. Opening an over-size golf umbrella, he retraced his steps of Friday night. The umbrella, years ago, had been a secondhand gift from his father, who might have received it from any one of his cronies who thought politics, like business, was best conducted on a fairway. "Too much sunshine," Martin Dorsey had told his son. "Never liked guys with tans, and most voters don't either. Makes you look like you take one too many vacations. Tans are okay if you're running for office in Florida."

Dorsey took the steps near the swimming pool, looking over his shoulder at the rain bursting on the surface of the chemical blue water. At the head of the steps, terraced into the easy slope away from Butler, he found the basketball court and a baseball field beyond. The court's demarcation lines were chipped yellow paint, scuffed from a thousand pairs of sneakers, taking Dorsey back some twenty years when his summers had been dedicated to crisscrossing similar courts all over the city. Before his knuckles had been smashed into the hardwood floor at WVU. When he worried about low post position and finding the backboard's sweet spot and not about insurance claims and mortgages and missing teenagers. But it was the ball field that captured his notice, especially the right-field line and the cyclone mesh fence that ran along it, holding back the cemetery. Dorsey moved toward it.

The cyclone fence, as Dorsey had predicted, was in desperate need of repair. Whole sections had been cut away, leaving jagged metal spikes twisting away from the support poles. These gaps, he knew, were escape routes, emergency hatches, ready-made for a fast getaway when the police hit the park. Dorsey chose one of the gaps, found a smooth handhold on a support pole, and hoisted himself up onto the cement footer supporting the fence. What he found was an unintended booby-trap, a good place to lose a few toes. Dorsey thought of it as the mother of all tetanus.

Extending out for nearly ten feet in all directions was broken glass. Ragged bottle necks, brown glass still strung together on the strength of label adhesive, and the clear glass remains of liquor half-pints. Dorsey had found the drinker's dumping ground. He could picture the park boys, and girls, finishing off sixteen ounce Iron Citys and tossing them over their shoulders and into the cemetery, like champagne glasses into the fireplace. The shards of liquor and wine bottles suggested to Dorsey that the party went on despite the change in seasons.

Sustaining an uneasy balance, managing the umbrella and crab-walking along the footer, Dorsey found clear ground and circumnavigated the glass field, wondering if he could retire on the proceeds of recycling the contents. The area he found himself in was a scooped out depression, and the mud sucked at his shoes. The long slits left behind by track-driven earth movers told him it was a harvest spot for landscape fill. Moving through the muck, each step a chore, Dorsey was reminded of old cartoons whose characters had their shoes stuck in tar or bubblegum. On the far side of the depression he struggled up a knoll and into a copse of trees. At the base of the trees was a heavy thicket, and again he had to work his way along one handed, holding the umbrella at arm's length.

In the midst of the trees and bush was a small clearing. And another surprise. The campsite took Dorsey way back—twenty years almost, into some empty field in the American South. Army basic training, field bivouac, one- or two-man pup tents. *Christ, how you hated that,* Dorsey thought. *Rain, just like this, and cold. Shitty food to eat and then no place to shit out that shitty food once it had finished with your insides. And here we have someone doing it on a voluntary basis.*

There was no evidence of a fire ever being built, so they were that smart, he decided. The tent itself, a greenish-blue geosphere with self supporting inseam posts, seemed capable of housing two occupants. A food bag hung from a tree limb, and Dorsey wondered if they had a concern about bears in Allegheny Cemetery. At the foot of that same tree was a stack of beer cases. Stepping into the clearing, Dorsey heard the dull whirr of the tent-door zipper being undone. An arm was extended outward, the hand turned with palm up.

"Fuck, man," a young female voice said. "Rain."

The arm went back in and was replaced by a chubby face belonging to what Dorsey figured to be a girl in her midteens. She scanned her surroundings, her face losing its drowsy complaisance when she came upon Dorsey. The face shot back inside and he could hear two voices, one female and one male, in earnest and mumbled discussion.

Hippie-ghouls, Dorsey thought, *confusing the cemetery with Yel-*

lowstone Park. I wonder if the park rangers know about these guys. The tent flap opened again, and a bare-chested boy—Dorsey figured his age at around twenty—shimmied out on elbows and blue-jeaned knees. He quickly got to his shoeless feet, toes sinking into the mud, standing just under six feet. Dorsey stopped running through his list of camping jokes when the boy pulled a hunting knife from a sheath on his waistband. *Oh, shit,* he thought, his sense of humor still somewhat intact, *good thing I brought along the umbrella.*

"Fuck you want?" the boy asked, menacing Dorsey with the knife, waving the blade with a slightly crooked arm. *Television style,* Dorsey concluded.

"Slow down, okay?" Dorsey said, backing up a step. "This is no big deal. I don't know you and I didn't come her looking for you. My coming across your little homestead here was strictly by chance."

The boy stepped a little closer, still brandishing the knife.

"On the other hand," Dorsey said, getting annoyed and hoping to get some information out of this pair, "I can take off now and come back a little later. With the police. And then you can explain what you're doing out here with your under-eighteen prom date. Probably a statutory rape charge, along with the trespass charge that the cemetery management might press. And from the looks of you—and your silly-ass tough-guy attitude—you're already on probation for some other dumb shit you were caught at. So, how's this gonna turn out?"

The boy's evil look receded, and Dorsey knew he had guessed right. Slowly, the knife went back into its sheath and the boy backed off, carefully planting each foot in the mud. Dorsey fell into step, keeping a few feet of safety between them in case the boy's change in attitude was only temporary. "Get in out of the rain," Dorsey said. "While I'm here, we should talk."

The boy pulled back the tent door flaps and motioned the girl toward the back wall. With the flaps open, Dorsey could see one sleeping bag, an air pillow, and a Baggie of pot. *But no Boy Scout manual,* Dorsey told himself. The boy sat just inside the entrance, protected from the rain, folding his legs beneath him. The girl moved forward and draped an arm across his shoulder. Dorsey found himself feeling as if he were an unwanted salesman, left out on the stoop.

"What's he want?" Dorsey heard the girl ask.

"How the fuck should I know?" the boy answered, then returned to Dorsey. "Yeah, what the fuck do you want?"

Holding the umbrella in place above his head, Dorsey crouched down, his free hand going into the mud to take some pressure off his bad knee. "Lighten up," he said, his gaze even with the boy's. "This might not take so long if you do. This girl that's gone missing, Maritsa Durant, I'm trying to see if I can't figure out what happened to her. You two know her?"

The boy shrugged off the question, but the girl perked up. "She was kinda neat, I liked her," the girl said. "But, boy, it's been a while since she left. Yeah, that was a while back."

"Left?" Dorsey asked. Not "disappeared," not "vanished," not "up in smoke." Left. She left, as if she had checked the bus schedule, packed her bags, and departed on her own.

The boy shot the girl a sour look. "She don't know shit," he said, addressing Dorsey but holding the girl silent with his eyes. "She's just gone; Maritsa's just gone."

"Gone with who?"

"Just gone," the boy said. "Happens everyday. Read the fuckin' papers, look at the TV news. Happens everyday."

Dorsey gave the boy his own hard-ass look, dismissing him. He shifted his concentration to the girl. "So you knew Maritsa. I've never met her, obviously. What was she like?"

The girl hesitated, looking at her boyfriend and then at Dorsey. Clearly, she found Dorsey more intimidating. "Like I said, she was kinda neat, cool. And she was smart; you could tell talking to her. And some guys said she was smart at school."

"Did she like to party?" Dorsey asked.

"Ah, yes and no," the girl said. "Not really. She was around some, but she didn't like to get high. She'd be around, and she used to just hold a beer in her hand. Mostly for someone else while they took a piss."

"So what was she doing around here?"

"Lookin' for her father. That's what some people said. Teddy's her father. I didn't know that for a long time, but that's what I heard. Teddy's her father."

Dorsey asked if she had seen Teddy lately and the boy took over. "That jag-off, he hasn't been around for a long time. Can't come around 'cause nobody wants him around. He owes money to just about half the people around here."

"How about Outlaw?" Dorsey asked. "Did he have much to do with Maritsa?"

"Outlaw's cool," the girl said before her boyfriend could quiet her. "I dig him, really. He's okay. With everybody. I think he liked Maritsa, like he felt sorry for her because of her parents. I remember he used to help her out, give her money sometimes, I think."

"They go off together?" Dorsey asked. "You said she left. She leave on her own?"

"Don't know." The girl looked again at her boyfriend and seemed to realize that she had gone on long enough. "Don't know."

Dorsey tried to switch back to Teddy but both insisted that they hadn't seen him in some time. It was clear that the meeting was adjourned. Dorsey stood up, shaking the mud from his fingertips and working some stability into his knee.

"Look," Dorsey said, "this is simple. I'm trying to find a missing girl. Not to get her in any trouble. Just to find her. To make sure she's all right. Nothing else. So if something turns up, let me know. I'm going to be around for a while."

He turned and made his way through the bush, picking up and ignoring several comments made to his back. *Homesteaders,* Dorsey thought, *modern Sooners, that's what they think they're doing. If you*

91

loaf around a place long enough, pitch a tent, call it your own. You have to wonder which one of these street lawyers stumbled across the principle of adverse possession.

He crossed back into the park, careful to avoid the glass dumping ground, retracing his steps through the baseball field and across the basketball court. The rain had begun to ease into a soft and steady drizzle, and Dorsey closed his umbrella, letting the rain glaze his scalp. *So they think she just left. Those two in the tent, they just weren't worried about it. About an unexplainable disappearance. Not worried that some freak might be riding around the neighborhood with an eye out for good-looking teenage girls. Girls that were never seen again. What the hell, girls disappear into the park, why can't they disappear from the park? As long as they have company. Outlaw, who helped out, who felt sorry for her because her parents were junkies? Or Daddy Teddy himself, who picked up his little girl from school?*

At the park entrance, fishing his keys from his trouser pocket, Dorsey heard a car horn and spotted a familiar blue Dodge pulling to the curb. The same one he had followed to the diner on Friday night. Janice Manning reached across the front seat and opened the passenger door, and Dorsey checked his watch. *How nice,* he thought, *to be followed so early in the morning.*

"Get in," she said, much more of a request than an order. "Had breakfast?"

Dorsey slipped through the door, wedging the umbrella between his knees. "Just coffee. Back to the diner?"

Janice Manning smiled. "I can cook; in fact I like to. My place isn't far, and, besides, I can give you the stuff I have on file about Outlaw."

Again, she looked terrific, Dorsey thought, regardless of the time of day. She had on washed-out jeans and a T-shirt covered by a red rain slicker, the zipper undone. Her short hair looked freshly shampooed and as if it needed little else. "Where's your other half?" Dorsey asked. "The one with the food in his beard."

"At this hour, home safely in his bed." Janice hooked a right onto Butler and drove along the park's lawns and the cemetery's stone walls. "He's got a family, so his hours are a bit more regular than mine. As long as I keep him up to date on things, he doesn't mind my freelancing. Besides, it gets results that we can both take credit for."

She went left at the Sixty-second Street Bridge, crossing the Allegheny River and out of the city. Once across she went right again and down a ramp that led into Sharpsburg. Opposite a huge grey stone Catholic church she pulled into a driveway that ran between two apartment buildings and parked among several other cars at the rear of the second building.

Janice killed the ignition and removed the key. "Early start in bad weather; you must like to earn your fees." She slipped out of the car, and Dorsey followed her to the building, where she worked open the security door. "Any leads on the girl?" she said. "Or did you take the entire weekend off?"

"After Friday night, I thought I deserved a little down time." Dorsey accompanied her along the first-floor hall to the front apartment, where she unlocked the door. "Besides, even detectives get weekends off. Now and again."

"Not this one."

"No shit," Dorsey said. "I would've never thought otherwise."

The apartment was shotgun plain, a series of rooms aligned like railroad cars. The living room had double windows that looked out on the front doors of the Catholic church. Next was a dining room and then a small hallway with side doors to both bedroom and bath. In the rear was the kitchen, where Dorsey settled into a chair at a rough wooden table while Janice went to the counter and poured water into a coffeemaker.

"Seriously, anything new with the girl?" Finished with the coffeemaker, she slipped out of the slicker and hung it over a hook near the rear door. With it off, Dorsey could read the printing on

93

her T-shirt's breast pocket: PENNSYLVANIA STATE POLICE MARKSMAN TEAM COMPETITION, 1984. *A finalist no doubt,* Dorsey thought.

"C'mon," she said, using that killer smile that Dorsey was coming to recognize. "What's going on with your case? I said the other night that I'd help if I could."

"And you did," Dorsey told her. "Friday night you were a big help. I was tailing the only lead I had, this oversized street king named Outlaw, hoping to find out something. So, to lend a hand, you and your trained midget assistant threatened to arrest me. And then to make matters worse, you took me to that diner and forced me to watch him eat."

"Having Dave as a partner has its drawbacks." She was rummaging through the refrigerator, her back to Dorsey. "He's a pretty capable guy, if you keep a knife and fork out of his hands."

Dorsey watched her carry eggs, milk, and bread to the countertop. *So,* he thought, *what does she want from you? And what would you like her to want from you? She wants to crack Outlaw, that's for sure, and anyone else from Butler Street she can get her hands on. And to be chief of police somewhere, probably director of the FBI in time. And what the hell difference does it make, if she helps you find the girl?* He decided to tell her about his morning encounter with the campers.

"Sounds like Dingle to me," Janice said after hearing the story. She had toast buttered and eggs frying.

"Dingle?" Dorsey said, sipping at the coffee she had set before him. "Where in the hell do they come up with these names?"

Janice Manning tended to the eggs, using a spatula to drip bacon grease across the egg yokes. "It's easy. Every Polish name gets the "ski" or the "kowski" knocked off it and maybe something gets added on. The guy's real name is Dinkowski. Maybe your name was Dorsekowski when your ancestors came off the boat."

"Dorsekowskiovachinski, to be exact."

She laughed and served the eggs on toast. "So, the girl gave you the idea that maybe Maritsa is off on her own?"

"Or with a friend or boyfriend or maybe even her old man." Dorsey watched her slip into the chair opposite his, appreciating the fluidity in her muscles, the movement so smooth that he had to wonder if her body really had bones or joints. "Old Teddy, he seems to have dropped out of sight as well."

"That's nothing new," Janice said, forking egg into her mouth. "Once, Dave Lyle and I thought we had something on him, and we cruised the park and the bars on Butler for weeks. No sign of him. And remember, we're supposed to be detectives and this is supposed to be our turf. People can't hide from us, even if they think they can. Like Outlaw thought he could on Friday night. That horseshit about Zima's backroom is old hat." Janice stabbed her fork in his direction. "Teddy couldn't hide from us. He was gone for a couple of months, is what we found out later."

"So," Dorsey asked, "where was he?"

"Never did find out," she said. "And he keeps going back there, wherever that is."

Dorsey concentrated on his food and a few moments of silence ensued. When he looked up from his plate, Janice Manning was giving him the smile again, a thorough going over that caused his stomach to shift. *Jesus, this woman. The changes you see. And she does it tight on cue.*

"You have some material on Outlaw?" he asked sliding his empty plate away.

"In a minute." She wiped her lips with a napkin. "This weekend you took off—how'd it work out, relationship-wise?"

To the point at last, Dorsey thought, an odd mixture of lust and fear welling up in him. "I'd say that I was given my walking papers, for the most part. No final decrees, but for the present I'm a free man, fully entitled to all the pleasures and severe depressions that accompany that status."

"Let the pleasures relieve the depression." Janice rose from her chair, rounded the table, and from behind his chair she leaned forward and looped her arms around his neck. "What would you say to an offer of getting laid?"

"Ah, all right."

Dorsey first stirred a little before noon. Janice had her face partially buried into a pillow, and he slowly realized that he had been awakened by this perfect woman's snoring. He slipped from beneath the sheets and started for the bathroom but stopped at the doorway to admire Janice. She was on her side, one breast falling into the other. Her legs were longer than Dorsey had imagined, and the muscles were those of a sprinter, the kind you saw at a track meet, tensed to vault the next hurdle. He realized that he had never before been with two different woman in so short a time. He wasn't sure if pride or shame was the proper emotion.

At the bathroom sink he washed the sweat and sleep from his face, examining himself in the mirror, wondering if Gretchen had the day shift. *Old habits,* he thought, *maybe they die in time. Hopefully they die before we do.*

Dorsey took a towel from a wall rack and worked it at his face. A little more awake, he began to take in his surroundings. The sink's splashboard was lined with lotions and shampoos, and Dorsey realized that this was the only room that reflected any femininity. Looking up from the sink, he spotted something in the mirror's upper left corner. Leaning forward on his toes, he saw that it was a miniature Post-it note with a THINGS TO DO heading.

"Jesus, what a nut. But it explains some things."

Janice Manning had only one thing on her list. GET NOVOTNY.

12

Dorsey sipped at his coffee and reviewed the notes he had prepared on his visit to the cemetery, undecided as to whether to refer to the campers as the Homesteaders or the Honeymooners. Dismissing the issue, he went back again to what the girl had said: Maritsa had left. *I'll bet,* he thought, *but she didn't leave alone. If that's how it happened. Christ, buddy, are you making progress on this one.*

The coffee had gone cold, and Dorsey went to the kitchen for a fresh cup. Back at his desk, he pulled the notes from the typewriter carriage and slipped them into the case file, which he tossed to the desk's far corner. He twisted backward in the swivel chair, slipping a cassette into the tape player, Erroll Garner's *Concert By The Sea,* a beauty from the late fifties. Straightening himself, Dorsey turned his attention to a second manila folder on the desktop, one given him by Janice Manning that morning. He wondered if he should type up his notes on that meeting, too.

He had washed and dressed quickly and returned to the bedroom where, from his own sense of modesty, he covered Janice with the sheet before nudging her awake. She roused almost immediately, shrugging away the bedclothes and hopping to her feet. Drawn to her full length, overwhelming as a nude, she kissed him quickly but softly, then made for the front room. On her return she gave Dorsey a copy of her file on Outlaw.

Dorsey had watched and listened as she dressed, mostly watching. She did it well, he thought, dressing slowly, taking care in the choice and application of each item. And she lingered after each one, stopping to talk for a moment, apparently giving Dorsey the opportunity to admire each stage in the process.

The return ride to the park and the Buick had been punctuated with her assurances to Dorsey that a dark connection existed between Dr. Novotny and Outlaw. "Read the file," she kept saying, "then we'll talk.

"And we *will* be talking," she had said, again with the killer smile. "Because you can bet I'll be calling."

The manila folder had a stenciled legend identifying it as concerning Dennis McCauley, aka Outlaw. Below the name, in parentheses, was RE: CONNECTIONS TO DR. NOVOTNY. Dorsey gulped his coffee and waded into the paper.

At the top of the heap was a summary sheet that appeared to have been designed on a PC. *Quick and dirty,* Dorsey thought as he read. Dennis McCauley was twenty-eight years old and had managed only two and a half years at Schenley High School. His dropping out was attributed to continual racial incidents, and Janice Manning's notes suggested that Outlaw/McCauley had been the instigator. Dorsey thought that portion of the notes had to be based on neighborhood legend and gossip, because he also knew that whites were desperately outnumbered at Schenley. He wasn't sure if he should think of the younger Outlaw as brave and foolhardy, or just plain stupid.

Next in the file were reports on several juvenile arrests, and Dorsey was again impressed with Janice Manning's powers. Juvenile arrest records were kept confidential, sealed once the offender had passed his eighteenth birthday. Which clerk had been bribed? And with what? Maybe just that smile alone.

The offenses were typical of the time—mostly car stereos and citizen band radios torn from dashboards in the St. Francis parking lot. There was one underage drinking charge, and all in all the record amounted to fourteen months of juvenile probation. The adult arrest record was somewhat more impressive, although convictions were lacking.

Once out of school, Outlaw must have gotten meaner, Dorsey figured. The adult offenses were violent ones. Assaults in or just outside of Butler Street bars, beatings administered to unlucky outsiders who had wandered into the neighborhood. There was a vandalism charge over his near destruction of a BMW with a crowbar. And when the city bused in blacks one afternoon to use the park's pool, Outlaw had broken the jaw of one of the chaperons. But nothing to do with dope.

But Janice Manning's file reflected an assumption that he was in the dope trade, at least with Dr. Novotny. Several amateurish photographs showed Outlaw entering the doctor's Butler Street office or standing at the street corner on Forty-sixth. At one point in her personal notes, Janice referred to Outlaw as Dr. Novotny's "Two-way conduit. One direction took drugs to the park. In the opposite direction, he feeds the doctor's personal appetites."

Erroll Garner's fingertips drifted across the ivory, and Dorsey sipped at the rim of his coffee mug, wondering what in the hell it was that Janice was alluding to. It was a tease, the entire file was a come on, Dorsey was sure. Like most everything else the woman did. But she didn't do it just to keep in practice. *Hell no,* he thought, *that one does not need practice. Her tease has a purpose, a goal. The means to an end. So, friend, feel better about yourself?*

Dorsey returned to the file summary and an item he had noticed earlier. It was a pair of addresses; Outlaw's present one and that of his family. The family lived on Fifty-seventh Street. Tenth ward. Uncle Davey's baliwick.

"You don't work the weekend at all? You detectives got some good union going for you."

Dorsey sat at Mrs. Leneski's kitchen table, wishing he was back at the office, safely lost in Erroll Garner's 1950s. He watched her pour coffee from the ever-vigilant pot. "Just this weekend. It was important to me." He took his coffee from the old woman and thanked her. "Anyway, you'll be happy to know that I've been on the job since the wee hours. In all that rain."

"So?" Mrs. Leneski sat herself across the table.

Dorsey sipped at the coffee, scalding as always. "Thought you might be happy with me. I've been checking out the park, just as you suggested." He told her of his morning encounter. With the Homesteaders, he had decided.

"So, did you call the cops? Maybe the people that run the cemetery? Those two belong in a cell somewhere. At least the boy does. So what'd you do afterwards?"

Don't ask, Dorsey thought. "Things got hectic afterwards," he said. "And the job is to find your granddaughter, not clean up the park. Anyways, I may need these people somewhere along the line." He took another light touch of his coffee.

"Goddamned park," Mrs. Leneski muttered. "Goddamned park."

"I need you to do something," Dorsey said. "You've been through Maritsa's room since she's been gone, right? With the police, maybe?"

Mrs. Leneski said she had and added a look of irritation at Dorsey's apparent treading over covered ground. "So what?"

"Do it again," he said. "Please."

"It could help?"

"There's a possibility, one you won't like." Dorsey told her the theory he had been considering.

"Then they tricked her, the sumbitches." Mrs. Leneski finished off her coffee in two swallows. Dorsey cringed. "Like they were taking her somewheres for the day," she said. Sumbitches have my Maritsa."

"Like I said, it's a possibility," Dorsey said, at a loss to come up with any other possibilities. "Go through her room slowly, carefully. Think about anything that means something to her, anything she might like to have near. And see if it's missing."

Mrs. Leneski, for a moment, sat quietly. Her hands played along the edge of the tabletop. "I go in the room a lot." She spoke so softly that Dorsey had to crowd into the table. "I don't go through her things. I never done that—not when she was still here or since. I made her do her own cleaning up and she was good." She went for more coffee, poured some for herself and for Dorsey without asking, then sat. "But I go in there a lot. Even before, when you rang the doorbell, that's where I was. You didn't know that. That's where I was. You find my girl, please. You find out what happened."

"I'm on it full time." Dorsey worked up a smile for her. "I'll even put in a few weekends, if that's what it takes."

There was no answer when he knocked at his uncle's door, so Dorsey went back to the Buick, taking Fifty-fourth Street across Butler in the direction of the river. As he neared the water, the row houses gave way to industrial buildings, mostly trucking terminals and metal shops. Wedged between two of them was a one-story cinder-block building with no identifying marks. There was a central door with windows to each side, both with curtains drawn. Dorsey parked next to a chained fence and went to the door, finding the buzzer along the jam. "Yeah?" The voice was electronically reproduced, and it took Dorsey a moment to locate the intercom speaker at the top of the door.

"Looking for Davey Sullivan?" Dorsey shouted at the speaker, hoping it was a two-way. "He in there? Ask if he's receiving visitors today."

There were a few moments of silence and Dorsey imagined the hushed conference among huddled heads that was going on inside. "Recognize the voice, Davey?" the bartender would ask. *Please say yes,* Dorsey thought. *It's getting hot out here.*

The voice returned with a perfunctory "Okay," followed by an electric burring as the lock was released. Dorsey pushed open the door and entered a scaled-down barroom. Miniaturized, it seemed to him. The counter was only a few feet from the door, and the back bar held just four liquor bottles arranged about the cash register. Along the side walls, as if for insulation, were stacks of beer cases, nearly to Dorsey's shoulder. Crammed into a corner, seated just below the mounted television, was Uncle Davey.

"Found me, eh?" Uncle Davey gestured Dorsey onto the next barstool. "I guess you really are a shamus."

"It was tough all right," Dorsey said, settling in. "When a bachelor Hibernian isn't at home, the first place to check is with the other Ancient Hibernians. Besides, I think you might have brought me here as a kid."

"That's possible." Uncle Davey glanced at the TV screen. The Pirates were in Philadelphia. "Always was a good place to watch the game. Especially these late afternoon ones, with most people at home or work."

Dorsey ordered up a Rolling Rock for himself and replaced his uncle's Iron City and whiskey sidecar. "Any score?"

"Phillies are ahead, two zip. We've had a few men on base, but never got them home." Uncle Davey knocked back his shot and pushed the tumbler across the bar. He turned to Dorsey. "So, what's up? You've got a home to watch the game in, but you put on a search for me. Help you with something?"

"Like to run a name by you," Dorsey said. "It's part of this job I'm on about the girl."

"Whatever I can do. Let's hear it."

Dorsey mentioned Dennis McCauley, and his uncle momentarily returned to the ballgame. Deliberately, he took a pack of Chesterfields from his hip pocket and lit up. "Do I know him?" he asked rhetorically. "The whole family, I know them all. The old man, he's my age. I know him and this Dennis and all his brothers. And excepting the old man, possibly, the whole bunch ain't no damn good. Take my word for it."

"I will," Dorsey said. He watched for a minute as the bartender filled a cooler and then left for the back room. "Talk to me about them. Tell me about this Dennis."

"The old man does roofing work." Uncle Davey took a pull of beer, and it was apparent to Dorsey that he planned on telling things as he chose. "Hard worker," his uncle said, "but he goes too heavy on the drinkin'. And his boys, he never gave them near enough time. None of 'em, all five, none of 'em finished high school. Maybe the oldest, but I think that was an Army GED. But that doesn't change things. They all drank like the old man. And they all had trouble with the law, stolen cars and I think they broke into a couple of places. Like I said, they're just trouble."

Dorsey took in what his uncle said. And what he didn't say. He offered no excuse for these people, these neighborhood people. Not even a local's loyalty, the reluctant acceptance normally reserved for the worst of the neighborhood's wayward. Not even a laugh for the familiar. *Christ, he thought, this family really must be no damn good.*

"Dennis is the fourth boy, I think." Uncle Davey watched the catcher snag a foul ball near the dugout before he continued. "No better or worse than the others, I suppose. But I hear he's supposed to be big shit down in the ninth ward.

"Hear anything special?" Dorsey asked.

"I never hear nothing special," Uncle Davey said. "I just hear what everybody else hears—and, nephew, that's enough for any-body. Dennis McCauley is like most rotten guys who make it through this world. He gets people to like him, despite what he is. Usually people that are younger that he is. You could almost say that he can get people to admire him. Well, at least pay attention to him. I'm sure he's a talker."

Dorsey finished his beer and switched directions. "Tell me,

who's your family doctor? You know, the guy you go to for check-ups, things like that?"

"Dr. Donahoe, like everybody else I know." His uncle looked at him inquisitively. "Worried about my health? Maybe I don't look so good, huh?"

"No, no. It's not that," Dorsey said. "It's just that I'm getting information that this McCauley has some kind of line in with a doctor down Butler Street aways. This one's named Novotny. Ever hear of him?"

"Sure I heard of him," Uncle Davey said. "He was your mother's doctor. When she had the cancer. He probably signed the death certificate."

13

Dorsey took a long hit from his ice water jug, then wiped his brow with a bare forearm. Grinning, he recalled his Grandmother Sullivan's warm weather advice. "Don't tell me," she had said so often, "I know what to do when it gets hot out. You're supposed to drink hot things, not cold ones. Hot ones'll cool you down. Do what you want, I'm putting on the teapot." Dorsey took another gulp of water. *Jesus,* he thought, *what a goddamned nut.*

In his seat inside the van's back door, Dorsey was stripped to the waist and peering through binoculars aimed at a front door half a city block away. The smoked glass of the rear windows cloaked him from outside view, and his perch was on three cases of beer he had neglected to unload before borrowing the van from Al. He had been in place for nearly forty minutes, and the van's closed interior was magnifying the early-evening heat by a factor that Dorsey could only guess at. The doorway he watched through his lens was that of Outlaw's apartment, one piece of a now chopped up single-family dwelling.

Dorsey shifted his weight to his left hip and again used his forearm to try to force sweat back into his scalp. Where his hair had gone thin it had melded into ropelike strands, accentuating the bare skin beneath. Reflected back at him from the glass, he wondered how much longer he had left on the hair-loss time line. And then he thought about his talk with his uncle.

Hate it when it seems close to home, he thought. *So much easier when the case is just about some guy, not some guy you already know. And when it's family it's that much worse.* Novotny had been Mum's doctor. Why? Or, for chrissakes, why not? So, they had passed up on their regular doc and went a little farther down Butler Street to Novotny. Most likely it had been the old man's choice, maybe. *Jesus, Novotny—who Janice Manning has a hard-on for, who has a reputation lower than sewer-water—was Mum's doctor at the end. What a fuckin' family.*

Outlaw's street ran parallel to the river, where the ground ran flat and the switch was made from residential to commercial. The curb opposite Outlaw's, where Dorsey was stationed, fronted a now-defunct foundry, a three-block-long crumbling structure of dusty brick and broken windows. It worried him to be sitting in such a noticeable spot, but the other side of the street was parked up. And putting a tail on Outlaw was the next logical step. After reading Manning's file. And after Mrs. Leneski's dinnertime phone call.

Dorsey had been leaving the house to pick up Al's van when she had called. "I said a rosary," she had said. "To help me. It helps. I don't give a damn what some people say, it helps. Then I went through all Maritsa's stuff."

"And? Something out of place? Missing?"

"A book," Mrs. Leneski had said. "Her favorite. I remember her talking about it all the time. And she talked about the person who wrote it, said she was a real screwed up young girl. I remember the book was called *The Outsiders.* What do you think?"

What the hell are you supposed to think? Dorsey asked himself again, his eyes trained the door front. *We have a match. The Outsiders.* S. E. Hinton, the young girl with so much direct experience and a talent to convey the significance. The greasers and the socs;

haves and have nots. The greasers, misunderstood tough guys who were hated for their social standing in town. The boys who hung out at the park at Forty-sixth and Butler. *Things do come together. And Maritsa left, she wasn't abducted. Took her favorite reading material and left. And most likely she didn't do it alone.*

Twilight set in, but the temperature in the van remained constant and Dorsey doused his head and chest with the remaining ice water. To ease his eye strain, he alternated his gaze from the doorway to the nine-year-old Electra parked in front. The license plate matched the numbers in Manning's file, and he was relying on this in his belief that Outlaw was inside the house. House surveillance was a crap shoot at best, but Dorsey had no other game to play.

Outlaw showed himself a few moments before nine, just as full darkness settled. Dorsey watched his bulky silhouette standing on the front stoop and saw a match flare as Outlaw fired a cigarette. Quickly, Dorsey slipped the binoculars into their carrying case, grabbed his T-shirt, and crawled into the driver's seat. Staying low, he saw Outlaw unlock the Electra's driver's-side door but stay outside on the asphalt, bathed in the weak glow of the dome light. Dorsey thought he had been spotted, but was relieved to see Outlaw, dressed in jeans and tank T-shirt, take several long pulls on his cigarette. Homemade, Dorsey decided, and definitely not tobacco. He turned over the engine in step with Outlaw, cranked the transmission noisily into gear, and, lights out for the first two blocks, followed the Electra.

The Electra went right onto Forty-fourth Street, and Dorsey figured they were headed to the park. But Outlaw went past Butler without turning, riding by Mrs. Leneski's house and Holy Family Church. Dorsey went by in turn and hoped that Mrs. Leneski was still hard at work on her rosary beads, beseeching God instead of leaving messages for him. At the next intersection, he held back a few moments, struggling into his shirt and cranking open the window for his first breath of air.

Near the traffic light on Penn Avenue by St. Francis Hospital, Outlaw pulled to the curb in a no standing area, and the Electra's hazard lights blinked on. Reacting a little too late, Dorsey was forced to drive past and make the turn onto Penn. Giving it the gas, he pushed the van and circled the block, finding a vantage point at the intersection below the Electra. Now, two teenaged boys were hanging into the driver's window, and the hazard lights had gone dark. The meeting lasted a moment, and although he had no way of confirming it, Dorsey was sure cash and goods had changed hands.

The next move was around the hospital and to the park. Outlaw left the Electra near the park's footpath, and Dorsey stopped farther up, by the ball field. He decided against another walking trip through the park and dug deeper into the van's seat to wait things out.

A breeze finally worked itself up, cool and carrying the sounds of living from the homes across the street. The murmured remains of front porch conversations backed by a modulated radio voice discussing the Pirate's standing in the Eastern Division. Dorsey felt at home, as if he were in his office, the windows open to Wharton Street. He yawned and checked his watch.

Nearly thirty minutes elapsed before Outlaw emerged from the park in the company of a teenage girl. They both held tall beer cans wrapped in brown paper sacks, and Dorsey went for the binoculars to confirm that the girl was not Maritsa. Instead, he found the female camper he had met that morning. *Hell of a long day,* he told himself.

The pair was standing at the edge of a streetlamp's glow, shadows partially obscuring them from the street, and it wasn't until the girl opened the car door before Dorsey had a true appreciation of the change in her. As she sat in the passenger seat with the door open, using the rearview mirror to check her appearance, Dorsey focused in on her with the binoculars and saw that someone had taken her out of the woods and into a hot shower, for starters. Then it had been a trim at a beauty shop and a makeup lesson. Dorsey felt as if he were spying on a makeover at a mall cosmetic counter. Outlaw was in a crouch by the passenger doorway, smiling at the girl. Not in a lurid fashion, Dorsey thought, more like one of encouragement—like a father whose little girl had just taken the training wheels off her bicycle. Outlaw pointed to a spot on her cheek, then found that same spot in the mirror, and with a circling index finger he apparently suggested that the girl apply more makeup. She complied, and with another warm smile, Outlaw closed the door and rounded the front of the car. Dorsey hit the ignition and worked the van's meat grinder of a transmission, ready for the next leg of the trip.

The Electra moved more slowly now, more cautiously it seemed to Dorsey, and he was obliged to lay back, again wondering if he had been spotted. They went left on Butler, and from the van's raised seat he trained the binoculars down at the Electra, several cars now running between them. Outlaw was driving with his right arm leisurely draped across the top of the front seat, and he seemed to be spending more time looking at the girl than the road. Dorsey could see him talking to her, the words intermixed with tender smiles, Outlaw stroking her hair. *Yeah, you better take it slow, with your concentration divided and all,* Dorsey thought.

The Electra hooked a right and crossed a bridge over the Allegheny River, leaving the city. Dorsey followed. In that same pattern they entered and left the working-class town of Millvale and into a suburban setting. Not a recent development with split-level ranches and weather-treated wooden decks, but older brick homes on smaller lots with shrubbery-enclosed lawns. *The kind of suburbs,* Dorsey thought, *that the first escapees from the city built in the late forties and early fifties. Before expressways and interstates and Jacuzzis blowing hot bubbles up your ass.*

They were on a secondary road when Dorsey saw the flash of the Electra's turn signal as it pulled into a short driveway. Dorsey drove on for fifty yards, dowsed his headlights, and made a U-turn.

Two homes down from the driveway he pulled onto the gravel at the road shoulder and killed the engine. Over the trimmed bushes at the lawn's edge he saw a porch light snap on, and then Outlaw laughed a greeting to a large figure of a man in the doorway. He held open the screen door for the girl, who was nearly hidden by the bush, then followed her inside. The porch went dark, and Dorsey crawled out through the van's passenger side, planning to get close enough for an address.

His T-shirt was the dark maroon he had worn while barhopping in Lawrenceville, and he felt secure in the darkness. The road was a remote one and traffic was nonexistent. He crept along the bushes, bent at the waist, coming to a halt at the side of the driveway. The rear bumper of the Electra jutted out into the road, and there was a dark-colored Cadillac, maybe two years old, ahead of it at the garage door. Dorsey slipped up to the porch railing and took note of the number, 611. *Great,* he thought, *now what in the hell's the name of the road?*

From the side of the house, brick with closed sash windows, came the hum of a whole house air-conditioning compressor, hindering Dorsey as he tried his hand at eavesdropping on the front room conversation. There was laughter—Outlaw's and the girl's— and the booming bellow of an older man. The words were barely audible, and Dorsey moved in on one of the windows, hoping for the best. Just as he did, the porch light went on and the front door opened on even more laughter. *These guys are having a hell of night,* Dorsey thought, scrambling around the Cadillac. He knew he'd never make it through the bushes or around the side of the house, so he went flat to the driveway and crab crawled under the Cadillac's front carriage. The harsh scents of metal and automotive oils assaulted him.

Face first in the gravel, he could only listen to the conversation being held on the porch. At first Dorsey thought the girl was being quiet; then he realized that she hadn't come back out. Outlaw was accommodating. He told the man not to worry, he knew he was

110

good for the money. "Maybe when I pick her up," he said. "If you have it on you then." The man said that would work, and he said it in a voice heavy with Slavic origins, reminding Dorsey of several merchants on Carson Street. There was a final chuckle and the man returned to the house. Outlaw left in the Electra.

Dorsey waited a few moments, time for several deep breaths and a thank God, then worked his way out from under on his elbows and knees. Back on his feet, he saw the lights in the front room go dim. Music began, loudly. Dorsey couldn't place it—heavy symphonic bass—and wished he had stayed awake in Music Appreciation 101. Between the music, the air compressor, and closed doors and windows, Dorsey figured he had a dead end and started back to the van. Fishing a pen and pad from his hip pocket, he squatted down to copy the Cadillac's license plate. The numbers meant nothing, but the emblem that preceded the numerals made Dorsey take a hard suck of air.

"Ain't this some shit." He was looking at a winged staff entwined by two snakes. "Has to be Novotny."

14

Sitting at the bar, the lone customer at such a late hour, Dorsey carefully picked bits of gravel from his elbow. Al was at the taps, running a washcloth along the levers and pipe spines. "Ask you a question?" Dorsey said, stopping to take a hit of his Rolling Rock.

"Sure, sure," Al said, his concentration remaining on the job at hand. "Might even have an answer to go with it."

"How'd your mother die?"

Al stopped his work and smiled. "Me and my three brothers, I think we did her in. Georgie in particular. He was a handful and needed a weekly beating to stay out of the juvenile detention house. He ended up a plumber. A good one. But before he got in the apprentice program, he took his share of years off that woman's life."

"Seriously," Dorsey said. "No shit, how'd she die?"

"Okay." Al ceased his work and carefully folded the cloth, slipping it into his apron pocket. He walked down the bar, coming even with Dorsey. "Seriously, huh? She was eighty-four when she passed on. Very quietly, peaceful as could be. A stroke, sitting in her favorite chair watching *Guiding Light* with the neighbor lady. Lovely funeral four days later; had to be one of the biggest this neighborhood can remember. Most of Sarah and Jane Streets in attendance. Kind of nice to see, if you know what I mean?" Al reached down into the cooler and produced another seven ounce Rolling Rock. "So, why the question?"

"I barely remember my mother." Dorsey gave a last rub to his elbow and turned to his beer.

"You don't think I already know that? C'mon, what's going on here?"

Dorsey brought him up to speed on the day's events and again laughed at his own disregard for client confidentiality where Al was concerned. *Christ,* he thought, *you'd go crazy if you didn't have this man to talk to. Saints preserve him. Saints preserve him, please.*

"She had the cancer, Carroll," Al said. "When'd she have it? The late fifties, early sixties? Everybody died of it then, no exceptions. Lucky ones died fast. Not so lucky . . . well, you went through hell first. Didn't make any difference who your doctor was. Even if there was a specialist around, all he did was watch you suffer and die and try to learn something from it. If that's your concern, who the doctor was, you're wasting your time."

"I just hate this shit, you know?" Dorsey took a long pull on his beer. "Took a long time to put that other crap behind me. Well, as much as I have. I just wish my family was out of this."

"It's a little bit of family history," Al said, "not your family. This ain't like the last time."

"Let's hope." Dorsey slipped from the barstool and drank off his beer in a final gulp. "One very long day, my friend. Straight to bed for me." He turned for the door. "Thanks again for the van."

Al went back to his cleaning. "Do yourself a favor and hop in the shower before you get between the sheets. You're pretty ripe, fella." He looked up as Dorsey opened the door. "I'll air out the van in the morning."

Out on the sidewalk, beyond the bar's air-conditioning, the humid atmosphere wrapped around Dorsey as he headed down South Seventeenth Street on foot. On the far side of the street was the basketball court, and he could picture the night two winters before when a tall black guy had stood beneath the near basket, the court obliterated by snow. His presence had been the opening of a death scene, nearly Dorsey's. A good friend went down instead, and Dorsey often wished he was a more religious man, one who would light a candle for Russie every Sunday.

Outlaw the pimp, he thought, jogging across Carson Street, avoiding a bread delivery truck. *With a clientele of one refugee doctor.* Dorsey had left the driveway but had remained in place at the van until Outlaw's return, several hours later. Outlaw's stay had been brief, and then Dorsey had followed him and the girl to the apartment where the evening had begun. The couple entered together, Outlaw's arm wrapped around her waist, and Dorsey took off, sufficiently disgusted for one night.

Janice's file had contained the remark about Outlaw looking after Dr. Novotny's needs. *So,* Dorsey thought, rounding the corner onto Wharton, *she knows about the girls.* So why not grab Outlaw as a pimp and the doctor for statutory rape, if indeed the girls were all the same age as his guest this evening. *Because she's a narc and wants a dope charge that'll do the doctor in for good.* Maybe. But dope charges didn't seem to stick to Novotny. Labriola had made that clear, and Dr. Riddle certainly alluded to Novotny's ability to dance through the raindrops. And why, in her file, was Janice Manning so coy about Outlaw supplying the girls. *Coy with the file or coy with you? To make you want to find out for yourself. One thing's for sure, she isn't coy about wanting Novotny's ass, badly. Her bathroom mirror even says so.*

Dorsey took Al's advice, stripping away his clothes as he climbed the stairs and made right for the shower. Soap stung at his elbows where he had performed his own crude surgery, and he let the hot water wash away the odor of his confinement in the overheated van. Cleansed, but dazed with fatigue, he worked himself into an ancient pair of Duquesne University gym shorts, a little taut at the waist, and went down to the kitchen. He hung on the refrigerator door, peering inside, and, finding nothing to his liking, went to the front-room office. Into the tape player he slipped a cassette and at low volume Mel Torme launched into "Sent for You Yesterday." With a fresh Rolling Rock from the midget refrigerator, he dropped into his swivel chair, stared at the ceiling, and tried to remember which case he was supposed to be working on.

Outlaw and the doc, they're only important to you where the girl is concerned. Whether or not either one of them ever gets cracked and does jail time isn't for you to worry about. That's for Janice Manning and Trooper Lyle, her trained chimp, to put in long nights over. Think of the girl, think of Maritsa. Does Outlaw fit in to the picture?

"Hell, yes, he does." Dorsey addressed a spot on the ceiling were water had leaked. If he was moving young girls, he might just know what happened to the best-looking one of the lot. Good looks combined with a golden but unschooled heart. The kind of girl who read novels for the whole truth, not just the occasional pearls that might just drop from the pages. And who thought she could change the greasers, give them the self-esteem they lacked—in her mind the *only* thing they lacked.

Dorsey came forward in his chair and rested his beer on the desk-top blotter, where he pinned his elbows, cradling his head. *And the next step,* he thought, *is confrontation. Your favorite. Push Outlaw, squeeze him. Use evidence of his whoring to press him for word on the girl. Say you'll tell the police. Say you'll tell the girl's—tonight's girl's—family.* That might be worse. Leave Novotny out of it for now. He might extend the power he had to protect Outlaw. Doubtful, because the bad guys rarely gave a sincere shit about each other when it came down to it.

Let's give it up for one night, Dorsey thought, looking toward a long and hopefully dreamless sleep. Turning in the chair, he ignored the opened mail he had collected earlier in the day, but the blinking light on the telephone answering machine pulled him back. Duty—and money—could be calling.

"Cut-rate or not," he said, "should have never bought the god-damned thing." He hit rewind, then play.

Ironbox calling, and sounding weak. "I would very much like to speak to you about your father. His condition, I mean. If you could call me at my place, whenever's convenient for you. We should get together to discuss these things. Privately, at my place. If that's okay with you."

His father's condition? Dorsey thought. What about hers? At his last visit, his father was nearly his old shitty self. But she had been a mess, or well on her way to being a mess. *Call her tomorrow, in the afternoon. When you get out of bed.*

"How are you?" The second voice was Gretchen's. "Just thought I'd call to thank you for the weekend, but I guess you're on the job. Or with Al and Henry." There was a brief pause. "I felt a little funny for a while," Gretchen continued, "the way I always feel after we talk, until it dawns on me that we're doing the right thing. Right? Anyway, it was a nice weekend. Think maybe you could come up here for a visit? I'm busy for the next few weeks, but maybe after that. When you're all finished with this case of yours, after that." Another pause. "Good luck finding that girl."

It's a life full of maybes, Dorsey thought, pressing the stop button. *Maybe we should visit, maybe in a few weeks. If you're free, maybe. And the central item: Maybe we're doing the right thing. Who knows? Maybe.*

He pushed off from the chair, switching off the ceiling light as he went into the hall. At the top of the stairs he killed the hall lights and turned for the bedroom. He heard two loud screeches from the doorbell.

"Now what the fuck is this?"

Slowly, holding the banister for support, he headed back down the staircase, thinking of all the private eyes he had come across in books, films, and TV. Would they answer the door in the middle of the night without their gun drawn and hidden from the caller's view? Hell, no. Those guys knew a dangerous doorbell when they heard it. But here you go bravely to answer the call, loaded for bear, armed to the teeth with your gym shorts.

He took a peek through the spy hole and sighed. "Yeah," he muttered, "what the fuck is this, huh?"

Dorsey opened the door and Janice Manning kissed his cheek, slipping into the hallway. Dressed in cut-off jeans and tank top, she looked as fresh as she had that morning.

"Well, you haven't changed much since our last encounter," she said, giving Dorsey an all too obvious once-over with her eyes. She held up a large brown envelope, fat with contents. "I brought you another file to read."

Yeah, sure.

15

Janice Manning departed near dawn, and Dorsey finally got his wish for a long and peaceful sleep. There were things on his mind, things to consider, but he managed to shove them aside. Phone messages, his confusion over Gretchen, young girls being served up to an old man at surely a handsome price, and a female state trooper with the nerve to show up in your life whenever she pleased and at any hour. And ready to hop into the first available sack with you. All that he put on the back shelf and went unconscious for nine glorious hours.

It was nearly two in the afternoon when Dorsey surrendered to daylight and pulled himself from the sheets. He pulled on his gym shorts and took a clean white T-shirt from the dresser drawer. From the top of the dresser he grabbed the brown envelope Janice had left behind, carrying it with him downstairs to the kitchen. He dropped it onto the Formica-topped kitchen table and fiddled with the coffeemaker. Once it was going, he went to the office to retrieve Mel Torme and returned to the kitchen, inserting the cassette into a portable stereo on the counter. Crouching down, he searched through the shelves below the counter for his frying pan.

What a performance, Dorsey thought, forking a clump of mar-

118

garine into the pan as he held it over the flame. *All charm in the middle of the night, the all-too-transparent excuse of business for dropping by. Calculated to be transparent and to be happily accepted despite it all. So you'd be willing to take her in, no questions asked. Questions like, Have you been sitting outside my place all night? Or, Have you been following me all night? And is that part of the timing, waiting for the lights to go out? You never ask because you never want to know. You just want. She fixes it that way. And then the sincerity that follows.*

In his bed, when they had finished, she was above him, her hands planted on his shoulders, elbows locked for support. She beamed down at Dorsey, and to him it appeared as if she showed no change, each hair in position, her skin without any flush. "Carroll," she said, "I want to call you Carroll."

"There's a few folks out there that do," he said. "Feel free to join up."

Janice jumped from the bed and scooted to the bathroom, her long legs covering the distance in a few strides. Dorsey heard a flush followed by running water. She came back with a bath towel, moistened at one corner, and washed his face.

"I like you, Carroll." She grinned. "Obviously."

"Yes, yes. It shows."

"Let me backtrack a little." She reversed the towel and dried where she had cleaned, then got to her feet, hanging the towel on the back of a chair. Still naked, she sat in the chair, her legs up on the bed over Dorsey's. "From the start, I figured you as different, a little special. Even when I thought I'd be arresting you in the park."

"Really?" Dorsey said. "I didn't notice any attraction until Lyle had finished slopping up his food and went for the phone. And even then, I just figured it as a pleasant relief from the gulping machine."

"I know what you mean," Janice said. "Dave Lyle would never

119

be asked back to a four star restaurant. But still, I knew this was going to happen for us. Right from the beginning."

What the hell is she talking about? Dorsey thought, pulling himself up against his pillows. *What is happening for us? for Chrissakes. She appears from nowhere, she gives you some information, then you get laid. That's happening?*

"You look surprised?" Janice said. "Aren't all your women this straightforward? Well, of course they're not cops, detectives, so maybe they can't see the truth for themselves. And if you can't see what's true, you can't articulate it."

Why don't you ask for what it is you want? Dorsey thought. "So," he said, "what's that in the envelope?"

Janice hopped from her seat and went to the dresser. "Men!" she said, "always business!" From the top of the dresser she pushed away her hastily gathered clothes and underthings, fetching the envelope. Returning to her chair, she tossed it to Dorsey who caught it against his stomach with a loud slap.

"It's everything I have on Novotny," she said. "Gave you the file on Outlaw, so I thought you'd like to see what his cohort was like. He's a trip."

"Really got it in for this guy, huh?"

She pulled in her legs at the knees and wrapped her arms around them. "We had him good. His ass was in the sling, finally. Then it mysteriously went to shit. And these city cop assholes are staying away. I want the son of a bitch. So does Lyle." Her mood did a quick shift and she gave Dorsey a wink, climbing back onto the bed. "Hey, you don't really plan on reading right now, do you?"

Dorsey left his breakfast dish in the sink, turned off the stereo, and took his coffee and Novotny's file to the office. *Well,* he thought settling into the swivel chair, *I sure will be doing some reading now. And then come up with a plan to put the heat on Outlaw.*

Anton Novotny, according to the file, had been born in Prague in 1914. With a father working as a college professor his family appeared well-off, in a middle-class way of speaking. When the Germans had rolled into Czechoslovakia in 1938 he was a medical student at the University of Prague. Young Anton finished medical school, probably with his father's slowly growing influence with the occupation forces, and joined a small practice near the city's eastern edge.

In 1945, with the Red Army pressuring the capital, Anton's father had become a deadly liability, and the family moved westward with the retreating Nazis. Maybe it was the Allied bombing, or the lack of food and medicine, but Anton had been the lone survivor of the journey, making it all the way to the American Occupation Zone. Both parents and a young sister had died on the way.

With a sip of coffee, Dorsey studied the typed sheets and wondered about the information sources. If Novotny's family had been Nazi sympathizers, he sure wouldn't have told anyone, especially if he had been trying to get into the U.S. after the war. It sure wouldn't have been on a visa application.

He pushed forward into the file material and found that Novotny hadn't come to America immediately after the war. In fact, he had been repatriated to Czechoslovakia under the short-lived Benesh government. Maybe he hadn't tried to get into the U.S.; maybe he had figured Benesh would last. *Well, fellow,* Dorsey thought, *you were wrong.*

The file was silent on Novotny's activities from the time of the Communist coup until 1955. At that point there was a reprint of an article from the *Pittsburgh Press* entitled "Freedom Seeker Sets Up Medical Practice." An accompanying photograph showed a thickset man with slick black hair and metal-rimmed glasses wearing a lab smock. The article recounted how Dr. Anton Novotny had survived a harrowing nighttime trek across the Czech border into Austria and a circuitous two-year journey through western Europe before settling in the U.S. He had opened his practice in the Lawrenceville section of the city two months earlier.

So, Dorsey thought, *the times changed and so did the labels. The*

*escape makes him an anti-Communist instead of the son of collabora-
tors. And being an anti-Communist makes you a hero in 1955. And
now, for that matter.* The source of information on the family was
rendered meaningless in Dorsey's mind. Because the information
was now meaningless.

The remainder of the file was a typed chronology of charges
without convictions. Allegations through the late fifties and early
sixties that Novotny had had a lucrative trade going as an abortionist. All charges dropped. The IRS raised a fuss in 1967 concerning his taxes, without success, and in 1971 Medicare said he
was a cheat. Novotny disagreed and won. Rumors of heavy traffic
in diet pills in 1973 went unproven. The last entry dealt with the
previous year's drug bust. The details revealed nothing that Detective Labriola had not told him.

Dorsey closed the file and wondered why Janice Manning had
not recorded any mention of Novotny's love of young girls. Surely
she knew about it. She knew everything else about the man, and
it was in the file on Outlaw. *More important, what the hell does she
want from you?*

He left the desk and went to the chaise, sitting at its edge and
looking out on Wharton. Some kids were outside, free at last for
the summer, chasing toward Oliver Pool. *You know what she wants;
she wants you to get the doc. Get him on something, anything. Mostly,
she wants you to tie him into the girl's disappearance. But that's starting to look like a voluntary disappearance.*

Go put the squeeze on Outlaw, he decided. *Find the girl and fuck
this Dr. Novotny business.*

16

Dorsey drove the Buick along Fifth Avenue past Ironbox Boyle's apartment building, taking the left onto Neville Street just before his old high school, Central Catholic. The area was clogged with double-parked delivery vans from grocery stores, florists, and furriers. All serving what Dorsey referred to as the Blue-Haired Ghetto.

After circling the block twice, he found a parking space near St. Paul's Cathedral, a huge grey stone Gothic structure. Flanking both sides of Fifth Avenue were some of the city's better rental addresses, older and elegant apartment buildings guarded by doormen who worked year round on their holiday tips. What they were protecting, Dorsey knew from too many visits through the years, were the elderly female recipients of a large share of the city's wealth. Lifelong professional women, the widows of male professionals, and the heiresses of steel and coal and railroad money; all of these populated these few blocks, making decisions that made and unmade bank managers and brokers.

The uniformed doorman admitted Dorsey and directed him to the elevator bank after telephoning the apartment. On the third floor he exited the car and turned right. Irene Boyle was in the hall-way, standing at the open door to her home.

"Thank you for coming so soon," she said, ushering him inside and shutting the door behind them. "I know how busy you are with your work."

"Temporarily," Dorsey said, taking a seat at the near end of the sofa. Her greeting reminded him that the Leneski case was his only case. At present, and only for the present, it was his career.

The apartment was of a configuration unseen in more modern construction. The parlor was long and thin, ending in glass double doors that led into a dining room. Beyond that, Dorsey remembered from earlier visits, was a kitchen and a balcony overlooking a courtyard. The furnishings were French Country and well-maintained by one of the horde of domestics who labored throughout the building.

Irene Boyle sat in an easy chair across a coffee table from Dorsey. "I'm sorry but I don't keep any beer in the house. There's coffee, and some soft drinks, if you like."

"Nothing, thanks." Dorsey sized her up and concluded that she wasn't as frayed as the last time he had seen her. She appeared stronger, more in possession of her mettle. And her bitchiness. *Even still,* he thought, *she's not the same. Tired, maybe. Ah, hell, with her devotion to the old man, she should be exhausted. A month in the country exhausted.*

"Good, let's talk." Mrs. Boyle leaned forward, lowering her voice. "Your father just isn't the same since he came back home. He's got me terribly worried."

"Ah, Irene," Dorsey said, "Mrs. Boyle . . . you don't have to whisper, the guy's not here. He's about three miles away, and right about now he's probably taking a nap."

Mrs. Boyle straightened herself, shot him a scowl, and continued. "Very well. Just the same, I'm concerned. And I thought you might be, too."

"Okay, let's hear it. Talk to me."

"He's so scattered," she said. "Maybe his hearing was affected by the stroke. Scattered, really scattered, when we talk."

Dorsey watched as she shook her head and her hand went to her mouth. "I can't say I see that," he told her. "Not during my visits. Last time I was there he was working on his checkbook. Looked like he was doing fine."

"Well, of course, he's fine when you're there. I think he must save up his energy to put on a show for you. And he eats funny. Not like he used to. So heartily."

"Since when?" Dorsey asked, becoming a little confused himself. "The man never weighed more than one fifty, one sixty maybe, in his whole life. He never ate much. And he was never home much to sit down to the table."

"Don't start with that. He worked hard for a lot of people, had a lot of things to juggle." She stopped for a moment, and a vacant look passed through her eyes. It was only momentary, but it put Dorsey in mind of Catherine Durant and her lapses. "He doesn't eat," Mrs. Boyle continued now. "And the music he plays on that office stereo. The damnedest stuff."

"Such as?" Dorsey started to wish that she did keep beer in the house. Anything to help get through this.

"Just things that are unlike him."

"Like what?"

"Just things," she said. "Music I'm not used to hearing. And at all the wrong times. He's just out of sync. Like most everything else nowadays."

Now what the hell is this? Dorsey thought. *There's only one thing, one person, out of sync. Only one.*

"It's just everything about him." Mrs. Boyle left her chair and went to the mantlepiece. "He's changing, going downhill."

For Chrissakes, Dorsey thought, watching her move about the room. *Take a look in the mirror, woman.*

125

"You have to take over," she said. "His care, I mean. I can't watch him go like this. You have to take over his care. It would be best, I should think, if you moved in with him full time."

"Let me stop you right there." Dorsey pushed off from his seat, deciding that this cockeyed conversation had had its run. "What are we talking about here? My father's a guy who had a stroke and gets around on a metal cane. And that's about all there is to it. He's sharp as a tack and he's probably the same political bastard he always was. So I really don't know where this is going. Except for one thing. *I* am not going. Not to my father's house."

Irene Boyle took a Kleenex from a box on an end table and held it there a moment, seemingly preoccupied with ensuring that the next tissue came through the clear plastic, ready for use. She played at it, and when satisfied she looked at Dorsey as if she was surprised he was still there. "Any regrets?" she asked.

"Pardon?"

"Regrets." She returned to her chair. "Regrets about life, about what you may have done. To other people. How you let them down?"

"Every day," Dorsey said, haunted for a moment by the face of an older man who once lived over Al's Bar. The thought sobered him, taking the sting out of his attitude toward the woman in the chair. "What's on your mind, Irene? Talk if you want."

"She was a good woman. We didn't make things any easier for her at the end."

"Who's this?" Dorsey asked.

"You probably think it was so long ago," Irene Boyle said. "But when you're my age, nothing seems so long ago. It's all part of your memory, and your memory likes to come back whenever it likes. You'll learn that."

"It comes in increments," Dorsey said. "You don't turn sixty-five and get maudlin overnight. Now, who is it we're talking about?"

Mrs. Boyle looked up into his eyes and then away. "Mrs. Dorsey, of course."

"Mrs. Dorsey?"

"Your father's wife." Mrs. Boyle gathered herself and spat out her next words. "Your mother. Okay?"

Dorsey dropped back onto the sofa. *Christ, you seldom have a chance to think of her; hardly ever given a reason to. And then there's a trip to her old neighborhood and they come at you, from all directions. All from this Leneski case. Like you told Al, you really hate this shit.*

"Please," Dorsey said, "please go on."

"As I said, we didn't make things any easier for her. She was so sick. What could we do? Things were the way they were and that's that. If it could have been different, if I or your father or anybody else could have changed it, we would have. Things can happen."

Dorsey reached across the coffee table and took her hand, both to soothe her and steady himself. *What the hell is going on?* he wondered. *Give me an answer. C'mon, Irene, clear your head and say it. Come clean with me.*

"Irene, please. What is it you want to say?"

She took a moment and then smiled. "I think you'd better be leaving now. You have so much work."

17

Rummaging through his cellar, Dorsey wondered why he hadn't moved his office down there for the summer. The walls were rough stone, the matching floor was dry, and the air temperature was ten degrees lower than that of the first floor. *Sure,* he thought, *all you'd have to do is completely rewire the place, run telephone lines, and get used to racing up the steps every time the doorbell rang. And remember, you're already covering a second mortgage, you've got a bum knee, and above all, you're lazy.*

He dug through an ancient workbench, property of the house's former owner, came up empty, and began working his way along the cellar walls. There were half-used cans of paint, woodstain, and lumber left over from a fence he had built at the edge of the backyard. Beneath the windows that showed Wharton Street at ankle level, he moved the shot-up mattress. The bullet holes, the results of Dorsey's long ago preparation to meet with a maniac, were singed at the edges and still had a smoky stench, eighteen months after the fact. The wall behind the mattress had several gouges in its stone where Dorsey had never bothered to dig out the lead slugs.

In the near corner, beneath a paint-splattered tarp, he found the chain, heavy gauge and four feet in length. Dorsey slowly wound it around his forearm, wiping away loose rust as he did. Turning and heading for the metal support pole near the staircase, he let several feet of chain slip from his hand. With a tight whipping motion, he slashed at the pole, sending paint chips and a high-pitched metallic ping ringing through the air. He repeated the movement, grunting with effort, then sat at the bottom of the staircase and examined the chain for damage. Satisfied that it had held true, he rewound the chain and secured it with a short length of electrical tape.

The search, and his preparation for the next day's piece of business, had kept his thoughts away from his earlier meeting with Ironbox Boyle. But now, in the cool air and surrounded by the silent and unadorned walls of the row house's foundation, the encounter replayed and replayed. "Scattered, really scattered," she had said, and Dorsey now wondered if she knew she was referring to herself. *What the hell is with that woman? And what is it that she thinks she did so long ago, to a woman on her deathbed? When you're under a death sentence, cancer gnawing away at whatever organs you might have left, what is it that another person can do to worsen the situation? But Ironbox thinks she did just that. And she thinks she wasn't alone in its doing.* Dorsey foresaw another meeting, another confrontation, with his father, and the thought sickened him. *The hell with that—for now, anyway. You've got a few other confrontations scheduled already, and if you're going to get sick, get sick over them first.*

A few minutes past nine the next morning, Dorsey stood on the grey stone steps of the Iron and Glass Bank, watching a young teller release the front door lock. Once inside, Dorsey found an assistant manager, established his identity, and followed him to the vault. Both inserted their corresponding keys into the safety deposit box and opened the locking mechanism. Dorsey cradled the metal box in his arm and was shown to a small back office where was left to himself, the assistant manager quietly closing the door behind him.

Dorsey flipped the metal lid and removed the velvet bags that had once held fifths of Crown Royal whiskey. Loosening the gold cord of the first bag, he fished out a pistol, a Meridian Break-Top revolver, and a box of cartridges. He loaded the weapon with care, remembering that the last time he had done so it had been to kill a madman. He also remembered that instead of killing the madman, a giant of a millworker whose only wish was to see Dorsey dead, he had unloaded the weapon into the wall of his father's office. Life has its twists.

He toyed with the second velvet sack, feeling the outline of the switchblade hidden within, then chose to return it unopened to the safety deposit box. *This is no time for even match-ups,* he told himself. *Stay healthy, that's the plan. When he has a knife, you bring along a gun. Fair knife fights went out with zoot suits and Cuban heels.*

The safety deposit box was returned to its aperture in the wall, and Dorsey returned to the Buick, heading across town. In Lawrenceville, he kept to Penn Avenue, which ran parallel to Butler for a time but then angled away, creating the expanding V that defined the neighborhood. He passed St. Francis Hospital and the psychiatric ward that housed Catherine Durant. Dorsey wondered about her condition, if she knew what day it was and how many days it had been since she had last been home. And if she knew about her beloved Outlaw—her own version of the American Hero—if she knew that he scrounged up teenaged flesh for at least one old man. And maybe more than one. Why not? Business had to expand to succeed.

Past the psyche ward, the landmarks started to bump into each other. Across a fence from the ward was St. Mary's Cemetery, a slice of ground that rode the hip of the much larger county cemetery. It was filled with departed Irish from the neighborhood, so crowded with the dead that a second Irish graveyard had grown up in Greenfield in the city's far East End. *Where Mum is buried,* Dorsey thought, then chided himself. *Not now, fella. There's a job at hand and you better keep your mind on it. And put your heart into*

130

it, as best you can. Here it comes, some more of this shit you hate. Stay on the case you're being paid for.

Dorsey continued along Penn Avenue in the Buick, an eight-foot stone wall to his left that made a seamless transition from St. Mary's to Allegheny Cemetery. To his right were several brick homes, which gave way to a plumbing contractor and several granite memorial businesses. Through picture-window plate glass, Dorsey could see the sample gravestones, fresh and impressive without the years of weathering they were guaranteed against. *Ah,* he thought, *the grieving process. Undertakers, coffin makers, stone carvers, and plot salesman. Keep up the payments on that insurance policy.*

The wall ended and was replaced with a length of heavy black iron fencing adding to the solemn, Gothic atmosphere. Dorsey drove through the open gates and down a sloping grade, using the continued downhill motion as his bearing. He passed the smooth grey walls of the crematory, negotiating the thin, winding road as it moved through huddles of gravestones whose ages at times defied estimation. Near a steep knoll topped by a duck pond, Dorsey pulled the Buick to the curb.

"Here we go," he muttered and checked the slugs in the gun's cylinder. He jacked the weapon closed and stuffed it into a hip pocket. From the floor of the Buick he took the chain, wrapping it several times about his left fist, estimating its heft. He left the Buick behind and headed for the campsite.

He found an observation spot behind several bushes and began to get himself pissed off. He jangled the chain and thought about Outlaw, the Pied Piper of teenaged Lawrenceville. Slick enough to convince young girls to give it up for old men. And to have fools his own age think he was hot shit. *But this ain't Hamelin. Outlaw takes the kids first and fuck the rats, they get to stay. Goddamned guy. He has this girl, so what about Maritsa? Wonder where she's been farmed out to?*

Dorsey stood on high ground and looked down into the copse

of trees that camouflaged the campsite. He let twenty minutes pass, working at his mood, enraging himself for the job at hand. Without picking up on any movement, and nearing his personal boil-over point, he started for the tent.

Even without rain for a few days the ground was still soft, spongy, and each time Dorsey raised a foot it was followed by the sound of mud sucking after it. When he reached the trees he took one last breath, shook his shoulders loose, and let a foot of chain drop from his fist. He charged the tent and ripped back the entry flap.

"Get the fuck out! Right fuckin' now! On your feet, assholes!" Dorsey beat the tent walls with the chain, his voice recalling that of his boot camp drill instructor. "Don't fuck with me!"

The twenty-year-old that Janice Manning had called Dingle scrambled out first and did a body roll past Dorsey, streaking his white T-shirt with mud. He made it to his feet with his shoulders hunched, quickly glancing around. When it seemed that he could find only Dorsey, he straightened to his full height.

"Yeah, yeah," Dorsey said. "You got it, it's only me, you fuckin' asswipe. Relieved, right? Thought it was the whole city narc squad sneaking up on you, huh? Well, fuck it. It's me, and I'm gonna kick your fuckin' ass all over this cemetery if you and that whore you keep in the tent don't give me what I came for."

Dingle grinned, hard-ass style, and jerked his head, flipping the hair from his eyes. Dorsey passed on the defiance and concentrated on Dingle's hands and belt line. The knife wasn't there. No blade and no sheath attached to a belt loop. *Good, good. The gun can stay at home.*

"Tell the girl to get out here."

"Fuck you, jag off." Dingle shot him the finger and a motion forward.

Dorsey tightened his grip on the chain. "Last fuckin' chance. She comes out and tells me what I want to know, like how many old men she's laid for Outlaw, and I'll walk away. Or, I can beat the living shit out of you then go in and yank her out by the hair. Which sounds better?"

Dingle looked at the tent entry and then back at Dorsey, indecision moving across his face momentarily. *Must really feel a commitment to this girl,* Dorsey thought sarcastically. There was a moment when Dorsey thought this might go easily; but then Dingle squared off his shoulders and hitched up his jeans. *Well, this is it.*

Dingle charged, head high and wild, fists ready to go, and Dorsey had the advantage and excuse he needed. With his long reach, he was able to lay the first swing across Dingle's nose, the last few chain links ripping at the far ear. The boy slowed a step and Dorsey pulled back to make his second strike, a downward motion that creased the center of Dingle's crown and forehead. Blood started its stream across the boy's face, and Dorsey flashed for a second on hygiene class advice on the bleeding potential of head wounds.

The boy clutched at his forehead but kept one hand free and closed in a fist. *Christ,* Dorsey thought, *maybe I will need that gun.* Dingle came again and threw a roundhouse. Dorsey ducked under the swing and whipped the chain again, this time across the shins. Dingle went down, now grasping at his knees, and rolled into a defensive ball. Dorsey gave him two more across the shoulders to drive home his point.

"Now stay put, please?" He turned his attention to the tent entry. Inside, a figure was huddled near the back wall. "Let's go! Out! Now!" Dorsey held out the blood-speckled chain for her inspection. "Like some of this yourself? Don't fucking put it past me."

Her head popped through first, cautiously, as if she were testing the weather. Dorsey rattled the chain and backed away a step, giving her room. She was dressed in cut-off jeans and what must have been, from its size, one of Dingle's T-shirts. Her hair was tangled and her feet were bare, mud seeping between the toes.

"We're going to have a talk." Dorsey gestured to Dingle and her eyes followed. She screamed, brief but high pitched. She went for

133

her boyfriend, but Dorsey held her in place. "We're going to have a talk."

With less force than he thought he might need, Dorsey led the girl to a tree and motioned her to a seat on an exposed root. He crouched before her, sideways to keep a watch on Dingle, who moaned but remained still, and gave her a few seconds to gather herself. Then he started in.

"I followed you the other night. You and Outlaw. All the time you were in the car together. Across the Fortieth Street Bridge, up through Grant Avenue in Millvale, and out to that house. The house where he gave you over to that old man. The big old man with the accent. The happy one with the loud music. I was in the driveway listening. I heard Outlaw when he told the old man good-bye. They were laughing, and Outlaw told him not to worry, he could pay up later."

The girl wiped at her eyes with the T-shirt's fat sleeve. She stole a peek at Dorsey, then looked away.

"See? I already know a lot about this. See what I'm saying?"

She nodded. She didn't look at him. She nodded again.

"You need to tell me more. That's what I want from you." Dorsey bent his left arm behind his back and allowed the chain to dribble onto the ground. "How long have you done this? With Novotny, I mean. How many times?"

"We didn't hear you comin'," she said, then looked at Dorsey. "You must've come around back. We always hear when somebody comes from the park."

"What's this?"

"The glass," the girl said. "We always hear it go crunch."

"Forget the glass," Dorsey said. "Answer my questions. You and Novotny, how many times?"

"Twice," she said. "In the last couple of weeks, I mean. A few times before that. But that was a while ago. Maybe a couple of months. There's been other girls around. Some of them probably did it, too."

"It's just for Novotny? Nobody else?"

"Just the doctor." She looked into his eyes; hers were wide with fear. Dorsey's stomach did a fast spasm as he wished away the last few minutes. "I heard about some other guys," she said, "but I think it was just talk. But other girls've been with the doctor. Maybe even the one you're lookin' for. I bet she might've. She used to be with Outlaw a lot. Most all the girls, he tried to talk them into it. Most of them go along."

"You think Maritsa did?" Dorsey asked, picturing the girl alongside a charicature of Outlaw, his face elongated, lupine. "You said she was different. That's how you remembered her the last time we talked."

"I can't say, really. I mean it's hard to say if she did or didn't. Some of us talk about it, the girls around here. But Maritsa, she wasn't like . . . like one of us. So we didn't talk so much. So I don't know."

Dorsey dropped back a step, checked on Dingle—who was still quiet—and gathered up the chain. "But she was with Outlaw, right?" he asked. "A lot. How about just before she came up missing."

"Maybe. Could be."

Maybe and could be, Dorsey thought. *From this place's language it translates to a yes.* "He ever take a girl somewhere else besides Novotny's?"

"Could be. Maybe."

Dorsey examined the chain links, wiping away some blood with his thumb. "Tell me, seriously. Why the hell do you do it? Just to keep the old doc happy and writing bogus prescriptions. No shit, why?"

"Do it for Outlaw," the girl said. "We get some money and he turns us onto some reefer."

"That's it?"

The girl braced against the tree trunk and rose to her feet. "He lets us stay here, too. He could get us kicked out, just kick us out

135

himself. He's a bad motherfucker. Nobody fucks with him around here. He lets us stay here. He says it's okay and nobody fucks with us."

It's as if the courthouse didn't exist, he thought. *No rooms full of deed books and mortgage registers and land titles that establish the chain of ownership. Hell, these people see the park as a land grant, and the cemetery is disputed territory at best. With a lake of broken glass as the natural boundary. This place exists in a vacuum. Goddamn it, this is the other side of the looking glass.*

"You'll be talking to your landlord pretty soon, I figure," Dorsey told the girl. "Don't give me any shit that you won't because you'll be running to him fast with some cleaned up version of what just happened here. Cleaned up as far as what you told me. So, you tell the lord of the realm that I'll be in Zima's late this afternoon waiting to talk to him. And tell him to take it easy. I'll be packing more than a chain."

18

Draped across the office chaise, stripped to the waist and with a cold, wet towel covering his face, Dorsey kept guessing at the value of his day's work. *There's a missing girl. Pretty, as innocent as they get these days, and sure as hell naive if she's keeping company with a guy like Outlaw. And there's a lonely old woman desperately holding on to her rosary beads. Stack that up against a guy named Dingle who lives in a tent in the cemetery with a teenage girl he lends out to an old lech. A guy named Dingle who now had chain marks on his forehead and shinbones. Stack 'em up. How's it look?*

From the floor where he had dragged it from the desk, the telephone rang; Dorsey let it sing out three times before he managed to free himself from the towel and sit up. He lifted the receiver slowly, untangling the looping cord. "Thanks for calling back," he said into the mouthpiece. "Didn't think you'd be free till later."

"Your message sounded urgent," Gretchen said. "Anyway, I had a break coming, and they let us use the lounge phone occasionally for long distance." She laughed and continued. "Until we over-abuse the privilege. Again. So what's going on?"

"Tough morning. I had to get mean again. To get the job done." Dorsey recounted his trip to the cemetery.

"Just as you say," Gretchen told him, "to get the job done. If you're saying there was no other way, then there wasn't."

"Sounds pretty simple," Dorsey said, working the towel across his neck vertebrae. "And kind of odd coming from you."

"What's this?" She asked. "You get to grow and I don't? I'm not as hard as iron just yet, but I don't preach goodness and light anymore, either. You've taken on a job with your eyes wide open and you're seeing it through. And that is not supposed to be easy. Even when it all goes smoothly, which this one obviously hasn't. I'm not saying you should be proud of this morning, just endure it."

"Then it's okay, you think?" Dorsey asked. "I'm all right after all? Huh?"

"That's why you called, isn't it?" Gretchen asked, and Dorsey sensed the smile at the far end of the line. "You're all right," she said, "and I'm glad you called me to ask."

"No one else to call." Dorsey was silent for a moment. "I may have to get mean again on this one. How's that sound?"

"Keep it to a minimum, okay?" Gretchen had a matching moment of silence. "Call me. Let me know how it goes."

"This weekend," Dorsey said. "I'll keep in touch."

Zima's held the afternoon air of a barroom: grey and diffuse with wisps of white cigarette smoke laying trails about shoulder height. Sunlight was restricted to the small front windows, with occasional invasions when the door swung open to admit a patron. The bar lights were on but dimmed by a rheostat, and the glow gave human flesh an ashen hue. Seated in the last booth, nursing his third Rolling Rock, Dorsey waved off the barmaid when she again offered him a lunch menu.

"It's pierogi day," the woman said. "Everybody eats the pierogi here. You have to order three of them, minimum. Cheese or potato. The prune are all gone."

"No thanks," Dorsey said, wishing his appetite hadn't been crushed by the job at hand. "I pass. Again."

138

"Suit yourself," she said, walking back to her bar station. "Everybody else around here does."

Maybe, he thought, *the message wasn't strong enough. Or maybe the guy just didn't give a shit. Could be he doesn't think you can cause him any problems. But then again, you already have. You've disturbed the peace in his self-proclaimed jurisdiction. You've caused problems for his tenants, his serfs. The Lord Sheriff has to take action. Don't worry, it may take a while. But Outlaw is going to put in an appearance.*

The waitress eased by again, checked the level of his beer glass, then turned to answer the ringing of the public telephone. From where he sat, Dorsey was in position to see the phone mounted near the bar's entrance, and he watched as the waitress carried on a hushed conversation. She covertly glanced over her shoulder several times in Dorsey's direction, quickly returning to her caller and nodding in agreement of something. Finished, she hung up the receiver, checked the street through one of the windows, and started down the length of the barroom.

"Hey," Dorsey called to her as she passed, "can I expect him in the next few minutes? Or should I order another beer and just keep on waiting?"

"What?" The waitress stopped just beyond his booth. Dorsey twisted around in his seat to address her.

"Okay, fine. Outlaw, the guy you were on the phone with? Or maybe a friend of his? No matter, really. Is he coming now? Or do I have to buy some of your goddamned pierogi to find out?"

The waitress came even with the booth and leaned in. "Okay smartass. It won't be long now. You just wait."

Dorsey watched her walk away and realized that he didn't care for the sound of her "you just wait." He patted at his waist, where his untucked T-shirt concealed the revolver, and took a deep, reassuring breath.

Several more minutes passed with a few patrons coming and going, a loud argument over the best way to pick the daily lottery number, and the waitress shouting that the kitchen was switching from the lunch to the dinner menu. Outlaw walked through the front door just after her announcement. His jeans and workboots were coated with a film of dust, and he wore a flannel workshirt with the sleeves cut off at the shoulder, exposing his thick arms. To Dorsey, he had the general appearance of a day laborer coming straight from the work site.

Outlaw signaled to the waitress and without comment dropped into the booth across from Dorsey. He smoothed back his hair and checked his ponytail, then took a long pull on the bottle of Iron City delivered by the waitress. "You fuckin' nuts?" he asked Dorsey.

"Yeah, I am," Dorsey answered. "You're making me nuts. Driving me crazy. Tailing you, watching you put the moves on little girls, and then give them over to a fat old man. Yeah, yeah, that can drive a guy right out of his fuckin' mind. Makes a guy nuts."

Outlaw hit his beer again, then turned and checked the faces at the bar. "Don't piss me off," he said, returning to Dorsey. "What's this about?"

Dorsey leaned into the table. "First of all, who gives a shit if you get pissed off? I'll tell you something to really piss you off. The other night, when you dropped off the little homesteader at Novotny's? I was right there when you left, a couple of feet away. Listening to the two of you giggling over the girl. By the way, did you get paid after all? When you came back for her, I mean?"

Dorsey sat back in his seat and watched Outlaw's hands. His grip on the neck of the bottle tightened for a few seconds, and the free hand gripped the edge of the table, as if ready to push off. But the moment passed and both hands loosened, allowing Dorsey to return his gaze to Outlaw's face. Even so, the potential for violence was not lost on him, and again he ran his fingers along the outline of the pistol.

"Okay, good," Dorsey said. "All I'm after is some straight talk. No bullshit."

"Fuck you, no bullshit," Outlaw said. "I came here to stick that chain up your ass."

"Sure you did," Dorsey said. "That's why you called ahead to see if I was alone. And that's why you're on your ass right now, drinking a beer. That's how it's done, right? You just show up, growl a little bit, and then the person you came for beats the shit out of himself. Do I have it straight now?"

"Pushin'. You're fuckin' pushin' me."

"I'll push ya," Dorsey said, "push you right into a jail cell. You and I both know that two state narcs want your ass bad. And maybe you think that whatever protection Novotny has extends to you. Well, my guess is that it doesn't. He didn't get past the Iron Curtain to get fat and happy by giving a shit about guys like you. These girls, I'll find them. Found one easily enough. And they'll give you up in time. Between that and whatever those narcs can put together, you're in deep shit. And Novotny will stay clean, as always."

Outlaw shook his empty bottle at the waitress. "C'mon, for Chrissakes, gimme another one. Jesus!" He turned back to Dorsey but held his silence until the waitress came and went, after slapping the bottle onto the tabletop. "If this is gonna be trouble, let's go back in the alley and get it started."

"Doesn't have to be," Dorsey said. "Just give me some straight answers, and it could be I'll be gone from your life—fast. Matter of fact, when I first heard of you, I was going to ask up front for your help."

"Who told you about me?"

"Catherine Durant. She sort of referred me to you."

"Crazy Katie?" Outlaw laughed. "What a nut. Saw her up at St. Francis, right? East Wing?"

"You got it."

"What she have to say?" Outlaw asked. "That I wear a cape and fly around at night with a ray gun?"

"No," replied Dorsey. "She just said that you were the man. The one to see around here."

Outlaw looked up from his beer, and Dorsey could sense the change. The shoulders seemed to square and he sat a little straighter. *Ah,* Dorsey thought, *what a little flattery can do for the posture. Let's see if it can get you where you want to go.*

"You're the mayor of Butler Street, right?"

"Now you got it."

"Okay," Dorsey said. "Tell me what I want to know."

"What's that?"

"Crazy Katie," Dorsey said. "Where can I find her daughter?"

Outlaw again checked the bar patrons before responding. "You're talking about the kid whose picture is everywhere you look the last couple of months? Christ, talk about milk cartons— she'll be on the back of every bottle of Iron City in a few weeks."

"This is no joke." Dorsey signaled the waitress for a beer of his own. "I'm here to find that girl. Her mother sent me to you for help. And after watching you in action the other night, and from what I hear around, you're the man to talk to." The waitress brought the Rolling Rock and took a few bills from the stack in front of Dorsey. "Don't get pissed off again," Dorsey said to Outlaw once she had left. "Maritsa Durant was hanging around the park. And she spent some of that time with you. This is a missing persons case. The narcs want you already; don't piss off a whole other set of cops, too."

"You think I gave her over to Novotny."

"It's a logical possibility."

"Shit, I wouldn't do that." Outlaw smiled. "If she was gonna be had, I'd have had her. Fuck that old man."

"C'mon, man," Dorsey said. "Where's she at?"

"Hell if I know," Outlaw said. "And don't try to hang that shit on me, either. She's gone, but damned if I know where."

Dorsey searched his face, wondering if there really was a way to tell if a person was lying. A tell-tale crease in the forehead or a deepening of a chin cleft. *No, forget it. Even if there were, this one, with all his practice, would be immune.*

"Then tell me what you do know," Dorsey said. "What was she like when she was around the park? How did she come to be there? Things like that."

Outlaw laughed again, a laugh that Dorsey was growing to dislike. "They come from all over, every day," Outlaw said. "For kicks. Because Daddy doesn't love them. Or they got a thing for bad boys. Poor misunderstood bad guys. Who nobody loves. You got it?"

Typical, Dorsey thought, *so damned typical. The leader is always the hidden skeptic. The one who never believes the line he professes. The one who gets the most mileage out of bullshit. Because he's the only one who knows it's bullshit.* "It's coming through very clearly," Dorsey said. "Which kind was Maritsa?"

"She felt bad for the world." Outlaw sipped at his beer. "Ask me, she should've been busy feeling sorry for herself. What with the parents she has. Psycho and Junkie."

It was Dorsey's turn to laugh, in spite of himself. "Psycho and Junkie—sounds like a law firm. But back to the girl. What were you doing with her?"

There was that laugh again from Outlaw, and now Dorsey was sure he hated it. "Tryin' to do," Outlaw said. "That's what it came down to. She came over to the apartment a couple of times, with some of the other girls from the park. Which makes it tough to get into her pants, right?"

"Take your word for it."

"So," Outlaw said, "I figured I'd invite her down to my place alone. And then, you know, I'd work things out. She's sweet, ya know? But just before I give her the invitation, she disappears. Gone up in smoke."

"Just like that?" Dorsey asked. "Here and gone? She didn't run off with somebody else from the park? She's not with some girlfriend, maybe?"

143

"Fuck no." Outlaw grinned. "That chick is gone. She must've been grabbed by somebody, maybe a wacko. Yeah, some wacko got her."

Not likely, Dorsey thought. *Not unless it was a wacko who sent her home first to get her favorite reading material. If this guy's being square with you, square all the way, he's not as on top of things as everybody thinks.*

"So you can't help, huh?" Dorsey asked.

"I could lie to ya, make ya feel better if that's what you want." Outlaw finished his beer and wiped at his mouth with the back of a hand. "But the truth is, I don't know shit. I don't know no more than Crazy Katie. So if you want fucking make-believe, go talk to her again. Or worse, go see Teddy. That burnout's always a barrel of laughs."

"Teddy's back?" Dorsey asked. "Teddy Durant?"

"Back from where?" This time Outlaw bellowed his laugh, and Dorsey wished he had the chain wrapped around his throat.

"You know where he is?" Dorsey asked.

"Sort of." Outlaw said, shaking his head. "You fuckin' guys. The cops and whatever the hell you are, that burnout always sneaks by you. Because that's what he is, a sneaking bastard. He never says where it is, exactly, but he claims he's got a place. Probably some shitty little apartment where he can hide out. And trust me, that guy usually has somebody he should be hiding out from."

"You said you sort of know where he is," Dorsey said. "Tell me about 'sort of.' "

Outlaw slipped out from under the booth table and got to his feet. He did a half turn to the door then stopped. "Ah, shit. If this can help the girl. Besides, I don't owe shit to that fuckin' Teddy. The place is supposed to be up in Polish Hill. Somewhere up there. Good luck up there, you think this place is tough to crack."

I've got my own good luck, Dorsey thought, finishing his beer. *Henry came home.*

19

This is completely out of hand, Dorsey told himself. *And listen, man, you're not going anywhere with this six-foot nympho.*

"How'd it go?" Janice Manning, dressed in jeans and an over-size T-shirt, sat on the Buick's hood. Over her shoulder, on the far curb of Butler Street, Dorsey spotted Dave Lyle in the unmarked Ford. He was working on a slice of pizza.

"What do you do with that guy?" Dorsey gestured toward the Ford. "Just give him something to gnaw on and then go off on your adventures?"

"Well," Janice said, flashing her teeth, "most of our recent conversations have not been designed for a third party. So he can have his third lunch while the adults have a talk."

Designed conversations, Dorsey thought; *ain't that the truth.* He opened the Buick and wound down the window, releasing pent-up, overheated air. "Which one of us have you been following?" He asked, leaning into the car door. "Me or Outlaw?"

"You, of course." She moved closer to the door. "You smell like beer. It's nice; I like when you've had a beer."

"Must be the secret to our happy relationship."

"Just a small part of your charm. But I still love it." She took a handkerchief from her jeans pocket and wiped at the nape of her neck. "Meanwhile, back to police work. Give me your impressions of Mr. McCauley."

"He's a shithouse rat." Dorsey checked the sidewalk for passersby, found none within earshot, and continued. "He's worth every effort you make to put him away. He takes neighborhood myths and tribal loyalties, things he doesn't give a shit about, and sells them at a profit. These dumb bastards think he's a hero while he laughs up his sleeve at them." Dorsey smiled. "How's that sound? Can I be one of the guys now? I happen to believe what I just said, but I thought you'd like to hear it, sort of prove myself."

"Free tonight?"

"No, I'm not, you dirty-minded little girl." Dorsey shook his head. "Work to do, I believe."

"Based on your talk with Outlaw? If it is, I like him even less. If that's possible. Besides, the finals are on TV again tonight. They're in Los Angeles."

I know, Dorsey thought, *and let's hope Henry isn't too tired afterward for a little adventure.* "Sorry," he said, "not tonight." He considered a few options and decided to let her in on his talk with Outlaw. "Claims that all he ever had to do with Maritsa was to try to get her in the sack. And she disappeared before he got his chance. He thinks I ought to talk to Teddy."

"You can try," Janice Manning said, "but that junkie is long gone to parts unknown."

"Not according to Outlaw." Dorsey told her of Outlaw's speculation about the Polish Hill hideout.

"Doesn't sound right to me," Janice said. "Junkie's aren't the brightest guys in the world."

"We'll see." Dorsey slipped in behind the steering wheel. "Any messages for Teddy? In case I talk to him?"

"Tell him congratulations on the disappearing act." Janice hopped to her feet. "I'll be calling."

Of that you can be sure, Dorsey told himself. *Of that you can be sure.*

Al waved to Dorsey from behind the bar. "He's upstairs waiting on you. Don't you get anywhere on time? Tip-off was ten minutes ago."

"Took a nap," Dorsey said, passing the bar and descending into the backroom. "Anticipating a long night. Things could go well into the evening."

"You boys behave," All called out and went down the bar to look after a customer.

Rested and fresh from a shower, Dorsey took the steps two at a time, entering the apartment to find Henry glued to the TV. His back was to Dorsey and again that pigtail caught his eye. *Beatnik, no shit.*

Dorsey slipped into his chair and found a Rolling Rock already popped for him and waiting on a TV tray. "Score?" he asked.

"Lakers by six." Henry's eyes never left the screen. "They got off to a fast start, which surprised the hell outta me. Really on the run. Figured they'd just keep setting things up for Jabbar. Fooled the Celtics for a while, too."

Dorsey got into the game for the rest of the first half, letting go of missing girls, old ladies with rosaries snaking between their fingers, and two-faced local heroes. He watched Bird and Magic alternately outdo each other, the gears being racheted to the next level again and again. The beer was smooth and cold to the bottom, and when Henry brought him another, it was done with silent thanks, the game remaining inviolate. The half ended with the Lakers ahead by three and Kevin McHale in foul trouble.

"You know who was really something?" Henry asked, settling deeper into his chair with a smile. "Kenny Durrette. Remember him? Schenley High School? I think he played at LaSalle in Philly after that. You ever play against him? Duquesne must've played LaSalle once in a while."

"Little bit before my time," Dorsey said. "Maybe by a couple of years is all. He was in the pros by then. Chicago, right?"

"Yeah, I think so." Henry sipped at his beer. "Shame about his knee. Him and a lot of others. But I used to watch him when he was a senior at Schenley. Went to all the games. Teachers probably thought I was a pervert."

"There were good players here," Dorsey said. He was reminded of names like Stokes and Twyman and Lucas. And then he thought of Leneski and Durant. "Listen, before the game starts up again, we need to talk. I need a hand with something."

Dorsey filled him in on the last few days. Henry sipped his beer, attentive, nodding as if pulling the information from the air. "So," Dorsey said, "I need a guide. Somebody who can show me the way and get information from the locals. Care to take a trip after the game?"

"After the game, sure." Henry pointed his beer bottle at Dorsey. "No problem; we can make the rounds tonight. But after the game. Priorities, fella. Priorities."

Henry insisted on driving and borrowed Al's van, despite Dorsey's suggestion that the transmission wasn't up to the terrain they had to cover. "It's nasty hilly over there," Henry had said. "The streets are steep, shit yeah. But you don't need a Land Rover."

Mashing the gears like an old trainman switching rail lines, Henry kept up a running commentary as he drove. "It's only half a hill, really," he said, pulling into the left turning lane at Bigelow and Herron. "Bigelow Boulevard is like a farmer's terrace, like in Italy, dug into the side of a mountain. Just this big slash made out of asphalt. A natural boundary, like a river or mountain range."

Dorsey, ignorant of the area and its history, remained silent and assumed the role of tourist. He found Henry to be a great moving commentator, securing his interest and capturing his attention. It was no different than a well-done travelogue or maybe an afternoon spent in a cyclorama. But this tour was all business, he reminded himself. Get his hands on Teddy.

A green directional light flashed, and Henry guided the van onto Herron Avenue and a severe downward slope. He worked the brakes and transmission, each of the apparatus squealing out in competition. "We'll stop there later if we have to," Henry said, pointing to a one-story building of orange-brown brick just below the intersection. "Private club, kind of a younger crowd, mostly. I want to stop at the Falcons first. And maybe one other place."

Dorsey sat with his leg straightened and braced against the dashboard while he searched for the seatbelt, fearing a free fall into the windshield. Then Henry took another left, and the van fought against an even steeper downgrade. On the far sidewalk Dorsey saw that pipe railing had been installed to assist pedestrians. The slope was deep but short, lined on either side with tall and ancient-looking apartment buildings that were once bursting with as many newly arrived Poles as could be shoved in. Dorsey thought of them as the immigrant version of college phone-booth stuffing. At the foot of the slope was a shelf of level ground, and Henry pulled the van to the left curb. Here the apartments ended, and the shelf was dominated by a church fronted by long stone steps, sectioned by wrought-iron handrails. The tops of the twin steeples were lost in the night, and Dorsey was awed by the church's immensity. He thought of it as nothing less than a cathedral, and Henry seemed to read his thoughts.

"Could've been called Carnegie Cathedral," he said, exiting the van and gesturing for Dorsey to follow. "That's the history of the place. Oral history. Andrew Carnegie, when he was trying to un-load his wealth and get into heaven, was willing to underwrite the whole deal. As long as his name went up on front." Dorsey joined him on the sidewalk and they wandered to the foot of the steps. "Can you imagine?" Henry asked him. "A Catholic church named after a mere mortal? And a Protestant at that? Not after a saint who's performed the requisite number of miracles before or after death?" Henry watched Dorsey until he shook his head. "Well, neither could these old Polacks. Put the place up all by themselves. Brick by brick, squeezed-out dollar by squeezed-out dollar. And named it themselves: Immaculate Heart of Mary."

"You've spent some time up here," Dorsey said.

"Yeah, dig it," Henry said. "C'mon, let's go."

On foot, they started away from the church, leaving level ground and heading downward. There were more apartment buildings but these were vacant, the windows and arched walkways secured by plywood sheets. Just before an intersection Henry took Dorsey by the elbow and guided him up a flight of badly chipped cement steps, grabbing the center handrail for support. The steps, about twenty of them by Dorsey's estimate, led to a tall building of dark stone. It was institutional looking, with four huge windows and a single outdoor light mounted above the double doors illuminating the winged insignia of the Polish Falcons.

Inside the doors was another flight of steps, and Dorsey began to wonder about the wisdom of building a community into the side of a cliff. At the top of the steps was a wedding hall; Henry led him along its wall to a side door that opened into a small barroom. Three elderly patrons sat at the bar, their necks craned, keeping track of the television mounted above the bar's far end. They sipped quietly at draft beer, occasionally checking their wristwatches. Dorsey figured they were gauging the time to see if another beer could be downed before heading for home and the eleven o'clock news. Opposite the bar, a younger man in his thirties played at a pinball machine that, to Dorsey, looked older than the three men on barstools. Henry ordered two drafts, handed one to Dorsey, and led him toward the pinball machine.

"Shit!" The man playing pinball shouted and gave the machine a mean shove, making it go dark except for the tilt sign. "You believe that shit, Henry? Goddamn, I had that sumbitch, and then one of the flippers goes lame. Ball goes right down the hole. What bullshit."

Henry nodded in agreement and shook the man's hand. He was a few inches shorter than Dorsey, once he had straightened up from the machine, but he carried a heavy gut that strained his Pitt T-shirt. He picked up his beer and a stack of quarters from the glass top, nodded Dorsey a hello after Henry's introduction, and the three of them took seats at the small wooden table near the wall. The table had the look of salvage to Dorsey. Pitted with knife strokes, cigarette burns, and the amateur carvings of several generations, it looked as if it had been pulled from a reform school.

"You're looking good, Tat, Henry said to the man. You look okay."

"I'm pretty, all right," Tat said. He grabbed at the folds of his waist. "Pretty fuckin' fat. How 'bout it, Hen. You back for a while?"

"Who's to say?" Henry replied. "Things are good so far. So I stay. Things change, I change my plans."

"Fuckin' Hen." Tat downed half his beer in one swallow. "Stay awhile, fucker. You're too old for that shit."

"Remains to be seen." Henry turned and ordered a second round from the bartender. "Friend of mine here," he said, gesturing toward to Dorsey, "he's a detective. A private eye."

"No shit? Like on TV?" Tat finished off the rest of his beer and accepted a fresh one from the bartender. He laughed. "This ain't prime time, is it?"

"Matter of fact," Dorsey said, "I'm on the job right now."

"Then we got something in common," Tat said. "I drink on the job, too."

"Works daylight at the brewery," Henry said, slapping Tat's shoulder. "Just down the bottom of the hill."

"Beer breaks," Tat said. "Cheaper than coffee or even water when you work in a brewery."

Henry took a pull on his beer and shifted in his seat to face Tat. He stated his business and asked about Teddy Durant.

151

"That emaciated bastard?" Tat asked. "I swear, if he was a nigger and had a belly on him he could pass for one of them Biafra babies used to be in *Time* magazine ten years ago. Seen him around, mostly just walking the street, going into a bar, maybe. Can't say I ever saw a girl with him."

"Are you saying you've seen him lately?" Dorsey asked.

Tat looked at Dorsey, then turned to Henry, who nodded for him to continue. "Yeah," Tat said, returning his gaze to Dorsey, "it's been recent. Last few days, even. Saw him on the street, like I said. Could've been comin' home from work. Me, I mean."

"Know where he's staying at?" Henry asked.

"Naw. But most of the times I seen him, he was coming out of Stumpy's with a six pack. That's the place on Melwood. You could give that a try."

"Already on my list," Henry said.

"When you get through there," Tat said, "c'mon back here and buy some more beers. Detectives on TV always pay for information."

Stumpy's was a bust. The bar was empty except for an elderly bartender who was busy closing up for the night. "Shut the cash register already," he said before Henry could get a word out. "It's locked and I can't ring up any sales. You gotta go somewheres else."

They went to the van and pulled onto Herron, this time on the incline. At the private club they had passed earlier, Henry parked the van halfway onto the sidewalk and killed the ignition. The engine rumbled on for a second or two, belched, then gave up. On the sidewalk, Henry rapped at the club's door, and when it opened he flashed a membership card at the attendant. The door was opened wider and Dorsey hustled in behind Henry.

The club consisted of one main room, half filled with rows of upright folding tables and matching wooden folding chairs, the club's initials stenciled across the back. Several card games were scattered about the room, and Dorsey watched the play as he followed Henry to the bar at the room's far end. Near each huddle of players was a beer pitcher and spent shot glasses, and Dorsey marveled at the players' ability to follow the cards and get loaded at the same time. *It's a knack you've never had,* he reminded himself. *So stick with your real strength, beer drinking.*

Henry joked with the bartender, whom he apparently knew, and Dorsey sipped at a beer, watching the games and fighting off the fear that he might have to find Teddy all by himself. Henry hadn't mentioned any other stops, and these guys looked too preoccupied to concern themselves with a lost junkie. *So where do you start? Ask Janice for help. Why not; she seems to have a file on everything else.*

"He says we should try the guy playing solitaire," Henry said, breaking into his thoughts.

"What?"

"The bartender," Henry said. "He's says we should talk to that guy." Henry pointed to a white-haired man sitting alone in the far corner. He was hunched over his game, one card in his hand that he seemed unsure of playing. At his side was a short beer glass and a bottle of Pepsi.

"I know the guy," Henry said. "Not real good, but I know him. Anyway, the bartender says he owns a ton of places around here. Kind of the local landlord. Buys up everything he can real cheap; fixes 'em up real cheap, too, then rents out. Might be of some help."

"Let's talk to him," Dorsey said. *He'll know something,* Dorsey told himself. *Unless Teddy is living in the backseat of a car or under a rock. Then again, you have to wonder what this guy might want for the rental on a car's backseat or the shady side of a rock.*

They went up the aisle between the tables and crabwalked on opposite sides of the landlord's table. He looked up as they approached, setting aside his cards and sipping at the glass of Pepsi. Henry did the introductions and they sat.

"Ready for another Pepsi?" Dorsey asked.

The man checked the level in his bottle and said no. "Besides,

I get gas real bad. Gotta watch how much of this stuff I drink. Beer's even worse, That's why I had to give it up. My wife used to throw me out of the house. Had to put in central air-conditioning. Keep the air recycling, ya' know? Otherwise, it got pretty ripe."

"Hoping you might be able to lend us a hand," Henry said and explained some about Teddy.

"Little girl's gone missing, huh?" the man asked. He took the deck of cards in hand and seemed ready to return to his game. "Have girls of my own," he said, "but they're grown now. But you'd have to be fuckin' nuts to let a guy like that anywhere near a kid. Even if the kid is *his* kid."

"So, you know him?" Dorsey asked. "Know where we can find him this time of night?"

The white-haired man placed a black eight on a red nine and reviewed the board, looking for another play. "There gonna be trouble? I don't like trouble in my places, even if it's the pile of shit I rent out to him."

Dorsey sipped his beer and thought of his revolver, now locked in his office desk drawer. And the length of chain that was in South Side, coiled in the Buick's trunk. *No, thank God. No more trouble today.*

"The job is to bring the girl home," Dorsey told the landlord. "It's been a long time since I've had any arrest powers. And I don't want any. So punishment is for someone else to parcel out. If the girl's with him, we take her and go. If he's alone, we talk."

"Just talk, huh?" The landlord freed up a king and moved it to an open spot.

"Well," Dorsey said, lifting his beer glass and speaking over the rim, "there is a kid involved. Even if, like you said, the kid is his."

"Besides," Henry said, "you've seen the guy. You figure he could give one guy trouble, let alone two?"

"Depends on how wacky he is," the landlord said.

"Yeah," Dorsey said, "but you wouldn't do business with anybody that wacky, right?"

154

The landlord looked up from his cards and smiled at Dorsey, shrewdly. "Exactly, I'd never do that. Not enough money in the world to make me do that." He gave them quick directions to the apartment.

Back behind the steering wheel, Henry momentarily resumed his role as tour guide. "One last thing to show you," he said, taking the van around the bend onto Paulowna Street, another slope that ran parallel to Herron. Midway down the hill he stopped in front of what to Dorsey was unmistakably a Catholic grade school. It was the classic architecture: a central tower with double doors and wings of schoolrooms flaring out on either side. From somewhere beneath the driver's seat, Henry produced a flashlight and shone it on the building's cornerstone. It read SCHULA POLONICA, 1895.

"The hell are you?" Dorsey asked, laughing. "Social drop out, hoops nut, or local historian?"

"Social drop out, for the most part." Henry clicked off the flashlight and pulled away from the curb. "I say that because the age of specialization is lost on me."

They worked their way back to Melwood and kept on past Stumpy's, leaving the church and the neighborhood proper behind. Where the homes ended, Melwood snaked beneath the Bloomfield Bridge and then the road went black with a lack of street lamps and with overgrown foliage that had responded to spring rains. *City weeds,* Dorsey thought, *the kind that grow eight feet high and don't give a shit about having to push away a paving brick to do it.*

With the bridge behind him, Henry slowed the van, and both he and Dorsey studied the left side of the road. It was difficult without lighting, but Dorsey spotted the single parking spot carved from the roadside weeds. The ground was worn clear by tire tracks, and a flight of cement steps led away from the spot. Dorsey gestured for Henry to pull in.

The steps were a sort of bridge spanning a small gully and once across it they found themselves on the roof of what appeared to be

155

a deserted factory. At the center of the roof, as if it were some type of afterthought, was a one-story brick structure. Long and slender, it went to the far end of the roof, and Dorsey figured it for a low-rent apartment, originally intended for the night watchman.

No lights showed inside and he made for the door. A mailbox was mounted next to it, and inside were two items: a stereo advertisement addressed to Occupant and, directly addressed to Theodore K. Durant, a letter from the Department of Public Assistance. Dorsey tore open the envelope and found Teddy's new DPA medical card. *You've got it right,* Dorsey thought. *Drop out of society, but only if you can continue to live off it. Using your head, Teddy.*

"Looks like nobody's home," Henry said. "Thinking what I'm thinking?"

Dorsey examined the door and found it secured by a padlock and hasp. He went back to the van, retrieved a tire iron, and worked it between the door and the hasp. Wood splintered from the frame and the metal pulled away, exposing two long screws that Dorsey figured must have gone in when the building went up. *Messing around with the mails and now breaking and entering,* he thought, *this is getting heavy.* Then he thought of the girl's face and Mrs. Leneski's determination and went in.

Dorsey ran his hand along the doorframe until he found the light switch. He flicked it and a bare lightbulb hanging from a ceiling wire dully illuminated a small kitchen. There was a run-down refrigerator, which Dorsey figured to be second- or thirdhand, and by the sink was an electric cooking ring. The sink itself was all rust and waterstains. Dorsey picked through a cupboard and found only canned food while Henry went to the adjoining room and turned on the lights.

"Holy shit," Henry said, half laughing. "Thought I'd left this kind of crap behind in San Francisco. About fifteen years ago."

Dorsey followed him in and found what he could only describe as a museum of late sixties–early seventies hard luck. A living room, of sorts, took up most of the structure and the walls were covered in rock posters. Joplin and Hendricks had one corner, which Dorsey figured for a memorial; Cream and Iron Butterfly had a spot between two windows; and the rest of the history lesson became too obscure for Dorsey's memory. Henry, on the other hand, seemed to appreciate it.

"Yeah, it's a throwback," Henry said. "Had a place like this myself, back when there was more hair on my head. Shared it with this girl who saw herself as an artist. Last I heard, she's selling cars at her dad's Oldsmobile dealership."

Dorsey moved about the room's furnishings, looking for anything obvious. There were some makeshift shelves filled with a stereo unit, albums, and several paperbacks. The chairs and sofa were vintage Goodwill, and the coffee table was littered with cigarette papers and a homemade waterpipe constructed from a tequila bottle, a two-holed rubber stopper, and two lengths of plastic tubing. Finding nothing at first glance, Dorsey checked the two rooms that ran off the living room's left side. The first was a small bathroom with a mildewed shower curtain and puddles of water standing on cracked linoleum. The second room was completely at odds with any of the others.

The contrast was startling. The room was a little larger than the bathroom and totally empty. And it had been thoroughly cleaned, scrubbed even; Dorsey could smell lingering traces of ammonia cleaner on the walls. The floor was bare, but small holes in the planks showed where a carpet and its tacks had been pulled away.

"Wonder what they had going on in here." Henry was in the doorway.

"How's that?"

"Must've been up to something," Henry said. "All this cleaning had to be for a reason. He sure doesn't give the same consideration to the rest of the place."

Dorsey stepped past Henry back into the living room and started a more thorough search. A set of dresser drawers at the far wall yielded only blue jeans, T-shirts, and loose marijuana seeds. The albums and paperbacks were innocent enough, and he turned his attention to the sofa and chairs, checking beneath the cushions. Henry followed behind and lifted the waterpipe, admiring the craftsmanship. When he did so, the coffee table jiggled and Dorsey checked the legs.

One of the legs was a half-inch shorter than the others and propped up from below by a paperback. The title was obscured, but Dorsey could see the drawing of three teenaged boys on the cover. He pulled out the book and let the table topple on its side. *The Outsiders.* S. E. Hinton. Ponyboy and family.

He showed it to Henry without explanation and then riffled through the pages, finding a place marker. It was a square of paper, about the size of a smallish index card. Dorsey knew it immediately for what it was. A sheet from Dr. Novotny's prescription pad, complete with name, address, telephone number, and Drug Enforcement Administration control number.

20

Drowsy from a long night of beer and discovery, Dorsey used the heel of his fist to work the sleep from his eyes as he drove onto Wilkins Avenue. Lingering at the edges of his thoughts on Maritsa and Teddy and Dr. Novotny were recent memories of Irene Boyle, confused and tearful over a past about which he had no knowledge. *Christ,* he thought, *I hate this family business even more than I did yesterday.*

The gate to his father's driveway was open, and Dorsey parked the Buick behind a late-model Toyota. At the door he rang the bell and was answered by a young male voice shouting that the door was unlocked. Dorsey entered, wondering what the hell was going on and if Ironbox had been replaced by a law-clerk type, and continued into the office.

"You working this thing? Really working it or just sitting at your desk?"

The young man was dressed in khaki slacks, button-down shirt, and white linen jacket, a style that Dorsey had come to think of as medical-casual. He was Dorsey's size but with even thicker shoulders, and he had a solid grip on Martin Dorsey's ankle, testing its strength by briskly twisting it in several directions. The elder

Dorsey was in his swivel chair, pulled into the center of the room for the therapy session, and clearly indignant at the question.

"What are you again?" Martin Dorsey asked. "A therapist, is that it? And what is that, exactly? It's my understanding that you're all a bunch of gym teachers who went back to school for a few years."

"I don't make fun of your work." The therapist finished with the ankle and went on to examine the calf muscles. He jerked his head in approval, apparently satisfied with the muscle's development. "It's okay, but a little more work wouldn't hurt."

Dorsey settled against the far wall and waited for the examination to conclude. The therapist moved on to the arm, checking muscle strength and range of motion. He then took a long look at the tripod cane, tightening several wing nuts and determining if the height was correct. Throughout, his father had the appearance of a man being held back from pressing business.

"Next week," the therapist said, scribbling notes on the case chart, "I want to see some improvement in that leg. Understand? The exercises are not optional. You can get a lot more out of that leg if you try."

"Would I be capable of booting you right in the ass?" Martin Dorsey asked. "If I really worked it, I mean."

"Hell, yes, you could." The therapist laughed and helped Dorsey's father out of the chair, which he returned to its place behind the desk. Martin Dorsey hobbled behind and retook his seat. He signed a slip given him by the therapist, who left with only the slightest nod of acknowledgment in Dorsey's direction.

"Sit," his father said, gesturing toward the guest chairs. "You appear to me as though you shouldn't be on your feet. Even more than I."

"Things took a hectic turn the last few days." Dorsey dropped into a chair. "You always give that guy such a hard time? Does he deserve it or are you just staying in practice?"

"You heard him," Martin Dorsey said. "These things have to be worked."

Dorsey shrugged in agreement and ran a hand across his face. "How've you been otherwise?"

Now his father shrugged. "Good as can be expected. The stroke didn't turn me into an imbecile, if that's what you mean. No cognitive problems, as the doctors call them, no change in personality."

"Didn't think so, but I had to ask." Dorsey told his father about his visit with Ironbox.

"Poor woman," Martin Dorsey said. "She's been slipping."

"Slipping?" Dorsey said. "Looks a little more serious than that. Talk about personality changes, she had at least three in less than a half an hour."

"No need to exaggerate." Martin Dorsey opened the desk's center drawer, considered the contents, and closed it again. "She's had a hard life and she's no doubt showing the effects, finally. It's very unpleasant to watch, I agree. And for her it must be frustrating. But let's not get dramatic, please."

"The dramatics were all hers." Dorsey chose his next words carefully, not sure if he wanted a response. "The other part bothers me some. A good bit, really. What she had to say about my mother's death. That's what she was fixated on."

Martin Dorsey looked fondly across the room at the bar. "Sometimes abstinence is the worst fallout of the stroke." He turned to his son and settled his gaze. "The woman has some guilt that she carries. Strictly of her own making. Her personal version of Catholicism has a lot to do with it. You know, wicked thoughts and desires are the equivalent of evil deeds?"

"I can follow that easily enough," Dorsey said, recalling eight years of Sacred Heart grade school. Eight years of guilt and anticipated damnation for scratching a few places when they got itchy. "She should have considered a life in the convent."

"It was suggested."

"Regardless," Dorsey said, again wondering if he wanted an answer, "what's the guilt over?"

161

Martin Dorsey propped his chin in his hand, thought a moment, then shook his head. "Ah, well," he said, "I thought it would be obvious. Consider her devotion as an assistant. Do you really think that it comes from political loyalty alone? No one loves the Democratic Party that much."

"You two have had a thing going all this time?" Dorsey almost jumped from his seat.

"Heavens no!" Martin Dorsey laughed but quickly turned somber. "I said her guilt was based on wicked thoughts, not deeds. Irene Boyle has made her feelings for me clear over the decades. She told me she loved me while your mother was alive, and I guess when your mother died she thought she saw her chance."

Dorsey shook his head in wonderment. He had thought of her as a neuter, a machine that cleared away any debris in his father's path. And who wiped away the footprints once he had passed. Now he was getting a new picture. Ironbox was no Ironbox.

"And what was your part?" Dorsey asked. "Your hands are clean on this one?"

"Physically, yes." His father seemed to sink deeper into his chair cushions. "I never returned her affections. But I used them to keep her working for me. To keep her working at her level of competence and devotion, I gave her just the right amount of appreciation to support her belief that she might have a chance. Nothing to be proud of, I assure you."

"Christy Almighty," Dorsey said. "What *do* you have to be proud of?"

"There are some professional accomplishments I can take refuge in."

"And you relate all her wild behavior to unrequited love?"

"Oh, sure." Again, Martin Dorsey hesitated. "You see—and this is a confidence not given lightly—Irene had a breakdown once before. It was just after your mother's death. As I said, she thought her chance had come, and when it became clear that this was not the case, well, you know how these things can be."

162

"Suicide attempt?"

"Not that bad, but she did have the breakdown and was hospitalized, very quietly, at St. Francis."

Hope she did better than Crazy Katie, Dorsey thought. *Must've, from the looks of things.*

"And when she was released," Martin Dorsey continued, "she took a long trip. Through Europe."

"Where she drove through the Po River Valley," Dorsey said.

"Where the trees grow tall and form a canopy over the road."

"Exactly."

Dorsey hit the doorbell three times without a response. Instead, a second-story window of the house next door flew open, and an elderly man stuck out his head. "Hey fella, you gotta go 'round back. She's out in the yard. You gotta go 'round."

"Okay, thanks," Dorsey said, looking up at the man from Mrs. Leneski's front stoop. "I'll try the back."

"Up 'round the block," the man said, coming farther out of the window, exposing his naked and sagging chest. "Up 'round the block, then back down the alley," he insisted. "You'll see her. In the yard, in the garden. Just keep lookin', you'll find her okay. She's in back."

Dorsey thanked him again and headed up the block and around the corner, passing identical row houses facing out on a curb lined either with parked cars or kitchen chairs that reserved the homeowners parking place. *Driveways,* Dorsey thought. *The promise of them had made millionaires of suburban developers. These folks had put out chairs and kept their money.*

The alley was an uneven, easy slope covered with grey paving bricks. On both sides were backyards similar to the one extending from Dorsey's South Side home. Long and thin, they were marked off by a variety of fencing, wood or steel wire mesh, and had either a paved or foot-beaten path through the center, leading to the gate. Mrs. Leneski's yard was enclosed by a newer looking cyclone fence,

163

and Dorsey figured it for the handiwork of her nephew, Ziggy. He undid the gate and entered, finding Mrs. Leneski on her knees in the dirt, lashing tomato plants to wooden stakes. This time, along with her housedress, she wore a pair of green work pants, and Dorsey wondered if they were leftovers from her days at Kress Box.

"You have news?" Mrs. Leneski asked, looking up from her work. She took a handkerchief from her pocket and wiped at her hands.

"I've got some news." Dorsey offered his hand to assist her to her feet, but instead she took firm hold of a metal wash line pole, bringing herself up in a hand-over-hand fashion, like a determined gym student. It left Dorsey with the impression that she had been employing this method for the last twenty growing seasons.

They sat in folding chairs near the kitchen door, where they were protected from the sun. From the back pocket of his khaki slacks, Dorsey produced the paperback. "Maritsa's, right?" he asked, handing over the book. "The one you found missing?"

Mrs. Leneski held the book flatly in one hand, running the fingers of the other across the faces of the teenaged boys adorning the cover. "Where'd you find it? She wasn't with it?"

Dorsey recounted his activities of the night before. Then he went back further, bringing her completely up to date. *She's paying,* he thought. *More importantly, she can take it.*

"So," she said. "The junkies, huh?"

"Yeah," Dorsey said. "You're right. The junkies."

Dorsey allowed a moment of awkward silence before he continued. "This Dr. Novotny, is he your family doctor?"

"Hell, no," Mrs. Leneski said, clearly coming back to the conversation without difficulty. "Everybody around here knew there was something wrong with him, goddamned refugee-hero my ass. Just another hunkie like the rest of us. And a sneaky one, you can tell. Everybody knew something was wrong."

"Still," Dorsey said," he has a successful practice."

"So," Mrs. Leneski said, "people have to go to a doctor some-where. I always hated Krupche, the man had a butcher shop on Butler. Always kept his thumb on the scale when he weighed your order. But what was I gonna do? Had to buy meat somewhere and the supermarkets weren't around yet. So I went to Krupche. Same with the doctor. People get sick and need a doctor in a hurry, they go to the guy just up the street, even if he's a bastard." She stopped for a deep breath that rattled her lungs. "Goddamned Teddy. He stole my little girl."

"He's part of it, at least." Dorsey leaned forward, planting his elbows on his knees and bracing his weight. "Not that it matters much, but I don't know why he did it. You say you never saw him around? And Maritsa never talked about seeing him?"

"Never a word," Mrs. Leneski said. "Sometimes, I figured he was dead, from the dope or from somebody else who hated him. And he wasn't supposed to see her, that's what the judge said. You gonna find him? That's what you have planned next?"

The prospect of looking for Teddy held no attraction for Dorsey. *The man has hidden from the police at will,* he thought. *But, maybe things are different now. Maybe he's been flushed out. And maybe he has a teenaged girl with him now. Maybe.* "I made a call to Strobec," he said, "the cop in Missing Persons? He now knows what we know and they'll be looking for Teddy. So will I. But first, I plan on paying an office visit to the doctor."

"You could sneak a look at his house; maybe he has her there."

"No," Dorsey said, leveling a stare a Mrs. Leneski. "I can't see her being there. If he had your granddaughter, why would he send McCauley after another girl?"

She dropped her head and looked at the book cover, making Dorsey wish this could be an insurance investigation. Just put the results on paper and stuff it in an envelope with proper postage. Never see the client, never a face-to-face accounting. Unless you happen to take him to lunch to hit him up for another case.

For a moment there was another silence, and only the chirping of a bird and the flapping of a neighbor's wet laundry hung in the breeze could be heard. The telephone rang from inside, mercifully for Dorsey, and Mrs. Leneski went to answer. Dorsey stayed in his chair, stretching out his legs and resting his head against the brick and morter wall. He smiled as he listened to Mrs. Leneski on the phone.

"Who are you again?" He heard her say. "Oh, sure, you, that's right. What is it? She's got insurance, I think." There were a few moments of silence and then Mrs. Leneski came to the rear door.

"You better get on the phone," she said. "It's the lady from up at St. Francis. Peg Malloy, the one who looks after my Catherine? She say's Teddy's up there visiting my daughter."

21

Forty-fourth Street is one way with parking on either side, allowing only a thin corridor of asphalt for moving cars. Children and dogs darted from the sidewalks, and the absentminded opened car doors into oncoming traffic. Dorsey knew the dangers and said the hell with it, crushing the Buick's accelerator underfoot and bursting up the street's incline.

Another face was to be revealed, he thought, another face in this case of the faceless. Dr. Novotny, whose voice he had heard and whose history was on file, but whom he had never looked in the eye. Outlaw, whom he had met only after a prep course supplied by Janice Manning. And now Teddy Durant. Dorsey had been in his home, had seen the dirt in his kitchen and toilet, and had heard only the worst about him from a dozen sources. He had to wonder if he would ever meet Maritsa Durant in the flesh.

Dorsey circled the main hospital and pulled to the curb at the East Wing, disregarding the no parking signs. Peg Malloy was at the entrance, accompanied by a security guard. "He's still here?" Dorsey asked as he shot up the steps. He looked at the security guard. "Your people are holding him?"

167

"For what?" The guard looked at Peg Malloy. "The guy's a visitor, right? Hasn't acted up, has he?"

Miss Malloy waved off the guard and gestured for Dorsey to follow her. "The guard was out here just to pass you through quickly." The two of them headed down a familiar corridor to her office. "We need to be clear on this," she said. "As far as we're concerned, this Teddy is a visitor like any other. He came in freely and he gets to leave the same way. Personally, I think the guy should commit himself for detox with twenty-eight days of rehab to follow, but we can't hold him without his signed voluntary committment."

"The police want to talk to him," Dorsey said.

"There's a warrant?" Peg Malloy asked. They had reached the office door, and she was fishing in her pocket for her keys. "You're not a policeman, and you don't have a warrant to arrest. We can't detain this man."

"So what's to do?" Dorsey asked. He followed her inside and sat in one of the plastic guest chairs while watching her cram herself between the desk and the far wall. "Where's he at? Someplace I can get a look at him?"

"I don't know what you plan on doing." Peg Malloy cleared some papers from the desktop until she found a laminated list of telephone extensions. "I called Mrs. Leneski to let her know about the visit because of the missing girl. Anyway, let me check something. Teddy and Catherine should be in the visitors' lounge. There's no secret observation point there, no two-way mirror to keep an eye on patients. So don't get the idea that you can spy on the conversation." She lifted the receiver and punched in four numbers.

Dorsey squirmed in his chair, his left foot vibrating off the ball and large toe. *Another confrontation,* he thought, *and this with little or no preparation. Without the righteous chain or the threat of it. What was it Gretchen had said? Better to keep this sort of thing to a minimum.*

Peg Malloy thanked someone and placed the receiver in its cradle, resting her head against the flurry of memos and announcements taped to the wall behind her. "That was the guard posted in the lounge. He keeps a respectable distance from the visitors; just makes sure that no one gets too riled up or out of hand. He says Teddy's still there. He looks pretty jumpy, but he's under control."

"I have to talk to him," Dorsey said. "He's been with Maritsa, there's no doubt. He knows what I have to know."

"We can go to the lounge, that's not a problem." Peg Malloy straightened in her chair. "But this has to be straightforward. No eavesdropping. You show yourself right away."

"Never had the pleasure of meeting the guy before," Dorsey said, rising from his seat. "So that's not a problem. Don't worry, I won't screw around."

Dorsey used the time spent walking through the hallways to the visitors' lounge to gear up. With only an angry sneer and implied threats, he had to break Teddy and find a missing girl. A beautiful girl, missing for months with her photo stapled to every telephone pole in the neighborhood. *You're doing this to save a young girl. It's for the girl.*

He followed Peg Malloy through metal double doors equipped with crash bars and found himself in a large dayroom furnished with older easy chairs and sofas, all of which had the worn look and cigarette burns of institutional use. There was a pool table near the center, but Dorsey didn't see any cue sticks or billiard balls and figured them for tempting weaponry. Next to the pool table, Catherine Durant was huddled in a yellow padded chair, her legs tucked beneath her and her face hung low, obscured by the black hair that fell around it. Before her, in what appeared to be a state of extreme agitation, was one of the skinniest men Dorsey had ever seen. Tat had been right; Give him a bloated stomach, and you might well have been looking at a famine victim.

Teddy's hair was a light brown, just a shade darker than blond, and shoulder length. Part of it was wrapped in a rubber band and the rest fell free, as if nervous hands had tried and failed at gathering a ponytail. His denim shirt was sleeveless and the jeans he wore were gritty and frayed at the bottom. But it was the thought of his body weight that Dorsey couldn't get past. *He's probably less than six feet,* he thought, *but the lack of fat and muscle lends another dimension, an illusion of an additional four inches of height. Even now, bent forward and pleading, he's another Ichabod Crane. A strung-out, on the run, Ichabod Crane.*

"You gotta have some," he was saying as Dorsey and Peg Malloy approached. "I gotta get the fuck away from here. Can't you talk to the old lady? She'd give you money. I need the fuckin' money, Cat. Right a-fuckin'-way."

"I'm worried about Maritsa." Catherine Durant spoke without movement, her gaze fixed on her lap.

"Ah, shit, she's okay," Teddy said. "Worry about me, huh? I gotta fuckin' take off, okay?"

"Pretty desperate, huh?" Dorsey stood behind Teddy while Peg Malloy went to Catherine's side, stroking her shoulder. "You must be," Dorsey continued, "showing up here. Hell of a chance you took, and look what happened. It was good, though, to hear that Maritsa is all right. Now just tell me where she's at. I'll go get her, and maybe you can just disappear into a doped-out blur."

Teddy turned on Dorsey, his eyes wide with what Dorsey first took to be surprise, then came to recognize as part of the shakes. Closer now, Dorsey picked up Teddy's unwashed scent and the sweat stains smeared across his collar. "The girl," Dorsey said, "your daughter. Listen, junkie, I don't give a shit about you or whatever it is you put in your arm or in your nose or up your ass. The girl, she was with you. Don't fucking lie to me. Tell me where she is."

Dorsey stole a quick glance at Peg Malloy and saw the distaste in her eyes as she led Catherine out of her seat and toward the double doors. *Take care of your charges,* he thought, *I'll try to do the same.*

"Stop fuckin' with me," Teddy said, backing off a few steps.

170

Dorsey followed. "I dunno what the fuck you're talkin' about." He rubbed at his eyes and pulled at his crotch like a nervous batter at the plate. "Lemme alone, man. You don't know shit about me."

"I don't?" Dorsey asked. Across Teddy's shoulder he saw the security guard rise from his desk at the far corner. The guard watched them, but made no approach. "Sure I know about you," Dorsey continued. "I know a lot. I've been to your place, that pile of crap in the weeds up on Polish Hill. The place where you kept your daughter. Her book was there, the one she took with her when she left home. She left home with you, right? So where's she at?"

"Fuck you, you ain't shit to me."

"That's not exactly true," Dorsey said, crowding him a little more. "I can make trouble, and I will. At the very least, there's going to be one very pissed-off judge in Family Court who will want you on a contempt rap. Not supposed to see the girl, are you? And that's just for starters. There's a cop named Strobec who smokes too much and is in a shitty mood because his boss wants him to quit. He's with Missing Persons and he's been looking for Maritsa, too. And he can put a hold on you. And that's too bad, seeing how you're looking to run away just now."

Teddy hesitated, apparently lost for the moment, and Dorsey thought he might have sunk the hook. But Teddy recovered quickly and spat at the floor between Dorsey's feet. "You don't know shit, asshole," Teddy said, adding a grin to his increasing arrogance. "Family Court? Get the fuck outta here. Who gives a shit about that? Them cops got more on me than you could ever keep straight. You don't mean shit to me."

Once again Dorsey wished he had that length of chain in hand. He swore he could use it now, without emotional preparation, without regret. Teddy had become more than a junkie, more than someone who had to be leaned on for a purpose, a good purpose. He was now a despised enemy. A Jap or Kraut for an earlier generation, someone to be mowed down for the betterment of mankind. Dorsey gathered himself for another attack.

"The girl." His voice was menacing. "You tell me where she is. Take me to her if you want. Whatever you like. But you're going to give her up. Right fuckin' now. Where's she at?"

Again the junkie was thrown, his eyes now taking on a twitch while he ran his palms along the stitching of his jeans. This time Dorsey was sure he had landed a strike. He waited a second or so, finding not a hint of rebound in Teddy, only the madness in his eyes. "Last chance," Dorsey said.

"Could be at Novotny's?" Teddy said, an apparent plea that Dorsey would believe him lingered at the edges of his words. "Really, no shit, that's where she's gotta be. That's where you should go."

"C'mon," Dorsey said. "Try it again. You're saying Outlaw pimped her over?"

"Outlaw ain't the only game in town," Teddy said, turning from Dorsey, clearly planning to take off. "Go see Novotny."

Teddy got in two shuffling steps before Dorsey took a handful of greasy shirtfront, spinning him around, amazed at how light he was to the touch, so easily handled. There was so much more to ask. Dorsey wanted to know about the rides home, the time in the apartment, the medicinally scrubbed bedroom, and the truth about Maritsa's whereabouts.

The knife must have come from his waistband, Dorsey figured, probably from the small of the back. It fascinated him that he could split his thoughts so well—watching the blade slice toward him while speculating on its origins. It made landfall, tip forward, into the underside of Dorsey's left forearm, then slashed forward, rooting out a wealth of blood vessels. Instinctively, he released Teddy's shirtfront and took hold of his forearm, trying to staunch the blood flow.

The security guard was at his side, working free his belt and applying a makeshift tourniquet. *"Get that guy!"* Dorsey told him, taking over the end of the belt and keeping the pressure constant. "I need that guy, need him bad."

172

"Doctor is what you need," the guard said, leading him to the doors. "ER's just across the street, far side of the building. You need to get to a doctor."

Yeah, Dorsey thought, *I need to get to a doctor. An old Hunky doctor on Butler Street.*

22

It was a role for which he had always considered himself far too intelligent, much too practical. And he had a packed house for the performance: Al, the ward nurse, and the vascular surgeon's chief resident. If it had been anyone else, Dorsey would have accused them of logging too many hours in front of the TV watching old movies. *Ah, the hell with it,* he thought, *play out the scene. Complete your rendition of the injured but devoted detective, too preoccupied to care for his own health and checking out of the hospital against medical advice.*

"It only nicked the artery," Dorsey said, pushing himself from the bed with his right hand, his left hand heavily bandaged from wrist to elbow. "Said it yourself, Doctor. So things aren't that bad. C'mon, man, there's a few things I need to do."

"There was serious blood loss." The physician was a thin man with yellow hair wearing wire-rimmed glasses. Seated in one of the room's guest chairs, with the ward nurse at his side, he flipped a page of the chart he held on his lap. "Oh, yes. Very significant. Your surgeon, Dr. Manfredi, he definitely would object to your leaving the hospital. You really have to stay."

Dorsey was on his feet now, going for the clothes closet and

174

holding the loose ends of his hospital gown behind his back. Al was standing in the room's far corner, grinning. "Listen," Dorsey said, "I'm going to make this quick because my ass is hanging out and it's cold in here. All that blood I lost, you guys replaced it. I know, because I have these nasty little holes in my good arm where you passed it through. Looks so bad I could be mistaken for one of the guys at the park down the bottom of the hill. And I'm not hooked up to anything else now, so all I'm doing is taking up a bed and turning down the food they serve around here. And besides, I have urgent business. Very urgent business."

"The wound," the physician said, "it could open up again. If it does, you'd be much better off in the hospital. I know that's a concern of Dr. Manfredi's."

Dorsey opened the closet and dumped his pants and shirt onto the bed. "If I bang my arm by accident or if it looks like it's beginning to seep, I'll get to an emergency room, okay?" He reached back into the closet and retrieved his shoes, socks, and boxer shorts. "One other thing, who the hell is this Manfredi, anyway? Supposed to be my doctor, but you can't tell that by me because I've never seen him. I guess he did a little work while I was unconscious, but again, don't look to me for proof. Must be important, though. He has you scared shitless." Dorsey took a handful of the partition drape then hesitated. "Sorry, Doctor. That was uncalled for. Sorry, really. We all answer to somebody. Anyways, a day and a half in this place is all I can spare."

The doctor stood up, adjusted his glasses, and looked to Al, apparently for support. Al nodded to the doctor, then turned to Dorsey, as if considering both sides of a debate. "My friend should be leaving now," Al said, turning again to the doctor. "Nine out of ten, I'd be on your side. I'm sure you're pretty smart guys, you and Dr. Manfredi both. And it's always best to be careful about these things. But there's a few other things, real important ones, hanging in the balance this time. It makes a difference, really. You'd understand if you knew."

The physician scribbled a fast notation on the chart, handed it to the ward nurse, and left without further comment. When he was gone, the nurse cracked a smile and told Dorsey to call Manfredi's office for a follow-up appointment. "And," she said, heading out the door, "you have to leave the hospital in a wheelchair. That's policy. Besides, once I tell everybody what just happened, there'll be plenty of volunteers to push you."

Al took the drape from Dorsey and closed it between them, pulling it along its ceiling track. "That doctor," he said through the drape's fabric, "he's really not a bad fella. Just sounds like his boss is a handful. And he's right; you should take it easy once you get the chance. But right now, you don't have the time. If it weren't for that little girl, I'd sit on your chest and make you stay."

"It wouldn't come to that," Dorsey said. "Just the threat would be sufficient."

"One other thing," Al said. "With your busted up right hand and now your chopped up left arm, you'll need some help. At least in driving. Henry'll be doing that for you. Already talked to him about it, and I've got somebody to cover for him at the bar. Henry can look out for you. Right now, he's getting your car out of the pound. Did I mention it got towed?"

Henry was waiting for them in front of the Wharton Street row house, slouched against the Buick's right front fender. Al pulled the van up even to him, shut off the engine, and tossed him the keys as Dorsey helped himself out of the passenger door. "Go on up to the bar," Al told Henry. "Ask Rose to pack some dinner for the three of us and c'mon back. Bring along a little beer, too. Couldn't hurt."

His bandaged arm held close to his side, Dorsey climbed the three steps to his front door as Henry drove away. With his right hand he searched his pockets, coming up empty and pissed until he heard Al come up behind him, shaking a key ring.

176

"How'd you think Henry drove the Buick from the pound?" Al asked, handing over the keys. "You really need a little rest, just to get your wits about you."

"Sorry," Dorsey said, undoing the lock. "I've been preoccupied, what with this case and my significant blood loss. I'll try to improve."

Once inside, Dorsey told Al to make himself at home while he took his first shower in two days. First he went to the kitchen and searched the cabinets until he found a plastic grocery bag without holes or tears. Upstairs, he stripped, slipped his left forearm into the bag, and sealed it watertight with a rubber band, triple bound at the elbow. Standing beneath the showerhead, listening to pipes rattle as hot water struggled up from the basement, he pushed away the last forty-eight hours. *Time wasted, spent in a hospital bed because you let a strung-out, emaciated doper cut you and get away. Away to who knows where. Which is a place you now have to go looking for. Because he says Novotny has the girl and that doesn't make sense. It has to be checked out, but it doesn't make sense.*

Dry and with his hair combed, Dorsey slipped into jogging shorts and a T-shirt and went downstairs. Al was sitting at the desk, sipping at a mug of coffee. Glen Miller, the Army Air Corps Band version, floated out from the tape player.

"Coffee's fresh," Al said.

Dorsey sat at the edge of the office chaise. "No thanks; I'll wait for the beer. Henry should be along soon enough."

"Did a few things for you while you were in the shower," Al said. "Didn't get the dressing wet?"

"I was careful." The front windows were open, screens in, and Dorsey had a soft breeze and the Wharton Street quiet at his back. "What kind of things, exactly?"

"Phone calls," Al said. "Made one for myself, too. Had to call in my order to the beer distributor. Otherwise, I called people I thought would like to know that you're safe at home."

Dorsey rested his bandaged arm on his knee, gently adjusting it into a comfortable position. "Let's have the rundown," Dorsey said, smiling. "Then I can decide if any thanks are in order."

"First, I talked to your client, Mrs. Leneski," Al said. "She felt real bad, and she's gonna whip up some food and send it over with Ziggy. She also says that you should know better. Said you have to punch Teddy in the nose before you talk to him. That settles him down and gets his attention."

"I suppose," Dorsey said, "that you gave my father a call?"

"We talked a little bit." Al set his coffee mug on the desktop. "He already knew, like he knows about everything ten minutes after it happens. He's all right. He said, though, that this Boyle woman was kind of shaken by it."

"How bad is she?" Dorsey asked, recalling their last meeting. *She was on the edge; let's hope this isn't the kick in the ass that puts her over.*

"Had to take some pills to calm her down," Al said. "Supposed to be okay now, though."

"Good, good," Dorsey said. "She's been a mess lately. Emotionally, I mean. Best thing would be to keep her on a steady high for a while. Maybe we should introduce her to the guys at the park, maybe get her a cut rate."

"Or maybe she should get together with this Novotny guy."

"Not that," Dorsey said. "Not for your worst enemy would you want that. By the way, who *is* your worst enemy?"

Al laughed. "You never met him. I put him in the middle of the river years ago." He lifted his mug and laughed again. "Seriously, though. I made one other call. To Gretchen."

"Thanks, man," Dorsey said. "Really, I'm glad you did. Even though I'm not glad you did."

"Understand completely. That's why I made the call."

"How was she?"

"Sounded nervous at first," Al said. "Especially when she heard about the blood loss and transfusion, but she got a handle on it

178

pretty quick. She was headed in for an evening shift and said she'd call you during her break. Said something about trying to get free this weekend, maybe come get a look at you."

Dorsey nodded, wondering if that was good news or an unwise possibility. *Ah, the hell with it. One way or another, we'll be reasonable people.*

The doorbell rang and Al answered it, admitting Henry. He had his arms around several large white paper bags and went straight for the kitchen. Dorsey and Al followed and took seats at the table while Henry unloaded the bags on the sink countertop. Two six-packs of Rolling Rock went into the refrigerator and a third was placed on the table. Henry found plates and tableware and served up a meal of roasted pork, sauerkraut, and mashed potatoes. Each grabbed a beer and for a while they ate in silence.

"So," Henry said, forking sauerkraut onto his mashed potatoes and mixing it in, "what's the plan? I'm gonna be the driver for a while, so you might as well let me in on things."

Dorsey began to speak, but Al cut him off. "Nothing today," he said through a mouthful of food. "You need to come up for air, take a rest. Tomorrow's soon enough."

Dorsey worked at his food with his arthritic hand. *No, tomorrow isn't soon enough,* he thought. *Not with Teddy making tracks and Novotny covering his ass a little more. But there's no choice. You're out of gas. And you need to think. You need the time to think and recharge.*

"In the morning," Dorsey agreed, "and not any time early, either. We have to start looking for Teddy all over again. And I've got to have a set-to with Dr. Novotny. And one other thing. If that Malloy woman will allow it, I need to talk to Catherine Durant. She had a lot of time with Teddy before I got there. It would be nice to know what all happened in their visit together."

"Thought you said he was looking for money." Al said. "Getaway money, I figured."

"That's the part I overheard," Dorsey said. "But I didn't get the whole thing. Maybe that'll be tomorrow's first stop."

"Buick or the van?" Henry asked.

"We'll use my car," Dorsey said. He sipped at his beer, then took up his fork, ripping off a ragged piece of meat from his plate. "The ride's less bumpy, and that's suddenly important to me." He lifted his left arm from his lap.

Al smiled through his food. "You just be mindful of that arm."

After dinner, Al and Henry cleared the table while Dorsey went to the office, beer in hand, and settled into his desk chair. Henry and Al soon followed, bringing the rest of the beer and storing it in the room's midget refrigerator. They watched a little TV until Al seemed convinced that Dorsey could survive on his own. There were some fast so-longs, Henry promised to be on his doorstep at ten the next morning, and they were gone.

Dorsey helped himself to a fresh Rolling Rock and cranked back his chair to meditate on the ceiling. *Teddy said the girl was okay. Teddy said it. Teddy the junkie. The junkie said the girl was okay. And what's the rule of thumb, how much of what a junkie tells you is to be believed? You take his statement, divide by four, and throw away whatever's left. Whatever condition that girl is in, she is definitely not okay.*

And if Novotny has her, what does that mean? Held prisoner? Chained to a water pipe in the cellar? Dead and dissected? No, no, Maritsa Durant was not okay.

What was it Teddy had said? The cops have a lot on him. Serious shit, that's how he made it sound. So if they did, why hadn't they tried harder to find him. How tough could it have been? Christ, face it. It took you and the world's last surviving beatnik one evening to almost pull it off. But what had Labriola said about Lawrenceville? The cops were laying off for a while. Did that extend to Teddy and, if so, why? Let's see if Labriola has anything more to say.

And is there a place in this mess for Outlaw? If Novotny has the girl, and he and Outlaw are asshole buddies, then old Dennis Mc-Cauley is shoveling shit in your direction. He's not a junkie, but it might again be best to divide by four and throw away the leftovers.

Good Lord, Dorsey thought, *you've got some ways to go with this thing, but where in the hell is that girl?*

The combination of a solid meal and beer did its work, and Dorsey fell first into a light doze, followed by his first deep sleep in several days. How long it lasted he wasn't sure, but when he awoke the windows were dark, and the only light was that of the street's mercury lamps. It was a few minutes before he realized that an insistent doorbell had brought him back to life. Mindful of his injured arm, he struggled out of the chair and went for the door.

Janice Manning had left her smile at home. In fact, Dorsey thought as she went past him into the office, she was awfully pissed off. *Maybe worse than that,* he decided. *She looks like a mental patient who hasn't refilled her prescription.* Standing at the center of the office, she had the appearance of not knowing which way to turn, which chair to take. Her neck was rigid, giving the illusion that she had grown three inches in the last few days. The skin was tight across her face and her eyes were wide. "I'm going to get that motherfucker for this," she said.

Thank God, Dorsey thought, *at least she's not here after sex.* "It's not that bad, really. Besides, don't get so excited about things. Really doesn't help, ya' know?"

Dorsey gestured her toward the guest chair, but she refused, shaking her head and pacing the room. He settled back behind his desk, watching her do laps around the room's periphery. She put him in mind of a lifelong smoker on her second week of a cure. She went to the windows, adjusted the drapes, and moved to the file cabinet, where she jerked open the top drawer, then slammed it home.

"All right!" Dorsey slapped the desktop. "The message is clear; you're one pissed-off lady cop. So sit down already. Have a beer if you want. But cut this shit out. Teddy Durant isn't public enemy number one. Christ, he's not even Dr. Novotny. And listen, it isn't like we're married."

181

With his last words she came to a halt and fixed her eyes on Dorsey. For his part, he couldn't come up with the words to capture what he saw in her eyes. It wasn't hurt and it wasn't the special anger returned at a lover's sudden insult. What the hell was it? Anger, but at what? She saved him from further analysis when she very deliberately went for a beer, then took the guest chair across from Dorsey.

"I want to get that bastard," Janice Manning said. With one hand she deftly fingered the beer's pop-top, cracking it open. "For what he did to you. And for a lot of other things, too, if it makes you feel better, safer. Safer from me, I guess. You're my first private detective. I suppose I underestimated your mania for independence. Sorry."

Mania, Dorsey thought. *You've been running into a lot of that lately. None of your own, however.* "Listen," he said, resting his left arm on the desktop blotter, "I never turn away personal concern, yours or anyone else's. It comes so seldom. You just happen to have a way about you. Like the way you go to extremes, right off the bat? It brings out a similar reaction in others. I'll bet you're hated as often as you're loved. Follow what I'm saying?"

She took a long pull on her beer, throwing back her head as if to allow the liquid to flow unabated through her system. When she lowered the can her head went with it, and for a moment she stared at her lap. Then, slowly, her eyes came level and sharp with Dorsey's, that melt-your-pants smile etched across her face. It was a transformation Dorsey had not seen before, and he knew it was more than the beer.

"I get involved fast," she said. "Socially and professionally. So regardless of what's been on your mind, this Teddy is one nasty little shit, one I've been after for a while."

"A nasty little shit that you and Trooper Lyle have been after for a while."

"Fuck Trooper Lyle," Janice Manning said. The smile left her face for a flash but was replaced by a much more playful grin. "He's in charge of driving the car and making plans for lunch. The rest I take care of. We don't get to work alone like a private eye."

"Even then it's unlikely." Dorsey thought of Henry but quickly thought better of it. The man comes through. "But back to Teddy. As much as you want him, I need him. Maritsa was with him; that's pretty clear. Why he had her and why she went with him, those are both still mysteries to me. As is the big question of where in the hell she is right now. So, along with talking to Novotny and Teddy's wife, Catherine, I'll be looking for him, too. Whoever finds him first lets the other know about it. Fast. Right?"

"Without question." Janice maintained her grin, sloshing beer about in its can. "We're on the same side, all right? When we get Teddy, we can have him on kidnapping maybe, along with all the other shit hanging over his head. And with any luck you'll have that little girl home with her grandmother. Sounds good to me."

The index finger of Dorsey's right hand picked at the bandage encasing his left arm. "Two things," he said. "Two things are putting a bug up my ass. How come Teddy was supposed to be so hard to find? I can see how Missing Persons could have missed him. Big case load and they don't know the territory. But you and Lyle—even between meals you should have found him. I did."

"You're good, that's all."

"That point's been proven wrong in the past," Dorsey said. "And the second thing. Why are you so personally dedicated to tying a can to Novotny's tail? As I understand it, it's been tried by a lot of people. And none of them has pulled it off. City narcs thought they had him, and that was part of your combined task force. How come you want to snare his ass all on your own?"

The playfulness fell from her face as quickly and easily as it had been adopted. "I hate him. I hate what he does." She finished the beer and placed the can at her feet. "Not just the pills, the dope. The stuff with the girls, it makes me ill. Personally. Old lechs with little girls reminds me of a family friend when I was a kid. An "uncle," know what I mean? He had some things on his mind, plans for me."

It explains the mania as well as anything else, Dorsey thought, *if it's to be believed. And don't forget, you never did get an answer on your question concerning Teddy's ability to avoid the police.* "Sorry to hear that," Dorsey said. "I wouldn't have guessed."

"You couldn't be expected to," Janice said. She got to her feet, putting the beer can on the desktop. "Besides," she said, the playfulness making its return, "I like to keep men on their toes. Keep them guessing."

And you succeed, Dorsey thought. *You certainly succeed.*

23

Henry reluctantly agreed to remain in the hall, and only after a long explanation and the promise of a chair to sit on. And then Peg Malloy objected to putting one of her office chairs in the hallway. Dorsey figured he had one hell of a day staring him in the face.

"You know what it's like to get—and then keep—a piece of furniture in this place?" Peg Malloy was framed by her office doorway, talking to Dorsey and Henry as they stood in the hospital corridor. "You have to sign a request form and wait. And six months later you get a plastic chair that's inventoried in your name. And then every six months afterward, you have to fill out a form justifying your need to have an extra chair along with everything else in your office. So," she was pointing at Henry now, "you look after that chair."

"Listen," Henry said. "We could save all this trouble if you'd just let me sit in on the meeting. I won't be any trouble. And I'm sort of a knowledgeable guy, ya' know?"

Dorsey shook his head. *Just sit in the chair,* he thought. *Please sit in the chair.*

"No way." Peg Malloy turned sideways in the door and dragged

185

out one of her plastic guest chairs. "I don't even like the idea of this woman being interviewed by your friend here. But there's a missing girl involved, so I'll take a chance. But there is a limit."

Henry took the chair and sat down, pushing it back against the wall. "Fill me in later," he said to Dorsey's back as he followed Peg Malloy into the office, closing the door.

"Well," Dorsey said, taking the remaining chair. "Now that the seating arrangement is decided, how is Catherine doing? She see much of what happened the other day? The part with the knife, I mean."

Peg Malloy squeezed behind her desk and sat. "We were lucky; I got her out of the room before it came to that. But hospitals, even psychiatric ones, have a grapevine. So she knows about it. But fortunately again, it's been a few days, so she's had time to take it all in and calm down. We've even been able to lighten her meds. Otherwise, I wouldn't have agreed to this."

"I don't like this, either," Dorsey said. "And believe me, I'm not crazy about getting sliced. This is just to help me find the girl. I just hope Catherine's lucid enough to be of help."

Peg Malloy pushed a lock of blond hair behind her ear. She spent a second rearranging some pencils she kept in a cup on her desk. "Honestly," she said, "I don't mean to be a beast about this thing. I'm concerned about Maritsa, believe me I am. And you haven't caused any problems—intentionally, anyway. But work is work, and there are rules I have to enforce. Rules which I believe in, by the way. So that's why I worry about the patients' rights, especially ones having to do with privacy and confidentiality." She smiled for a second. "How's the arm?"

Dorsey started to tell her that it wasn't so bad, but he was interrupted by a knock at the door. As in their first meeting, the door was opened before a response could be given, and Catherine Durant was shown in by an orderly. Dorsey gave up his chair and wedged himself into a corner of the tiny office, resting his bandaged arm atop the filing cabinet. The movement made it ache, and he wondered just how tough a private eye he really was.

"Who's the guy out in the hall?" Catherine asked. She was dressed in jeans and a hospital scrub top. "Another patient?"

Dorsey started to laugh and stopped when he caught a sharp look from Peg Malloy. "Sorry," he said.

"He has an appointment with me once we're done," Peg Malloy said. "Now, you remember Mr. Dorsey, correct?"

"Heard about your arm," Catherine said. "It's all they talked about in here the last few days. Teddy's carried a knife for a long time. These guys ripped him off a few years ago. Over some grass, I think. That's how come he's got the knife. Sorry. I would've told you if I thought things were gonna go that far."

"It's okay," Dorsey said. "The cut's not so bad."

She had been looking up at him as she spoke, and Dorsey studied her eyes—once he got past the beauty that her daughter had inherited. They seemed calm, much more tranquil than when Teddy had been berating her. And it wasn't a drug-induced tranquillity, Dorsey was sure. Not like their first visit, when she had rambled and digressed in a thousand directions. *No,* he thought, *she's really behind those eyes this time. Maybe we can get somewhere.*

"I don't want to upset you in any way," Dorsey said, "but I'd like to eventually get around to discussing your visit with Teddy. But let's take it light at first. I wanted to mention that I took you up on your advice. I went to see Outlaw."

"Yeah," Catherine said with a shrug. "That was my idea."

"Not a bad one." Dorsey smiled. "Not a great one like you initially thought, but it was a help. It led me to Teddy. I was able to find out where he was staying."

"At the shack?" Catherine asked. "In the alley under the bridge?"

Dorsey stole a look at Peg Malloy who nodded her head, prodding him to continue. *My God,* he thought, *is this Catherine the same Catherine? Hell, it sure isn't Outlaw's Crazy Katie.* "You know about the place?" he asked. "Last time you wouldn't hazard a guess as to Teddy's whereabouts."

"Last time was last time," Peg Malloy said, interrupting. "As should be evident, things have changed for Catherine. Changed for the better."

Okay, Dorsey thought, *the new term is "changed." Nobody "gets better" anymore because that might remind them that they used to be a lot worse off. Well, hell, thank God for the change.*

"Your daughter, Maritsa, she'd been staying at Teddy's place." Dorsey quickly waved off the eagerness on Catherine's face. "I didn't see her there, but please, don't get me wrong, she's been there. Recently, I suppose." He went on to tell her about the missing and found book.

Catherine smiled at Peg Malloy and then at Dorsey. "See? Teddy said she was okay. It's true then. She's all right. You think so, don't you?"

"Nothing to indicate otherwise." Dorsey spoke slowly, word choice becoming important. "Nothing I know of suggests she isn't. But, that's her health we're talking about. She's still seventeen and she's still missing. She was with Teddy and she has no business being with him, at least as far as Family Court is concerned. It looks to me like the court had good reason for that. I know you're glad to get any good news about your daughter, but doesn't it bother you at all, her being with Teddy?"

"I'd thought of all the other possibilities," Catherine said, "and they were at lot worse than her being with Teddy. I thought somebody took her. Hurt her. Killed her, maybe. Face it, Teddy is her father. So at least she was with someone who loves her, right? Teddy loves her."

No, Dorsey thought, *no, he doesn't. He might want to, he might think he does, but he doesn't. He can't. He's a strung-out user with one objective in mind. No, that's wrong. Not in his mind—in his heart. He cares and he acts for one thing. The next high.*

"The other day," Dorsey said, "when Teddy was here, me and

Peg Malloy, we came in after the two of you had been talking for a while. From what I could gather, he thought you might be able to help him out with some money. He looked bad, Catherine. Sort of on the ragged edge, if you know what I mean. Desperate. Hell, he must've been to come here. Tell me all he had to say. About the money and anything else."

Catherine looked at Peg Malloy, apparently for advice. "This man isn't from the police," Peg Malloy said. "Or any other authority. But he has been hired by your mother and he is looking for your daughter. Your choice. Either way is fine, I think."

Catherine Durant shook her head as if she were shedding her reservations. "Oh, Teddy." She turned to Dorsey. "He was crazy, wild. The way you saw him. That's the way he gets—a lot. He kept saying that they were moving in on him. That they had all they needed to put him away. That they had had it for a long time and that they had finally gotten around to him. It was his turn, he kept saying. It was his turn. And that's why he needed cash, all he could get. To get away."

"They being the police?" Dorsey asked, wondering if he himself were part of "they." *Maybe not,* he told himself. *You found his place, but he was gone before that.* "The police, right?"

"Seems so."

Dorsey paused for a moment, then pushed on. "Teddy, like I said, he took a hell of a chance coming here. And it was a chance that didn't work out. So I doubt he would have ever come back. Which means, if you could have scrounged up some money for him, you'd have to find a way to get it to him without his coming back. How was that supposed to happen?"

"We never got that real straight," Catherine said. "But I can sort of figure it out. Somebody would have come for it, like they were here to visit me. I would have passed it to him." She turned to Peg Malloy. "To be honest, it happens all the time here. Only it usually works the other way. People sneak things in, know what I mean?"

189

Dorsey chuckled to pull Catherine's attention away from an embarrassed Peg Malloy. "How else *could* it work?" he asked. "Can't be too many things you have in here that the general public is dying to get at."

"You got that right."

"So, back to what we were saying. Who would have come for the money?"

"Huckie," Catherine said. "Huckie would have probably come."

"Who's this?" Dorsey asked. He thought of Janice Manning's rules about local nicknames. Huckowski? Hucacynski? Hucnarovich?

"He's a friend." Catherine laughed. "In fact, he was our best man. He's real good, real reliable. Has his own place on Forty-second Street. He's on a methadone program out at the VA hospital."

Well, Dorsey thought. *Reliable. On methadone, that free and dependable source for the luckiest junkies.* "Listen, Catherine, I need to find Teddy again. So I can find Maritsa. So I can pick up the trail. I've got another lead to follow, but Teddy could explain it all. Shit, I'd even forego any charges about my arm if he helps out. Where do I look?"

"Teddy's looking for help. He'll go see Huckie. You ought to try Huckie's place."

Dorsey slipped into the Buick's passenger seat with a sense of disorientation, groping for a steering wheel that wasn't there. *This,* he thought, while Henry got in the opposite side, *will definitely take some getting used to.*

"You've got the address?" Henry asked, pulling away from their spot in the parking garage. "We should talk to the guy, I suppose. But if he's like I think he is, methadone junkie and all, he won't say shit."

When they got to the exit and the attendant's booth, Dorsey handed over the ticket and some dollar bills to Henry. "We should

190

watch him for a while instead," Henry continued, paying the attendant and pulling out onto the street. "That way we can maybe spot Teddy coming by. We should try that, at least for a while."

"We are going to try that," Dorsey said. "Well, *you're* going to try that. On your own for a bit. To start with, anyway. After we get you in place, I'm going to hustle my ass up the street to see if I can get a few things done in the meantime."

They shot down Forty-fifth Street, passing cemetery walls, churchyards, and row houses. The houses were mostly brick but a few vinyl sided ones were sprinkled in, and Dorsey thought of them as missing teeth in an enormous jawbone. A few turns later they reached Forty-second and following some hesitation, Dorsey directed Henry to a spot at the curb.

"Wish we had the van for this," Dorsey said, thinking he would have to change vehicles if the surveillance dragged on. He pointed out the address that Catherine had given him, a smallish house on the far side of the street with an aging wire fence surrounding a few inches of sparse grass and dirt that led to an arched walkway. He gave Henry a quick physical sketch of Teddy.

"Good," Henry said as Dorsey struggled out of the car. "If any of the walking dead show up, I'll know it's him. Bring me a Coke, okay?"

Dorsey's left arm was aching again and he held it to his side, his head down, carefully placing each step on the uneven brick sidewalk. At Butler he turned left, passed a few storefronts, and came to the remodeled facade of Dr. Novotny's office. He peered in through the glass door. Seated in the waiting area were two elderly women; the receptionist's desk was unattended. Dorsey had been working, unsuccessfully, on a cover story to bypass the receptionist and was glad for the extra time. Keeping his left arm near his ribs, he went inside.

The room was furnished with two sofas that met at the room's far corner, and the two women sat at the far ends, as if each suspected the other of a contagious disease. Dorsey nodded quick, unreturned hellos to each and sat where the sofas met, asking himself if he was afraid to show any favoritism. He looked the room over, hunting for magazines of any vintage, and found none. Beyond the single door, which he took to be that of the examination room, he could hear a telephone ringing. It was then that Dorsey realized that the receptionist's desktop was a blank. No calendar, no billing forms, no appointment book.

"Any idea about when the girl gets back?" Dorsey asked. He was addressing both women, swiveling his head as if at a tennis match. The woman to his left turned away, preferring to stare at the blank wall. The woman to his right giggled.

"You hear that?" she said. The telephone in the next room was ringing again. "He answers the phone himself. There ain't no office help. You have to pay office help. Gets the phone himself, interrupts whatever he's doing and goes for the phone. Could be doin' God-knows-what, have his finger who-knows-where, but if the phone rings, he goes right for it. Somebody should report it to the telephone company."

Report what? Dorsey thought. *Somebody's supposed to call Pennsylvania Bell and tell them there's a guy out here who doesn't wash his hands before he uses his own phone? But the lack of office help was good news. Just walk into the examination room when your turn comes. No smart-ass receptionist telling you to take a hike until you're bright enough to call ahead for an appointment. And for Novotny, no receptionist who might end up as a witness in some drug trial.*

"Does all his own bills, too," the woman said. "Makes you pay cash before you can get out the door, most times. Now, he don't charge as much as the young ones do, and that's good, but you gotta have the money with you. Most times. Unless you got the Medicare, and only if he knows you real good. That Medicare makes for paperwork, and I don't think he likes that stuff. Taxes, know what I mean?"

Before Dorsey could get off a noncommittal remark, the other bookend spoke. "He's not so bad," the second woman said, "not like you make him out to be, anyways. He was good to my sister when she had the cancer. He couldn't do much for her, but he was good to her."

"He wants the money right away," the woman to Dorsey's right said.

"So give him the money. He's entitled. Besides, you've got it."

Dorsey braced himself for an all out catfight, geriatric-style; then the examination-room door opened, and a third elderly woman stepped out, closing the clasp on her purse. As soon as the doorway was clear, Novotny's defender shot into the examination room, slamming shut the door.

"Her sister never had the cancer," the remaining woman said once the doctor's last patient had exited out onto the sidewalk. "Her sister's liver was blown up like a balloon. She looked pregnant at sixty-seven. It was the liquor that did it. Hard liquor. All her life she was at it. Everybody knew. Everybody."

Dorsey closed his eyes, rested his head against the wall, and wondered if seven thousand was enough for this job. *Maybe a raise is in order, what with all this horseshit.* He decided against it, but he did plan on asking Mrs. Leneski if it was the cancer or the liquor. If everybody knew, she definitely knew.

The phone rang several more times, but the doctor must have been working quickly. It was only a few minutes before the woman came back out, avoiding the other as she left. The next examination seemed to take even less time, and the second elderly woman was gone. Dorsey got to his feet and entered the examination room.

It was larger than he had expected and apparently furnished for a division of labor. At the far end of the room was the exam table clothed in white linen but showing no sign of use. There were several cabinets laden with pharmaceuticals and instruments. Much nearer was a wooden office desk with several metal filing cabinets behind it. Somehow stuffed into a chair between the desk and cabinets was Dr. Novotny, head down and reviewing a chart while he finished off a candy bar.

Jesus, Dorsey thought, *this guy is fat. Man, is he fat!* Seated in an ancient-looking bentwood swivel chair, the doctor had the look of having been forced into it, his ass pinched with fat forced up and billowing once it was past the restraint of the chair. He wore a lab coat and necktie, but it was clear to Dorsey that the shirt's top button hadn't been closed in years. The man's jowls were so heavy that Dorsey wasn't sure if they ever really ended.

"What happened to your arm?" Dr. Novotny closed the chart he was reading, crumpled the candy bar wrapper, and tossed it in a wastepaper bin. His voice was soft, and Dorsey couldn't seem to connect it with the laughing fiend he had overheard when he was facedown in his driveway. Years in America had eroded Novotny's accent, but traces remained, especially at the end of his sentences, which seemed to trail off into the air. "You should go over to the table. I should look under that bandage."

Dorsey rolled his sleeve up to his shoulder and sat at the edge of the examination table. He watched the doctor lever himself out of the chair, his upper body lurching forward as he used his flattened palms to push off from the desktop. The movement was accompanied by wet-sounding breath, as if oxygen had to route itself through a moistened washcloth. Dorsey tried to avoid it, but he thought of the young girls. *You fat bastard! You sick fat bastard!*

"So, again," Dr. Novotny said, "tell me about the arm. A bad cut, right? Not so long ago, either." The doctor took a pair of angled scissors from a cabinet drawer. "So, tell me please?"

"Thought you would have heard by now." Dorsey dug into his right hip pocket and came out with the blank prescription sheet he had found in Teddy's Polish Hill apartment. He flipped it onto the table's linen.

Without a misstep or wasted motion, the doctor returned the scissors to the cabinet drawer and faced Dorsey. "This is about what? You have a prescription blank; I don't know how you got it, but you have it. Tell me, what is this?"

"This," Dorsey said, "was being used as a bookmark by a teenage girl. The kind you like. Only this one is missing. And she's the daughter of one of your regulars, Teddy Durant."

"I know Teddy." Dr. Novotny wedged himself back behind his desk and crammed his way back into his chair with what was obviously considerable effort. "And that explains you, somewhat. You are the one Teddy stabbed, or cut—whichever. You are correct, I am aware of your incident at the hospital. Teddy himself told me of it. You were very lucky; I can see that."

"The surgeon said the same thing," Dorsey said. "Now, I want to talk about the missing girl. And if I hear from you what I need to hear, then no one else has to hear about the flesh that Outlaw delivers to your door."

Dr. Novotny shook his head, his jowls flapping along, exaggerating the movement. "This wouldn't work, I should warn you of it. If you know anything about me, you know I wasn't born in this country. And that means that this is not the first time someone has come to my door with threats. Where I am from the government's agents and the government's thugs have been to my office. Or to my home. And always with threats of how they will deal with me. So, at face value, regardless of what you slap down in front of me, I don't see you as being of much account."

Dorsey drifted across the room and dropped into the one chair in front of the desk. It was true that Novotny was a man used to dealing with threats, and with authority. He knew both sides of intimidation and seemed to have mastered them both. And he mastered them by dealing. *He'll talk to you,* Dorsey told himself, *if he thinks you're worth it. He's asking you to prove your worth, to show that you are of some account. Otherwise, he would have thrown you out already.*

"I'm not the police," Dorsey said, lifting his hands, palms out. "No badge, no authority. Except maybe a few personal contacts.

Like with the city narcs. The ones who are avoiding you since your last brush with the law. You've got pull somewhere, Doctor. And I don't give a shit about it. I'm being paid to find a girl, Maritsa Durant. And her junkie of a father says you can get me to her. So, that's why I'm here."

"I can't help you," Dr. Novotny said. "I know the girl you are talking about. You can't walk two blocks around here without seeing her picture five or ten times. It's in every storefront window. But I've had nothing to do with her."

"You've had a few things to do with some other girls her age." Dorsey recounted the night he had followed Outlaw.

"Very good, Detective," Dr. Novotny said, again failing to show any emotion. "Some problem? You want me to say I'm sorry? Because I indulge myself in those things I enjoy?" Once more he shook his head, jowls following in a prolonged motion. "An occupation of one's country by an outside enemy or an illegal regime, as in my experiences, causes deprivations. Many deprivations. And when these occur during one's prime, you have a tendency, later in life, to make up for lost time. There was war and tyranny in my youth. There is none for today's young people. They can afford to share their good fortune with me."

Dorsey still thought he could deal with the man, but he was liking it less and less. He had a rationalizer on his hands, a man without even a submerged sense of guilt. A man so lacking in a conscience that lies had no value. There was nothing to hide, no closet skeleton, no secret too dark. So he told everything. If he was asked and not quoted.

"You talked to Teddy," Dorsey said. "He told you about my arm, about our little two-step. And it was during that go-round that Teddy suggested I see you about his daughter. And he had your prescription blank at his place. Again, do you know anything about the girl?"

"Nothing."

"So tell me about you and Teddy. And the prescription blank."

Dr. Novotny hesitated for a moment, then shrugged and smiled. "Oh, all right, I can tell you some. You seem to know some already. Teddy's been here in the office several times. Not very often, he's so erratic and untrustworthy. He made some pickups for others. So, as far as the prescription blank is concerned, he could have taken it on any number of occasions. It doesn't surprise me you know. He is what he is. Every bit of him. He would even lie about his daughter, sending you here looking for her."

"What about your latest talk with him?" Dorsey asked, gesturing with his bandaged arm. "When he told you about this."

"He was crazed," Dr. Novotny said. "Very, very agitated. And, like you, he thought he could frighten me. Only he wanted money. Which I did not give him."

"Threatened to tell the police about his connection to you, did he?" Dorsey asked. "And that's only a slight matter to you so it wasn't much of a threat. He's not a bright one."

"Yes," Dr. Novotny said. "He is not a bright one."

The conversation lulled for a moment and Dorsey was unsure how to proceed. From Butler Street, muted by the walls and the waiting room, he heard an emergency vehicle siren followed closely by another before they died away. *The girl,* he thought, *Maritsa. That's the point of this whole thing. In front of you is a dope dealer and a statutory rapist who can beat the system at will. And he doesn't know where the girl is because he'd tell you if he did. Goddamned Teddy, that heartless, soulless junkie bastard. He send you on a wild goose chase. You've got to find him. He had Maritsa and you have to find him.*

Dorsey dug a business card from his wallet and slid it across the desk. "You don't give a shit about much and that's okay with me. None of my business what you do, and if you burn in hell for it all, well, that's okay, too. But you've got nothing to gain by protecting Teddy or from stopping me from finding the girl. So why not call me if he comes by? Or if you hear anything about him or his daughter—maybe Outlaw might say something in passing. It could happen. And it wouldn't mean a thing to you, just to give a call."

Dorsey rose from the chair as the doctor looked over the card. "Carroll Dorsey," Dr. Novotny said, "you're the one who was all over the news a while back. Your father's Martin Dorsey?"

"Why not ask about my mother?" Dorsey said. "They tell me she was your patient. One of the many you've lost over the years."

"Your mother," Dr. Novotny said. "A little anger is understandable. But she was a very sick woman when she came to me. Very little could be done, except to keep her comfortable."

"Now there's a question." Dorsey was at the door, his hand on the knob. "How was it she came to be your patient? After she saw the Irish doctor up the street all her life?"

"You think so little of me because of the drugs," Dr. Novotny said. "It's not always such a bad thing. People need relief. Your mother's cancer, it was very bad, extremely painful. And back then, in this state, not every painkiller was given legal sanction. Even for doctors. And some prescribed amounts brought questions. I thought of myself as taking a wider view. She was dying, horribly dying. She was brought to me because I was willing to address that suffering."

"Brought to you? By who?"

Dr. Novotny smiled, nodded, but didn't seem ready to speak. Dorsey moved toward the desk but came up short when he heard the office front door ripped open, followed by rushing footsteps. The examination room door opened in turn, and Dorsey spun about to find Henry bracing himself in the door frame, gulping for air.

"C'mon, we gotta get back there!" he said. "They just did Teddy!"

198

24

Late-evening breezes flowed through the office windows, fluttering the sheer curtains and nipping at the stitches of his now-exposed left arm. Seated behind his desk, a Rolling Rock cradled in his right hand, Dorsey watched closely as Henry worked at his wound. The desktop was draped in clean towels, and from a Thrift Drug shopping bag Henry produced several rolls of gauze, Ace Bandages, and hydrogen peroxide. Al, apparently unconcerned, was perched at the edge of the chaise, sipping at a mug of coffee and looking out at a dimly lit Wharton Street.

"Careful, now," Henry said, gently positioning Dorsey's wounded arm across the towels, stitching facing upward. Dorsey compared it to the surgeon's art work that decorated his knee, concluding that this latest effort reminded him of a baseball's needlework. It was the first he had seen of it, but it was okay; it was far from being his first scar.

"This dressing should have been changed before," Henry said. "Bad cuts, boy they can give you a time of it. Believe me, I know. Seen some bad ones."

"Korea?" Dorsey asked, watching Henry shake the bottle of hydrogen peroxide before he snapped the seal. "Army medic or just personal observation?"

"Personal observation and experience, but not in the service." Henry said. He hesitated with the antiseptic, then continued. "Back in my people-smuggling days, we had to do a little doctoring of the merchandise. Those Chinese, jeez, some of them were a mess. Sick, different kinds of injuries, you name it. Keep in mind, the truck ride down the West Coast from Canada was just the last leg of one long-assed journey for most of them. We had guys who'd been hurt two weeks earlier in Hong Kong, and there they were, bleeding all over the back of my truck. And some of those trucks were rentals. Think about it. How you gonna explain a lot of dried blood stains to the U-Haul manager and get your deposit back?"

Dorsey grabbed Al's attention with a loud, exaggerated cough. "How are you on this?" Dorsey asked him. "You trust this guy to look after your best friend? Namely me?"

"All the confidence in the world," Al said, addressing them both. "Now that I've heard about the smuggling business. I've never known Henry to be a bullshitter, not on any level. So if he says he smuggled illegals into the U.S., which is probably how most of our ancestors got here, I believe him. And if he says he knows his way around a mangled arm, I believe him."

Henry tilted the hydrogen peroxide and carefully soaked a fist-sized wad of cotton. He grinned. "Shall we proceed?"

Dorsey nodded in the affirmative, then threw back his head and poured beer down his throat. The Rolling Rock was well chilled, nearly ice, but it stood little chance against the intense pain as Henry pressed the medicated cotton to the sensitive wound, carefully and thoroughly, making sure that all potential sites of infection had been coated. When the beer can was empty, Dorsey whipped it across the room, striking the far wall just above the TV set.

"Fuck, man!" Dorsey screamed. "Jesus, did that hurt!"

"Really should give it another going over," Henry said. "Really, it'd be the right thing to do."

Dorsey looked squarely at him, turned his gaze to Al, then locked on Henry again. "I haven't gone back to the bank yet. I haven't been to the safety deposit box to return my belongings. And that means I have a loaded, untraceable revolver in my desk drawer, which I will use to prevent you from doing that again. There you stand with your cotton wad in hand. Here I sit with a well-functioning firearm. Your move."

Henry slipped a grin onto his face and dropped the cotton into the wastepaper basket. "I believe my work here is nearly done. Just need to get this thing bandaged up."

"Sounds good," Dorsey said. "Another beer, too. Please?"

"For both of us."

Al drank off the last of his coffee and set the mug on the floor. "So, what are you gonna do now?" He gave Dorsey a moment to respond. "Seriously, what are you gonna do with this thing now?"

Dorsey accepted a Rolling Rock from Henry and cracked it open with a one-handed motion. Henry sipped at his own beer, then began gently applying gauze to Dorsey's left arm. "What am I going to do?" Dorsey asked. "I'm not entirely sure. Not at all."

"Back to square one?" Henry suggested. "That's what you're trying to say?" Dorsey lifted his left arm, allowing Henry to smooth the gauze and begin the Ace bandage shell.

"For the most part," Dorsey said. "I've got to look over all the old ground, revisit some people. But that's not always so easy. Know what I mean? Some people you can only push around, intimidate, once. You're a new threat only once. Time passes and you're always on the scene, so you become part of the scene. Just another everyday hassle that people have learned to deal with. The elements of surprise and the unknown are lost."

Al took his coffee mug out to the kitchen and Dorsey kept his attention on Henry's handiwork, telling him to forego the wrapping between his thumb and first finger. "Stop the bandage at the wrist. I like to be able to move my fingers." He smiled. "Like to scratch my ass with either hand."

"Freedom of movement—my dearest belief." Henry finished off the wrap by securing it with clips and several loops of white tape about the wrist and at the elbow. Dorsey worked his fingers, approved their movement, and switched his beer to his left. After a short sip he declared the procedure a success.

Al came to the office door. "Time I got back to the bar," he said. "Rose's been minding things while I'm down here, and that's not always good. Night crowd, ya know? Sometimes people stay a little too long and forget their manners. For me that's part of the job, but Rose shouldn't have to put up with it." He turned to Henry. "You coming, too? We really should get things ready for tomorrow."

Henry set down his beer and told Dorsey to finish it for him. "There's kegs need moving and cases to stack. Easy on the arm," he told Dorsey. "Skin around the stitches needs to crust up some before you return to competitive weightlifting."

Dorsey remained in his chair, listening to the front door close and the firing of the van's engine as they left. He finished his beer, eyes closed, then shook himself awake and pulled the Olivetti to the center of the desktop. From the center drawer he took some typing paper and fed a sheet into the carriage. He entered the day's date and resumed his case notes.

They had run along Butler to the corner and down Forty-second, Dorsey chasing Henry as he flagged him on, looking like two little boys in a race. Across from the Buick, fronting the house that Henry had been sitting on, were two police wagons and a patrol car. Two uniformed officers were unrolling the yellow plastic ribbon that declared the house and sidewalk a police crime scene. When they came even with the Buick, Dorsey caught Henry and pulled him to a stop, demanding a quick briefing.

"When they pulled up," Henry had said, "I had no idea they

were cops. You know, the car not being marked and all? And they just sat there for a while, watching the same house as me. I thought it was a buy, a deal in the making. But then they got out, and I remembered you describing those two, especially the tall woman. And it was kind of funny—the little twerp with the red beard, he finished off a Twinkie as he was getting out of the car."

"They just go for the house?" Dorsey had asked. "Knock at the door or just crack the lock?"

"The woman, she headed for the walkway between the houses; looked like she was going around back. Before she does though, she stops and says something to the beard. She must really wear the pants in that family because the beard just nods and stays put while the woman goes into the walkway. He looked a little antsy though, and he pulled out his gun. For a while nothing is happening and it feels like time is passing and maybe the crisis or whatever has passed. Then the shit really hits the fuckin' fan. Fast, ya know? That woman, who looks like a real ass-kicker to me, she lets out with this scream and she shouts for her partner."

"Then he flies in to the rescue?"

"Ah, yes and no." Henry was watching the police secure the plastic crime scene barrier, and then a coroner's wagon drove down from Butler. "He went in all right, but you could tell his heart wasn't in it 'cause he hesitated. But then there was a second scream and he took off with a head of steam. Shuffled his feet to get going, like he was Fred fuckin' Flintstone. And then I hear the shots, two or three maybe."

Dorsey motioned Henry into the Buick, setting him behind the steering wheel. "Stay put," he told him, looking in through the open window. "You may want to be a witness, but then again, there may be a good reason not to be. Your story might not jibe with the party line, and nobody does well in that position. Let's see what I can see."

Dorsey drifted across the street, moving between two sidewalks that were beginning to crowd with neighborhood onlookers.

Mostly elderly men and women, retirees, they spoke in what they apparently thought were whispers—the exaggerated voices that arose from failed hearing. Dorsey caught short bits and pieces. Mrs. Monevich used to live there with the two kids. But she died and the second son, the ironworker, he made it into apartments. And let those bums move in. Oh, the noise. And the dope. Like nobody knew they were selling dope in there.

The rear doors of the second police wagon were open, and Dave Lyle was seated at the rear bumper, apparently collapsing into himself. His head was up, though, and his eyes were wild, darting about in search of something. *Hope,* Dorsey thought, *he's looking for hope and reassurance. Because he's the one that pulled the trigger.*

Janice Manning seemed to hover at her partner's side, whispering in his ear, her hand lightly massaging the nape of his neck. When she looked up, Dorsey saw the tear tracks through her light makeup. He was somewhat shocked; he would've never expected tears from her.

"It's not what we wanted," Janice said as she came to Dorsey. "But we got him just the same. Teddy, I mean. Had a tip he'd be here. Never expected him to have a gun."

The surgical thread in Dorsey's arm twitched at the suggestion. "You're okay?" he asked. "Lyle looks bad."

"Give him time," Janice Manning said. "C'mon, I'll show you."

Dorsey fell into step behind her as she parted the uniformed officers and led him through the walkway. Teddy's body was sprawled on the brick footpath, at the far end of the walkway. There were two bullet holes, one to the chest, direct hit on the sternum; the other was a jagged renting of the throat. Dorsey was surprised by the width of the bloody pool by the body. He wouldn't have thought that a rail like Teddy could've carried more than a pint or two.

Several detectives arrived and ordered them out of the crime scene. One was a state policeman and Dorsey watched as both Lyle and Manning were relieved of their sidearms. Another detective exited the walkway carrying a small revolver in a plastic evidence bag. Teddy's gun, Dorsey thought. A cheap hunk of metal, .22 caliber at best. Not much firepower for going up against the state police. Manning and Lyle were ushered into an unmarked car and taken away. With Dorsey's invitation canceled, two uniformed officers sent him packing, and once back in the car he told Henry to take off before the media arrived. "They've been unsympathetic in the past," he told him.

Dorsey pulled back from the typewriter, his arthritic hand having had enough. He rolled his chair to the bookcase and chose a cassette, inserting it into the tape player. Billie Holiday sang out, eulogizing Teddy, her fellow dead junkie.

From the filing cabinet he retrieved the Durant case folder and returned to his desk. He sipped beer and inserted his fresh notes, then looked over the entire contents. Time to begin again. But where?

Teddy had had the girl for a time. Teddy who somehow had a gun and got the drop on superwoman when she came for him. *Well,* Dorsey thought, *maybe Teddy was vastly underrated. He got the drop on you, too, remember. So let's not sell him too short. He lasted a long time in the dope world. And that's not a friendly environment.*

But Maritsa had been with him and now she wasn't. And Teddy is no longer with us, as they say. The last person known to have seen the girl is dead. Henry was right, Dorsey thought reluctantly. *You have to go back to square one and start fresh. Well, not entirely fresh. There's Outlaw, the boys at the park and in the cemetery, the Butler Street bars. Here we go again.*

He had taken the first steps already. There had been the late afternoon call to Mrs. Leneski to let her know that Teddy was out of her life forever. "We're all better off without him," she had said. "If only it had happened years ago. Now, where's my grand-

205

daughter?" And the call to Peg Malloy, who could break the news to Catherine as she saw fit. Peg Malloy was to call with Catherine's reaction, and with a time for Dorsey to question her again.

Dorsey had never killed anyone. He had experienced the opportunity and he had experienced the desire. But never the aftermath, the deed completed and irreversible. *Poor Lyle,* Dorsey thought, *he's had the whole sickening thing. Charging in to save his partner, about to be killed by a junkie. How goddamned heroic. There'll be a medal in this for him. A citation signed and presented by the governor himself. You're a hero, Dave; now just get the picture of a bullet-riddled Teddy Durant out of your mind.*

Back to the file, he told himself, lifting a pencil, beginning a list of people to see. Arbitrarily, unsure of who knew what or who would be willing to tell what they knew, he began to rank his priorities. Then he gave up and concentrated on the beer and Billie Holiday. Like a unionized construction site, a new high-rise going up: A fatality shuts down the job for a day.

The tape clicked to a halt, and Dorsey flipped it over to the B side. Lady Day continued on and he went deeper into his funk, looking at a long, lonely night and wanting nothing else. And so the telephone rang.

"Yeah, hello. Dorsey."

"We better talk, right away."

The voice didn't connect at first. "Outlaw?" Dorsey asked. "Dennis McCauley?"

"Outlaw," the voice said. "Just leave it with Outlaw."

"So, we have to talk, huh?"

"Fuckin' right we do," Outlaw said. "You, me, and another guy. Tonight. Right fuckin' now. As soon as you can get your ass over here."

25

Dorsey pulled the Buick to the curb near the bottom of Forty-sixth Street, across from the park. Waiting, he listened to the eleven o'clock news give Teddy's death twenty seconds of notice. *Congratulations,* Dorsey thought, addressing himself to the recently dead. *That's more attention than you ever got alive.*

He had chosen to leave Henry out of this. The conversation with Outlaw had given him an uneasy sense of closure; the boiling point was being reached. He wanted no one between him and the heat. From the glove compartment he took an oversized flashlight, checked the battery strength by flicking the on-off switch, and killed the Buick's ignition. He took the revolver from the car seat and slipped it into his waistband, covering it with the tail of his sport shirt. Once on the street, he locked the car doors and entered the park.

Outlaw stood within the glow of the first lamppost, the spot of his initial meeting with Manning and Lyle. Smoking a cigarette, he was dressed in white painter's pants and a tank top; Dorsey took it to be the latest addition to his hard-ass pose portfolio. Slowly approaching the circle of dim light, Dorsey clicked on the flashlight and checked the area. They were alone.

"Said I'd meet you by myself." Outlaw dropped his smoke and ground it out with his heel. "Said I'd take you to him."

Dorsey turned off the flashlight and, waving it like a weapon, approached Outlaw. "Trust is for assholes. Around here, anyways. Let's get started."

Outlaw gestured for him to follow, and they climbed the short flight of cement steps and came level with the basketball court and baseball field. At the top of the steps, collapsed into a snoring huddle, was a boy in his late teens. Outlaw stopped and looked down at him, allowing Dorsey to come even with him. "What a fuckin' mess." Outlaw chuckled and slapped the boy lightly on the top of the head. "C'mon," he said to Dorsey, "we're supposed to meet him over by the fence."

They crossed the basketball court, now bathed in low light from a streetlamp attached to a telephone pole, and passed into the darkness of the baseball field. Dorsey could hear several conversations, mostly loud and drunk, and picked up on the dark silhouettes gathered in small groups against the cemetery fence. *Ghost-drunks,* Dorsey thought, *ghost-junkies. The young that would remain just blacker marks in a dark night all their lives. Stains hardly noticeable in comparison to the backdrop. Jesus Christ, is Maritsa here?*

Outlaw angled toward the cemetery fence and Dorsey stayed in step, carrying the flashlight in his left hand, tightening his grip as best his injury would allow. He wanted his right hand free to go after his gun if the need arose. *You're outnumbered here,* he reminded himself. *Stay close to the equalizer.*

"Right there," Outlaw said, pointing toward a solitary figure seated on the fence's cement base. "That's him, fuckin' right." He raised his voice. "Dingle?"

"Yeah, man." Dingle's speech was slow and he raised what looked like a beer bottle in salute. "C'mon man, it's me. Right here, man."

A few feet from the fence Dorsey gave the flashlight a quick hit and checked his surroundings. Dingle, wearing a T-shirt and cut-offs, sat on the cement with the remains of a six-pack of bottles at his side. Behind him was one of the empty spots in the fence, the steel mesh peeled back between support poles. Dorsey clicked off the flashlight to jeering voices asking him what the fuck he was doing.

"This is one scared motherfucker," Outlaw said, helping himself to one of Dingle's beers. "And I'm kinda worried myself. We gotta be straight on something, you and me; we gotta be straight. What I said before, about not knowing nothing about the girl and everything, that was true. Then. Things are different now." Outlaw gestured toward Dingle. "This motherfucker was lying to me."

Dorsey slipped over to Dingle and sat next to him on the cement. He watched him drain the last of a beer and toss the bottle backward over his head. The crash of glass on broken glass followed. "So," Dorsey said. "Who's going to start?"

"Teddy had the girl at his place," Outlaw said. "This guy knew about it. This guy was in on it, too."

"In on what?" Dorsey asked. *It wasn't a kidnapping,* he thought. *The girl went on her own with her favorite reading material with her. Teddy convinces his daughter, somehow, to run off and join him in Polish Hill. For what?*

"Teddy wanted to fuck over Novotny." Dingle shoved his blond hair from his forehead and reached for another beer. "We used to party up at his place, in that alley in Polish Hill? Good place, especially in the cold weather. Teddy used to talk about it all the time, gettin' Novotny. He hated the sumbitch."

"For what?" Dorsey addressed the question to Outlaw who shrugged it off. "He wanted to fuck over a source?"

"The fuck do I know?" Dingle said. "He wanted to, that's all. Talked on it all the time; beat my fuckin' eardrums in. Like it was a fuckin' crusade. Didn't make any sense, but that's what he was about."

Of course it didn't make sense, Dorsey thought, *because it still doesn't make sense. Even if he had a reason to hurt Novotny, Teddy*

209

wouldn't do it. He was too busy looking for his next cheap high. Besides, the last person he went to for help was Novotny. It smells like bullshit, self-serving bullshit. Cover-up bullshit; but from what?

"Teddy had a plan, right?" Dorsey asked. "His daughter figured in it, right?"

"Yeah," Outlaw said. "Teddy knew about Novotny and the girls. Don't get me wrong, I didn't know what these guys were up to. I didn't know shit about this till today."

"Relax," Dorsey told him. *Jesus Christ,* he thought, *this is the mayor of Butler Street?* Dorsey turned to Dingle. "C'mon, man, give up the story. What were you boys up to?"

"Teddy wanted to feed his daughter to Novotny." Dingle chuckled and took a pull on a fresh beer. "Pretty fuckin' sick, right? He had this idea that she could get to Dr. Novotny, sort of become his regular, ya know? Maybe she could get into his little place on sort of a permanent basis. Learn all the doctor's dirty shit, and then Teddy could fuck him good."

What the hell's the difference? Dorsey thought. *We sell our kids dope and then our doped-out kids sell their kids, and this mess next to you tells you what's sick and what isn't. Like you have to be told.*

"Teddy was a good talker sometimes," Dingle continued. "Had a good line of shit when he wanted. And, you figure, no matter how fucked-up a father you are, you should be able to fool your own little girl at least once."

Dorsey thought of all he had learned about Maritsa. The good-looking seventeen-year-old with high marks from all her teachers. Service clubs for after-school activities, deep concern for others. The teenaged idealist. And that picture was further supported by what he had been told by Dingle's tentmate.

"So," Dorsey said to Dingle, "Teddy starts hanging around the high school to see Maritsa, maybe convinces her that he's reformed, at least a little bit?" Dingle nodded for him to go on. "They start to be friends, and Teddy always reminds her to keep their new relationship a secret from her grandmother. And then, when Teddy is convinced in his slimy little mind that Maritsa is set up and ready to respond, he tells her about Dr. Novotny. About how the doctor is Satan's personal representative in Lawrenceville and about how he happens to be responsible for every stray pill and syringe on this side of the Allegheny. This sound about right?"

"Fuckin' right it's right." Dingle pulled himself to his feet, looking off into the cemetery's blackness. "He just talked about the doctor at first. Really kept it up, from what he told me. Drummed it into her head. He never let on about gettin' her together with Novotny, not for a long time. But he did start telling her that he was going after Novotny."

"And she was frightened for him, worried about him," Dorsey said. "Which was what he wanted. Couple that with her nature, and you knew something would happen. That she would eventually come to her father and ask him if she could help. He never had to approach her; she came to him. Not with a plan, but with a worried and willing heart."

Dingle flashed a quick smile, then suppressed it. "Teddy was good. He didn't tell Maritsa anything until she took off with him. So, she was hooked when he let her in on the plan. No place to go, I guess she figured. How could she go home and explain everything to her bitchy old grandmother?"

You would think of her as a bitch, Dorsey thought, *you dumb-assed bastard.* "So," Dorsey said, turning back to Outlaw, "where are you in all this? C'mon, you deliver the doctor's goodies; was Maritsa on the drop-off list?"

Without a word, Outlaw took Dingle by the hair, spun him about-face, and laid a fist across his chin. Dingle's knees buckled for a second, but Outlaw held him up. Dorsey wondered if he was getting used to a daily beating and hoped it would continue.

"You tell this guy the truth," Outlaw said, his face inches from Dingle's. "Don't fuckin' lie. Don't dare fuckin' lie." He released Dingle and shoved him in Dorsey's direction.

"Outlaw was in the dark on it." Dingle steadied himself on a fence post. "I did that. Teddy asked me 'cause he knew Outlaw was Novotny's man. So I told Outlaw I had a girl he could have for the doctor. Never said who she was."

Dorsey watched Dingle try to gather himself, then turned to Outlaw and considered flashing a spot of light in his face. He thought he might like to study his features, to see what contortions they were in. But he knew what he'd find from listening to Outlaw's voice, from seeing the way he had slapped Dingle around. *This man is scared,* Dorsey thought, *scared shitless and trying to distance himself from the thing he was frightened of. And guess what?* Dorsey told himself. *It isn't you.*

"You took her to Novotny?" Dorsey asked Outlaw. "Goddamned liar, thought you never saw the girl. Fuckin' pimp. You're a fuckin' pimp."

Outlaw took a tenuous step forward, and Dorsey got to his feet, transferring the flashlight to his right hand. "Stay put, asshole. You're scared to death of something and you better damn well stay that way. Don't lose your head over this thing. Because with what I'm hearing tonight, I'll take your goddamned head off for you. A chunk at a time."

Outlaw stood motionless, and Dorsey sensed he had hit home with his threat. But what the hell was behind this? What was so threatening? "Let's get it straight," he said to Outlaw. "You delivered the girl or you didn't."

"Never had the chance." Outlaw spoke slowly, his voice dropping. "This guy, him and Teddy, they canceled out at the last minute. Really pissed off the doctor. But like I said, they just said they had a girl. They never told me who it was."

Dorsey turned his attention to Dingle, who had hoisted himself up onto the concrete. "Rug cutting time, fella." Dorsey hopped up next to him. "What happened to Maritsa and where's she at?"

Dingle looked lost for a second, then tugged at the top of his cut-offs. "I gotta piss. I gotta go piss right back here."

Dorsey said he was coming with him and turned to Outlaw,

telling him to stay put. He wanted to get them apart and find out what they were afraid of. And he wanted to concentrate on Dingle. *You've already beaten the shit out of him once,* Dorsey reminded himself. *You can dominate him easily, push him where you want. Hell, he's still got your scars on his face.*

Beneath their feet was the hard crunching of glass being reground and packed. Where it began to dissipate, Dingle spread his legs and pissed while Dorsey again flicked on the flashlight, giving the area a check. Something had changed. The tent had been struck and the campsite raked. "Getting ready to take off, huh? You and the girl?"

"She's gone." Dingle closed his zipper and adjusted his belt. "Hell with her, you don't care. You want me to finish telling you about Teddy's daughter."

Dingle started back toward the fence, but Dorsey stiff-armed him with the flashlight, sending him back a few paces. "That's right," Dorsey said. "First you're going tell me what happened, and then you're going to tell me why you're telling me. You two didn't bring me out here in the middle of the night to moon over Teddy and confess your sins. Not just for the hell of it. Now, get started."

"Even after all the talking to her, she was real nervous when it was time to go see Novotny." Dingle rubbed at his breastbone where Dorsey had landed the flashlight. "So, Teddy figured she might feel better if she got a little high first. Just a couple of beers, she wouldn't go for anything else. But even that was too much. She had some beer and fell asleep, passed out, kinda. And it's time to get going, so she's got to wake up. So we shake her and she pulls herself together some, but she's still real groggy. So Teddy—and this was Teddy's idea and he done it himself—he tries a couple of these things."

Dingle fished a small brown prescription bottle from his hip pocket and handed it to Dorsey, who hit it with the light. Amyl nitrate vials. Poppers. Crack one open under the nose, and you and

213

your heart got the rush of a lifetime. The label read from a crosstown drugstore. The prescribing physician was Novotny. Dorsey figured it as a forgery taken from the stolen pad, the kind of thing you could expect from Teddy. So what if Novotny was his drug source? Fuck him.

"It was bad, really bad." Dingle shook his head. "She did this fast sort of jump—weird, like it started in her chest instead of her feet. Then she falls back and this blood started, just a trickle at first, coming out of her mouth. Then it starts from the nose. Aw, shit, did it get bad."

Dorsey staggered back a few steps and back into his days with the district attorney's office. He had seen more than his share of dead junkies, cold and on slabs, and he had spent all the time he ever cared to reviewing their autopsy reports. But one came back loud and much too clear: Amyl nitrate, the guy thought it'd be a fast rush, a kick in the ass that he'd bounce back from. But he didn't, because the sorry bastard didn't know about his congenital flaw. Thoracic aneurysm, a spot on the wall of his aorta that was much too thin, far too weak, to take the slam that the drug delivered. And it gave way, ruptured, and the blood poured into the chest and then out—everywhere. Dorsey saw the report before his eyes and then another vision took over. A room in a rattrap of an apartment on Polish Hill under the span of the Bloomfield Bridge. Two guys on their knees, Teddy and Dingle, scrubbing away at the bloodstained floor and walls. The faint smell of ammonia crept into his nose. That junkie, the one in a million physical type, he killed himself. Now these two, they did it. They killed another one in a million.

"Dead?" Dorsey asked.

Dingle wiped at his lips with the back of his hand. "It was bad," he said. "Fast, but nasty."

"The body," Dorsey asked. He was already thinking of the grandmother. "Where the fuck is the body?"

"Right here," Dingle said, scattering the glass with his toe. "We put her under here. Knew the glass would keep getting deeper, keep

214

spreading. Funny, when you think about it. Who'd expect to find a dead body in the cemetery?"

Dorsey smashed him across the chest with the flashlight, then vomited.

Dorsey gave him two more shots with the flashlight and left him flat on his back, praying for ground glass to dig into his neck and legs. Steadied and determined, he made for the fence line, hoped down onto the baseball field, and signaled for Outlaw to approach. At a distance of six feet, Dorsey shifted the flashlight to his left hand, drew the pistol with his right, and shot Outlaw in the foot.

"Fuck, man!" Outlaw screamed. Instinctively, his wounded foot danced out from under him and he fell as he reached down to grab at the bullet hole. All around him, Dorsey could hear the response from the muzzle flash and gun report as the ghost-junkies called out and their black silhouettes shot through the escape routes into the cemetery. Dorsey ignored them—knowing that in their world it was every man for himself and there was little chance of anyone coming to Outlaw's rescue—and made his approach. He kicked Outlaw once in the face and shone the flashlight in his eyes. The muzzle of the revolver, smoke trailing away from it, was pressed into the bridge of his nose.

"Now that I have your undivided attention," Dorsey said, calmly, "there's a question I put to Dingle but to which I never got an answer. Dig this: This gun is in no way traceable. It disappeared years ago from the police impound. It's colder than your fuckin' heart, you useless piece of shit. I pull the trigger, then drop the gun in the river, and there's not a jury in the world that could convict me. And, best of all, you're dead. That's the best part for me and the part you better keep foremost in your mind. You follow?"

"Yeah, yeah," Outlaw said, nodding his agreement, pressing into the business end of the revolver. "I'm with you. Really, whatever you say."

"Just shot you in the foot," Dorsey said, "and now you're scared shitless of me. But not before. Before something else had you on the run, something else had you and that other asshole—who's not feeling so good either right now—get me out here. Tell me what it is. Tell me now." The revolver's hammer reared back with a metallic cranking sound.

"You saw it," Outlaw said. "That's what I heard. When Teddy got it. Who the fuck wants to end up like him?"

Dorsey eased the hammer down and drew back. "Lyle? You fuckin' guys are worried about Dave Lyle? Last I saw of him he had the look of a whipped dog. Didn't look pissed-off and there wasn't an ounce of fight left in him. Besides, he's a puppet on a string."

"Fuckin' right he's a puppet." Outlaw grinned through his pain. "You got that right. So now you're gettin' the picture, huh?"

26

It was around four in the morning when Dorsey got away from the park and cemetery. Portable arc lights had been brought in to illuminate the burial site, and a small earth mover worked over the sea of glass. The body, wrapped in heavy green trash bags, came up with the fourth scoop. Dorsey walked off before the bag was opened.

Detective Strobec took down Dorsey's version of the night's events. How Outlaw and Dingle had confessed, identified the burial site, then had a change of heart and attacked Dorsey. The shooting of Outlaw and the beating of Dingle were self-defense. Strobec suggested that Dorsey make himself available to defend South Korea. On his own.

Pulling away in the Buick, Dorsey dug into his pocket and took out the prescription bottle. The murder weapon—one of them anyway, the one with Novotny's name printed across it. *That's one of the killers,* Dorsey thought. *Now let's visit the other.*

He drove along an empty Butler Street past the cemetery wall and the turn-off for Uncle Davey's. He wished he could stop there, get his uncle out of bed for coffee and a talk. To tell him what he had found in this backhanded homecoming of a case. And to tell

217

him where he was heading. *No, my friend,* he reminded himself. *You're the private eye, the social loner, advocate of individual justice. You get paid, so do your job.*

The girl was dead, had been for a while, and Dorsey couldn't reconcile himself to the idea. All the facts on file, all the interview notes, the flyers that could be seen behind store and barroom countertops and stapled to telephone poles—they had kept her alive. She was a celebrity, and all of those photo handbills had been nothing more than media coverage. The bio kept in the newspapers' files. Well, the obituary could now be written. And maybe that would make it official.

At Sixty-second Street he turned left and rose onto the bridge that crossed the Allegheny. Teddy was dead because he had pulled a gun on a cop. Teddy, who had sliced him just days before with his handy blade tucked neatly into his pants.

Blade men were blade men. They dug knives; that's all there was to it. The way the metal glistened and the way it evoked cringing fear in others. Fear of an animal that kept violence at a brutal level; fear of the scarring it might leave behind. Very simplistic, all blade men were that way. Teddy was a blade man.

And then he changed preferences, in just a few days' time.

Dorsey thought of the gun he himself had used on Outlaw. Snatched years before from the police evidence bin while he was still a law enforcement officer, taken at the advice of an older partner who had warned him that every cop needed a throwaway piece. *Every cop. Not just you, stupid.* Dorsey wondered if Teddy's gun had even been loaded. *Before* he was killed, anyway.

Poor dead Teddy, reunited with the daughter whom he had loved enough to feed into corruption's furnace. And Dingle said Teddy had done it because he had a bad case for Novotny. Because he had hated him over some unknown slight. *Bullshit. Teddy didn't want to get Novotny. He just wanted to get high. To stay alive, sure, but only if he could do it with a buzz on.*

When Dorsey reached the far end of the bridge, he went right and used the Catholic church as his guiding landmark. Lots of people, lots of cops, wanted to get Novotny. The task force, Dorsey recalled, they wanted him and thought they had him, too. *Now let's see the one person who* really *wants Novotny.*

Dawn was still an hour away as Dorsey parked in front of the church. From the highway edged into the hillside above the town, mercury lighting gave off a distant, sad glow, mingling with that of the streetlamps, depressing him even further. Dorsey checked his gun and then checked the apartment windows where at least two lamps were lit. He stepped out into the street, rounded the building through the parking lot, and hit the buzzer at the security door. A responding buzz sounded, and the door was released. She must be expecting you, Dorsey thought.

The apartment door was open when he got there, and he closed it after entering. Gun in hand, Dorsey followed the lights to the front room. Janice Manning was seated at a writing table before the window, her back to Dorsey. Dressed in a long white robe, she turned her chair about and faced him. "You don't need that gun with me," she said.

"No, not a gun," Dorsey told her. He slipped into an easy chair across from her. "A tank or two—now, that would make me feel more secure. You know where I just came from, right? You're the type that's always connected to the best of grapevines. You know what's happened."

She seemed to sit a little straighter, her hands folded softly in her lap. She crossed her leg and let the robe fall from it. Dorsey stayed with her face, studying it, looking for her reaction to being caught. All he saw was defiance. And pride. *That's it, goddamn it, pride. Pride on an unbelievable scale. What a psychopath.*

"You get them all to do your dirty work, right?" Dorsey rested his gun in his lap, willing to keep it there as long as Janice's hands stayed in sight. "Teddy pimps off his daughter to set up Novotny for something or other. Then when that goes bad, you get Teddy and this idiot Dingle to bury the body."

219

"Put her under glass," Janice said. "That was the joke they made."

"I'm in fucking stitches."

"At least your arm is."

"Back to your story," Dorsey said. "The latest chapter. I start to catch up to Teddy. In fact, I mention to you that I'm looking for him in Polish Hill. And when I find his place, he's not in it. No doubt because you told him I was on my way. But instead of just lying low or getting as far away as possible on his own, Teddy goes a little wacky. He sees Catherine at the hospital and I get cut. Then he bugs Novotny for money. And he hides out in that house on Forty-second. Maybe he's ready to settle down some, but you can't take the chance. So you and Lyle raid the place looking for a junkie who is known for his recent violence. You go in first, pull some shit with Teddy, and then scream for Lyle. Who falls right into your plan and puts a few holes in Teddy. Convenient. Always someone else to carry the load for you."

"It's a skill," Janice said. "Manipulation is an art."

"How'd you get Teddy to go along? You didn't take him to bed, too? Just the thought—shit."

"Teddy had troubles, legal troubles." Janice kept up her pose, showing not a crack in her self-satisfaction. "He did some break-ins up on Polish Hill. He was after TVs, VCRs, that sort of thing. He did one where an old lady was home. He never touched her, but she saw him and dropped dead from a heart attack. Felony murder. I had him cold for it with the woman's goods. I owned him after that."

"So you cooked up this plan to get Novotny, using his daughter," Dorsey said. "Maybe you saw her around the park a few times and she looked like good bait. And you wanted Novotny. And you knew about Outlaw and the girls. Shit, you hinted at that in the file you gave me. Maritsa was just right for the job. Too good-looking for Novotny to give up after one night. Just the kind he'd like to find in his house most every night. And she would tell her father everything that went on in that house. And Teddy would tell you. You'd get Novotny, just like the bathroom mirror says."

Janice Manning lost her smug expression, but quickly recovered. "I forgot about that," she said, smiling. "I should have kept the fucking strictly at your place."

"What about my role?" Dorsey asked. "Sure, you wanted to know what I was finding out, but that's not enough for you. What'd you have in mind for me? How was I supposed to move things along?"

"Some of that was totally up in the air." Janice recrossed her legs and closed the robe. "I did like the idea of you having such a powerful father. Novotny has some pull, somewhere. I thought if you got caught up in this thing, your father could help. And then later, when things changed, I figured you might be the one to get rid of Dingle. Maybe Outlaw, if necessary."

"Now, on that last part you came pretty close," Dorsey said. "Those two boys are just a little less than healthy right now. But with Maritsa dead, I could have finished the job. Thought you might have a gun out when I came calling. I was hoping I'd get to shoot you."

"Sorry." Janice held up her empty hands for inspection.

Dorsey pulled up from the chair. "Aw, hell. Been a long night, full of surprises, and I need my rest. I'm due at the Public Safety Building tomorrow morning to give a deposition on all this. I've got my file, the prescription bottle to make Novotny sweat, and enough conjecture to see you get in some hot water. Your cop days are numbered, and with any luck, a lot worse will happen to you from the law. You're right—my old man has a lot of pull. That I know, sadly, from personal experience. I'll see what punishment he can arrange for you."

"Don't bother yourself," Janice turned back to the writing desk and lifted a notepad. "My statement is prepared."

Dorsey stopped in the doorway, sagging in fatigue against the frame. *Is she that crazed, that self-involved? Good Lord,* he thought, *is immortality her last refuge?* "I think I know what you're getting at. Care to tell me I'm wrong?"

Janice Manning's eyes were on the notepad and to Dorsey she seemed pleased with what she had written. "I have no intention of losing a fight. Not with a lowlife like Novotny. This work has meant everything to me, you should know that by now. Look at the lengths I've gone to, the efforts I've made in chasing down the fat bastard. It's the *next* to last move I have."

Dorsey shook off the idea. "Up to now, this whole business hasn't cost you a thing. There've been sacrifices, human ones, and they've all been made to your ego. You want to be the second body found tonight, go ahead. But don't be noble. Your suicide is to get you off the hook. You're not noble; you just can't face the music. You just want off the hook."

"It's a beautiful piece of work," Janice Manning said, setting the notepad on the writing desk, giving it a gentle pat. "Everything I know about Novotny, everything he ever did. And all my efforts to put a stop to him. And how all my efforts were turned against me. By the city police and politicians and fools like you. It's the story of all my work. It's my story. And it's my ending."

"Pills, gun, or razor?" Dorsey asked. "Just out of curiosity. Gun, right?"

"I'm a cop."

"Gun, then," Dorsey said. "Figured you for the type of soldier who falls on her sword."

He pushed off from the door frame and turned to go. Janice laughed and called after him. "Hey hero, you're not going to try to stop me?"

Dorsey stopped cold. *My God,* he thought, *I want out of here. Don't look back,* he told himself. *The face of evil or illness, what's the difference? You can't change it and you can't stop her short of a strait- jacket. Don't look back. Let it die.*

"No," Dorsey said, his eyes fixed on the corridor wall. "I won't stop you. Made a promise to myself a long time ago, in parochial school. Promised that when I died, I'd leave the world in better shape than I found it. Stopping you would break that promise."

Outside, slouched behind the Buick's steering wheel, Dorsey gave some thought to waiting for the gunshot. The sky was going red and orange in the east, daybreak was close at hand. *The hell with it,* he told himself and turned over the ignition. *Why force yourself to witness an execution at dawn?*

27

Dorsey drank hard that morning and slept long into the late afternoon. After coffee and a long shower, he dressed in a dark suit and tie and drove to Lawrenceville.

Mrs. Leneski was in black, too. In the kitchen, across the Formica tabletop, he gave her all the details. The back door was open to an afternoon breeze, and Dorsey heard the flap of laundry drying in the open air as he went through the litany of villains. Some dead, some in pain, one practicing medicine.

"This policewoman," Mrs. Leneski asked, "she dead for sure?"

Dorsey looked into his half-empty coffee cup. "I got a call on it this afternoon from Strobec. People in the next apartment reported the shot, and the state police made the identification. She's gone."

"That's good." Mrs. Leneski took his cup to the sink and poured out the remains. "You hate my coffee. With your work over, you don't have to hide it no more." She came back to the table. "This Lyle, he didn't know a thing? He's a fool?"

"He's a fool," Dorsey said. "Truly a fool. Teamed up with a cop he thought was going places, that's how I figure it. Thinks he'll ride the coattails. And she keeps him in the dark. Even gets him to kill Teddy for her."

"I would thank her for that," Mrs. Leneski said. "If she were still alive. I would thank her. Then I would kill her."

Dorsey told her again how truly sorry he was for her and Maritsa. And for Catherine, whose hospital stay now seemed to have no end. He told Mrs. Leneski that his written report would come to her in a few days.

"I don't want to read anything." She looked away, somewhere far away, then continued. "Don't send me nothing. You don't have to tell me my little girl is gone when I already know it. Just tell me about Dr. Novotny. Will you kill him?"

"No," Dorsey said. "I just haven't the stomach for it. I'd like to; I wish I was one of the ones that can do those things. Sometimes I wish that; other times I know better. No, I can't kill him. That's a job for someone else. If you look, you'll find someone who can. That's always for sure."

"I'll look." Mrs. Leneski held Dorsey's gaze for a moment, then dropped her eyes to her hands, folded on the tabletop. "Funeral's day after tomorrow, at ten in the morning. The church just across the street. You gonna come?"

"I'll be there," Dorsey said.

"That's nice."

Around eight that evening Gretchen returned his call. With his legs thrown across a desktop littered with crushed green beer cans, he told her all that had happened and all that he had done. And what he had not done.

"So it's finished," Gretchen said over the line. "Those poor people, all of them."

"Some of them," Dorsey said, then rethought his comment. "Sorry, I don't want to pick a fight. You're right, it's finished for me. Just the deposition tomorrow. And then I shut it down."

"Novotny, you'll tell what you know about him?"

Dorsey fingered the brown glass prescription bottle. "Oh, yeah. He'll play a big part. And then we'll see what good it does. Maybe your Dr. Riddle is wrong. Maybe we'll get to this Untouchable. Maybe."

"Hope so."

Dorsey suggested that he would be free to get away next weekend, that maybe he could come to Franklin. Gretchen didn't think much of the idea.

"It's not good for us after a thing like this," she said. "You pour out your remorse on all the bad things you had to do, wanted to do, and I get nervous. Because, sometimes, I can't stand these things you do. Okay?"

Sure it's okay, Dorsey thought. *Having no choice, not being able to change the soul of another, that has to be okay. That's why you drove away from Janice's early this morning.* "I understand," Dorsey said. "Let's give it a couple of weeks, how's that sound?"

"Reasonable," Gretchen said. Dorsey laughed, and she said she thought he'd like that. Fast good-byes and the hang up followed.

Dorsey brought his feet to the floor and took the trash bin in hand. With his bandaged left arm he swept the desktop, mowing over the beer cans and toppling them into the bin. He adjusted the blotter, squaring it at dead center, then rose and started for the kitchen. Two steps into the hallway the doorbell rang. At the door he peeked through the glass, thinking he would once again be dodging TV and print reporters.

"You're kidding," Dorsey said, opening the door. "I didn't think you even knew my address."

Martin Dorsey entered the house, relying heavily on his tripod cane, and made for the office. Dressed in dark slacks and a short-sleeved dress shirt, he took one of the easy chairs in front of the desk. Dorsey lingered at the front door, noticing a late-model Oldsmobile parked just beyond his Buick. Behind the wheel was a young man whom Dorsey recognized as his father's physical therapist.

"Hire that fellow full time?" he asked his father, closing the door and retaking his seat behind the desk. "Taking over for Ironbox?"

"I need a hand with things," Martin Dorsey said. "Carl is a pretty handy sort. Besides, I pay better than Visiting Health Services."

"Never doubted that." Dorsey pulled the swivel chair close into the desk, as if for protection. *What the hell was going on?* he wondered. His father did not visit. He just did not. Martin Dorsey conducted business on his own turf, on his home field. Dorsey recalled some advice his father had given him years ago. Never play an away game.

"I've heard about the outcome of this Lawrenceville business of yours," Martin Dorsey said. "My condolences to the family. I'm sure this was not how you had hoped it would end."

"She was dead long before I ever heard her name," Dorsey said. "And, well, there's hardly anything of a family left to feel bad for. It's done. Just tomorrow and then it's done."

"Tomorrow." Martin Dorsey fussed for a moment with his cane. "We should talk about what you'll be doing tomorrow. Your deposition in this matter. There may be a problem."

"Not for me," Dorsey said. "I've had my statement taken a hundred times. But it must present some kind of problem for you. You're here, and that tells me that something is bad wrong. For you, at least. You never go out-of-doors unless it's to fix a problem."

Martin Dorsey again played with his cane. "You'll be giving the district attorney's office your version of events. I suppose that will include whatever it is you know about Dr. Novotny. Correct?"

"There's only so much to tell." Dorsey watched his father, intrigued. He seemed uneasy, pained, as if he for once was not pulling the strings. *This,* he thought, *could be bad.* "He's mixed up in this, and there may or may not be grounds for charges, but yeah, I'll be talking about him. And his prescriptions." Dorsey produced the prescription bottle from the center desk drawer. "He provided the murder weapon."

"This discussion of the doctor in your deposition, is it essential to resolving this case? Certainly, if this girl's father caused the death, any discussion of Dr. Novotny could be kept to a minimum."

"There's no reason to hold back on him," Dorsey said.

"Yes, there is a reason," Martin Dorsey said. "The reason is very important."

Dorsey thought back to his conversation with Detective Labriola. Novotny had been nailed, they had him good. Then evidence disappeared. And witnesses got lost. And the narcs were told to stay off Lawrenceville for a while. Who has that kind of pull? The kind of pull to keep Novotny out of trouble for thirty years. *Jesus Christ,* Dorsey thought, *it's sitting right in front of you. Dr. Riddle was right. Novotny is an Untouchable.*

"You're it, huh?" Dorsey asked his father. "Dr. Novotny's protection, his guardian angel. You fixed this dope business for him and some taxation problems a few years back and God knows what else. And for some reason I'll never fathom, you took my mother to him so she could live out her last few months in a drugged-out haze."

"I hadn't realized you knew about that," his father said. "But then again, Dr. Novotny did say you two had met. He called me, you know."

"I do now," Dorsey said.

"You have no concept of your mother's suffering. Specialists, they played by their self-proclaimed rules. A patient could get this for pain, but not that, and not enough of this to do your mother any good. I knew about Novotny and had him care for your mother. Europeans, they seem to take an alternate view of these matters. Well, I owe the man some favors. And in my business, favors are the legal tender. Novotny and I discussed this matter."

Dorsey stayed at the chair's edge, letting his father's words process through his mind. Novotny had helped his father, illegally, and it'd been payback for almost thirty years. Dorsey shook his head. *It doesn't ring true,* he thought. *Favors are paid back, sure, but it's done on a favor-for-favor basis. Not repeatedly for thirty years, like the monthly mortgage payment. This business with Novotny should have had a clean slate long ago. This isn't a debt; it's blackmail. Help like this is extorted, not asked for.*

"He really has something big on you," Dorsey said to his father. "Not some long-ago sedation for a dying woman. Novotny has the goods on you and he has you by the neck. I can tell. I know the feeling."

"I'm here to ask for your help," Martin Dorsey said. "Actually, I'm offering you an opportunity to protect the people I believe you still care for. That's a rare thing. The older we get, the more we want just to be left in peace."

Dorsey remembered the last time someone had said that to him. Ironbox Boyle. It was during one of her more lucid moments. *Yeah,* Dorsey thought, *the kind of moments that have been growing fewer and fewer for her.* "Tell me what it's about. Ironbox is mixed up in this, right?"

"Irene is at the center of this." Martin Dorsey hung his head for a few silent seconds then continued. "I told you about the breakdown. Again, Dr. Novotny was involved. Irene was using morphine, can you believe it? I think it started after a hospital stay or some such thing. She fell into its use when she was depressed. Actually, it was Novotny who came up with the cure. The trip to Europe? That was part of the treatment."

Again, Dorsey worked through the data, filling in holes and finding that others defied completion. He took the case from Mrs. Leneski and Novotny got wind of it, probably after Dorsey's first encounter with Manning. That could have gotten back to Novotny through who knows how many people. So, Novotny started calling Martin Dorsey and Irene Boyle knew about the calls. And with each call she got a little less stable. *Good Christ,* Dorsey thought. *That's the fill in, but what about the remaining blank spots? Thirty years have passed and this threat doesn't pack the punch it once did. And your father, would he really go to such lengths, take such extreme risks, to protect anyone but himself? Hell, no. There's more. He did something.* Dorsey flashed on his last meeting with Ironbox: "We didn't make it any easier on your mother," she had said.

"Tell me the rest," Dorsey insisted.

"There is nothing else."

"Sure there is," Dorsey said. "Don't know if I'm going to help you either way, but I want the truth before I even consider it. What really happened?"

Martin Dorsey left his chair and did a lap around the room, stopping to check the dust on the top of the file cabinet and adjust the position of the chaise. Humping about on his cane, he reminded Dorsey of a wounded animal, weakened and captured, waiting for the death stroke. It was a role not designed for Martin Dorsey. *But still,* Dorsey thought, *who's to say?*

"I suppose you know about the old days." Martin Dorsey retook his seat, lowering himself with care. "By that, I mean before abortions became legal. That was another service provided by a few doctors on the sly. Novotny, of course, he was one of them. Knowing him, he probably congratulates himself on his vision and forward thinking. Well, an abortion had to be done."

"Irene Boyle?" Dorsey asked. It seemed obscene to call her Ironbox at that moment.

"Yes," Martin Dorsey said. "The mental breakdown business, although it probably had some validity, it was a cover we came up with in case some hint came out."

Dorsey wasn't sure he needed to pose the question. "The child was yours?"

"I've felt bad about it for a long time."

One last question, Dorsey thought. *The last and most reluctant.* "Mum, she was still alive?"

"I said that I felt bad about this," Martin Dorsey said. "I still do. Irene, well, she was a comfort. She wanted to be one and I saw no reason to feel otherwise."

Dorsey dropped into his swivel chair, pushing back from the desk. Martin Dorsey, Commissioner of Allegheny County, almost

230

thirty years back. A county that included Pittsburgh and river valleys with a string of milltowns. Loaded to the overflow with Irish and Poles and Italians and every kind of Catholic Slav. Catholics. Traditional no-meat-on-Friday Catholics. And then there is Martin Dorsey, the man who cheated on his dying wife. The man who put his secretary through an abortion. *My God,* Dorsey thought, *Novotny had you by the political balls.*

"He can still hurt me, hurt Irene," his father said. "He could hurt the memory of me, which really means something to me. At my age, what's left? And Irene, she might just go over the edge. Carroll, what is it that you plan on doing?"

Dorsey snapped on a picture of the fat doctor's face. *Bloated evil,* he thought. *Drug pusher, childfucker, abortionist, and totally unrepentant. Worse, he feels justified because he lived through a war. One that his side lost. Well, the hell with him. He's had it his way for a long time. Thanks to you, Dad.*

"Remember your mother, how'd she'd feel about this," Martin Dorsey said, playing his ace. "She's gone to her peace. Better for her that way."

It was the use of his mother in this conversation that reminded Dorsey why he hated his father. "I remember her."

"Carroll, what are you going to do?"

231

28

Late the next afternoon, Dorsey pulled the Buick into the gravel in front of the Hibernian Club. Dressed again in his dark suit, he went to the door, announcing himself through the intercom. The electronic latch was freed with a buzz and he entered.

His uncle was seated at his stool in the bar's corner, his back resting against a stack of returnable beer cases. The cigarette in his left hand was held by two fingers with oval nicotine stains, contrasting with his light complexion. He smiled at Dorsey and waved him on.

"We usually don't enforce the necktie rule until after six in the evening." Uncle Davey clapped a hand on Dorsey's shoulder, directing him onto a barstool. "But you're always welcome." He ordered a Rolling Rock for his nephew and told him how sorry he was about Maritsa.

"It all just went bad," Dorsey said, pouring his beer. He thought about Mrs. Leneski's proposed search for a hitman. "And I don't think we've seen the end of it. I've got a feeling about that."

They both concentrated on their beers for a few minutes, Dorsey waiting for the bartender to find himself some work in the backroom. Uncle Davey drew on a fresh cigarette, pushing the smoke back out in short bursts that rose and mingled in his reddish-gray hair. In their reflections in the back bar's mirror, Dorsey studied his uncle and saw his mother's pale blue eyes.

"There's more to what happened," Dorsey said to the reflection. "You're entitled to know."

Uncle Davey shifted on the barstool and faced Dorsey, who told him everything he knew about Novotny, Ironbox, and his parents. Uncle Davey calmly had two smokes through the telling.

"How'd you play it today?" his uncle asked him. "With the boys downtown."

Dorsey sighed and let his shoulders drop. "I kept Novotny as clean as I could." He downed his beer and wished for another. "Made it sound like the guy's name just happened to come up in the investigation. The prescription bottle with his name on it? That's in a dumpster by this construction site by the South Tenth Street Bridge. These two guys from the park, McCauley and the other one, they may tell a different story, but they won't be believed. Even if they have some flimsy evidence, my old man can fix that. He's cleaned up worse messes than that." Dorsey looked his uncle in the eye. "Novotny's still got it coming, and I know from where. But it's better if you don't know."

"How about you?" Uncle Davey asked. "Any trouble about you shootin' McCauley?"

"They have my gun, and they're pissed about where I got it, but it'll be okay," Dorsey said. "Might even get the gun back. If I stick to my story, I'll be okay."

Uncle Davey turned to the bar and sipped at his beer. He dashed his cigarette against the edge of a round metal ashtray and looked at Dorsey. "You did the right thing. You do realize that, don't you?"

"No, I don't," Dorsey said, "and I don't know as it makes a difference if I did. Novotny's a fiend." Dorsey gave his shoulders a shrug. "That's the only way I can describe the guy. I talked to him, face to face, and we weren't discussing medicine. He's a goddamned fiend, and I haven't done shit to stop him."

"First things first," Uncle Davey said. "And the first thing is your family. You had to be loyal to your mother's memory. And to your father and the Boyle woman, believe it or not. You had to protect them because you were in a position to protect them. That's where your father was always dead wrong."

"Tell me," Dorsey said.

"Hell, yeah, your father was a smart guy, understood a lot of things. But the first of those things he missed out on. Loyalty to family and neighbors. Like they say, loyalty to your community. Your old man missed that one. What he had, anything he had, was for sale. It was up for trade. So he doesn't have a family now. The guy is as homeless as a bum taking up a cot at the Salvation Army shelter. Sorry bastard."

"That's how you see it?" Dorsey asked.

"See it for what it is," his uncle said. "That's how I see it. People look out for each other and that begins in your own house and your own street. And that ain't always perfect. Look at that goddamned park. You think that drug shit could really go on if people didn't look the other way? Because one old lady doesn't want to get some other old lady's grandkids in trouble with the police. Maybe get them sent to prison where they belong? Hell, no, no way. Because those two old ladies have been through forty, maybe fifty years of struggle together, so they look the other way when it comes to the next couple of generations. Because they're loyal. A little mixed up sometimes, don't always act in their own best interest, but there's times—most times—when it works pretty well. Like when food or money runs low or maybe there's a fire. Or maybe, like with you, there's a hurt that can be avoided. A shame that the family can keep to itself."

The bartender came back in and Dorsey ordered another round. He sipped at the Rolling Rock and looked at his uncle. "So it's okay then. What I did?"

"You're a good boy," Uncle Davey said. "Carroll, you're a good boy.

234